ALWAYS ANOTHER SUNSET

PREVIOUSLY "ONE LAST SUNSET"

KC LUCK

This book is a work of fiction. Names, characters, places, and incidents are products of the author's imagination and/or are used fictitiously. Any resemblance to actual events, locales or persons either living or dead is entirely coincidental.

Copyright © 2022 KC Luck Media

All rights reserved, including the right to reproduce this book or portions thereof in any form whatsoever.

1

Unable to stop herself, Bella Wood dropped her forehead to the keyboard and let out a long growl of frustration. Enough was enough. The blinking cursor on the laptop's blank screen mocked her, almost scolded her for not writing all day. Six hours spent in her chair, at the desk, trying to write. She wasn't going to look at the damn thing any longer. Rising from the desk without a glance back, Bella cut across the small studio she had rented three days before and stepped onto the lanai. Four stories below, the famous Waikiki Beach thrived with early summer excitement as sunburned tourists headed home for the day along Kalakaua Avenue, dodging trolley busses and rented cars, all convertibles naturally. In the distance rolled the ocean—turquoise blue water accented with white caps racing toward the famous beach. The day was starting to fade, and as she looked on, another spectacular Hawaiian sunset was already in the making.

She willed herself to enjoy the view and not think about the weeks passing without progress on her next book—a sequel to her debut, runaway bestseller, *Catching the Moment.*

The novel hit the lesbian romance bestseller list only six months before. Unfortunately, writing it wasn't easy. As much as they professed to love the story, her fans were growing restless, and emails from them sounded more demanding than ever. Readers were desperate to know what happened next to their beloved characters. *If only I knew*, Bella thought, feeling a constant knot of anxiety tightening in her chest. *But I have no idea*. Every possible plot that popped into her head over the last few months seemed flimsy and contrived. She would sit and write what felt like something promising and then abandoned it when she realized there was nothing worth reading there. *Boring*.

Add in that Bella could not shake the idea that anything but another blockbuster would dissatisfy everyone, and she was paralyzed. The thought she might disappoint her fans petrified her. So, in the end, she wrote nothing worthwhile at all. Thousands of words were simply deleted.

At least tomorrow I'll have a reason for not writing, she thought, slipping into one of the cushioned, wicker patio chairs. They were nestled around a small glass-topped table, cute and a little romantic, assuming she was with the right person. Leaning her back against the cushion, Bella took in a deep breath at the thought of finding anyone special and then sighed. *Whoever that is*. Being a lesbian romance writer, fans assumed, or rather, expected, a fantastic love life behind it. For Bella, nothing could be further from the truth.

People, real people, not the brave and flirty ones she dreamed up and wrote about, made her nervous. In the real world, meeting someone for the first time left her tongue-tied and ready to flee. Just another thing her readers would never know about her, because she worried they would love her less. *But tomorrow, I'll be different,* she thought. *Tomorrow, I'll be brave and do something exotic. I'm going on an adventure.* The colorful, glossy pamphlet that inspired her rested on the table beside her, accompanied by an empty wineglass faintly stained with pinot noir from last night. The wine had proved to be the extra inspiration she needed to leave a message at the number in the pamphlet to sign up. When the nice, young-sounding man called her back at lunchtime, Bella almost changed her mind, but at that moment, anything seemed a better alternative than the blank computer screen and taunting cursor. So, tomorrow, at dawn no less, Bella Wood was embarking on something significantly far out of her comfort zone—a sea kayaking adventure.

Sitting at the computer on the old metal desk at Oahu Paddle Adventures and working on the day's paperwork, JC Monroe's blue eyes glanced up from the screen when someone stepped through the small building's backdoor. Blake, her teammate for the day and favorite employee, had wrapped up his chores outside. "Kayaks are rinsed and stowed for the night, and I locked up the shed. Anything else you need done before I head out?" he asked, already grabbing his red, waterproof gear bag and heading for the front door.

JC waved her hand toward the exit. "Thanks. You can take off," she said with a smile. "Same time tomorrow."

Blake gave her a grin, his teeth flashing white against his tan skin. "Sure thing, JC," he said and then he was gone, while she refocused on finishing her last task. She nearly had the day's customer insurance waivers filed in the computer, then she would lock up the hut that served as the company's headquarters and head home. The idea of settling in a lounger, putting her feet up around the small pool in her backyard, and enjoying an ice-cold Kona Longboard sounded like a good one. Although, for JC, every minute spent in the Hawaiian sunshine was a good one. Even today, which had proven to be tougher than normal, she loved the tropical paradise she called home. Back-to-back, three-hour kayaking tours, with the first starting at eight in the morning, were part of why the day was a struggle. It didn't help that the groups were larger than expected for so early in the season and that no one showed much natural skill at the sport. It was all she and Blake could do to keep everyone upright in their kayaks and paddling in one direction. At least the weather cooperated, only misting the group with one 'pineapple shower' as they were leaving Moku Island. The island was a popular seabird haven just off the coast of Lanikai Beach on Oahu's windward side and served as the midpoint for the paddling adventure.

Thinking of the small bit of rain they experienced, she remembered the weather forecast notification for tomorrow sat in her email inbox. Clicking on the Gmail icon on her screen, she took a look and frowned. A significant weather front was coming in. High winds and heavy rain were predicted to arrive late in the day, so it might not impact the tours, but it was still something to note as the ocean swells in front of the storm would be higher than average. Canceling tomorrow's activities crossed her mind, but she felt that might be overreacting. The weathermen were so often wrong, especially about the severity of storms. She decided to peek at the next day's appointments before making any kind of decision. Another big, inexperienced group could be trouble, and she didn't want any surprises.

Opening the client registration program, JC scanned the list of people signed up. Thankfully, the day's A.M. and P.M. groups were more manageable. In fact, the morning one was really small. Only three people had registered for the tour, and no one had signed up for the afternoon. Not great for business, but after wrangling a dozen in the day's first group, she was happy to see it. The afternoon might still fill up, but if the weather moved in faster than expected, that excursion would need to be rescheduled. The tourists wouldn't be happy about it; no doubt some would cancel outright because they were only on the island temporarily, but JC put safety first. *We will just have to play it by ear*, she thought and went to close the list when a name caught her eye. *Bella Wood.*

Not the most common name in the world, so not entirely impossible it was the person she knew. Still, odds made it unlikely the woman was the same one she remembered from college back on the mainland. The one JC had a wicked crush on through four years of English classes together. They were always 'just friends' and devoted study partners. For JC, the infatuation was so much more than friendly that she used her electives to take the same classes Bella had enrolled in. Suffering her way through courses about Faust and Shakespeare, she endured the confusing plays and poems in old languages if it meant they could hang out with each other afterward. *Could Bella Wood actually be in Hawaii and going on a tour? With my company?* She felt a flutter in her stomach at the idea, but then frowned. *No way.* JC considered herself fortunate, sometimes would even say a charmed life, but she knew even she wasn't that lucky.

2

*B*ella bit her lip as the white passenger van rolled into the nearly empty parking lot near the beach where she and the others would launch their adventure. For the tenth time she considered bailing out of the whole thing. *What am I doing?* she asked herself. Never a strong swimmer and not a big fan of the water in general, Bella going out on the ocean on a floating piece of plastic was crazy. *Not to mention dangerous.* The idea she may actually drown before the day was over popped into her head, and the scary thought was the final straw. She didn't care if the company wouldn't refund her money or even give her a ride back to her building—she was ready to admit to everyone that kayaking was not something she could do.

The driver, a polite young man named Blake, pulled into a parking space and shut off the engine. "Here we are," he said with a smile as he turned to look at his passengers. "Everyone excited to hit the waves?" Bella swallowed hard. She hated conflict and knew her sudden decision not to go would be unpopular. Still, quite possibly, her life depended on explaining she had changed her mind. Before she could raise her hand and begin to rationalize her desire to quit, the young couple, honeymooners as they had announced during introductions, exclaimed they could not wait. Their enthusiasm was so great that the new husband opened the sliding door to the shuttle even before Blake could come around to do it for them.

Suddenly, Bella felt her hand being grabbed by the bubbly bride. "Come on," she said with a laugh. "This is so incredible."

Never one to put up a fight and not sure what else to do, she let the young woman pull her along until she stood with them beside the van. With an aching stomach, Bella tried to distract herself by scanning the parking lot around them. They were not alone, and her eyes stopped at the sight near them. Blake began giving a few instructions, but he could have been speaking Greek for all Bella heard. Her focus was entirely distracted by the athletic, tan woman, with blonde hair pulled back into a ponytail, unloading kayaks from a trailer attached to a black Jeep Wrangler. Stenciled in gold on the side of the vehicle was Oahu Paddle Adventures, and Bella's decision to abandon the trip was temporarily forgotten. If that goddess was going with them, the trip might be worth dying over. Watching the woman for another minute, Bella felt the strangest sensation of déjà vu. *Like I've seen her before somewhere*, she thought, but before she could process anything, she heard someone calling her name.

"Ms. Wood?" Blake asked and, feeling herself blush at being caught staring longingly at a stranger, Bella forced herself to pull her eyes away and refocus.

"I'm sorry. What were you saying?" A broad grin flashed on Blake's face. Friendly and warm, but also perhaps a little knowing.

Clearly Bella was not the first person to ogle his partner. "Just explaining we will be fitting for life vests first, then learning some strokes with the paddle before heading out. Okay?" he asked.

Unable to stop herself from simply going along with what was happening, she nodded. "Yes."

"Perfect," Blake said before motioning in the direction of the blonde and the jeep. "Here comes JC with some vest options for everyone to try on."

JC? Bella thought. The initials brought back a rush of memories. College. Studying for quizzes on Shakespeare's sonnets. A friend who Bella had wished would kiss her almost every day of the four years they spent together. *But that's not possible...*

Suddenly, the goddess from the trailer was standing beside her. For a second, the morning's rising sun was behind her, so the woman's face was shadowed. There was no way to discern her features. It could be anyone, but then she turned. Bella saw who it was, and her heart nearly stopped. "Hello, Bella," JC said with a smile, and Bella was whisked back in time. The same gentle voice, the same beautiful smile, the same gorgeous blue eyes… it seemed impossible. The woman she once had an incredible crush on stood right in front of her.

As JC had walked across the parking lot with the life vests, she studied the dark-haired woman standing with the others. She was tall enough, maybe curvier than in college, but there was something in her stance that made JC think it could possibly be the Bella she once knew. When she came up beside her, and their eyes met, the world seemed to stop. JC was looking into the face of her old college crush. In an instant, fifteen years were wiped away. There they were together, in a parking lot, on a tropical island, in the middle of the Pacific Ocean.

Stunned, JC forced a smile and a hello and was amazed she was able to get the words out. Especially considering her mouth went dry the minute she realized it really was Bella Wood from college. Unfortunately, she didn't know what to do next. Everything seemed to move in slow motion, except her heart, which galloped a million beats a minute.

Thankfully, Blake came to the rescue from where he stood with the others. "Hey, you guys know each other?" he asked, lifting an eyebrow at JC when she didn't answer or move to hand him any life vests. Stepping closer, he took the lot of them from JC's arms, while looking back and forth between Bella and her. His furrowed brow proved he was more puzzled than ever. "Everything okay?"

As if his question broke the spell that had frozen them, JC watched Bella cover her mouth with her hands, but she didn't say a word. Her eyes were wide and filled with emotion. For a split second, JC wondered if maybe everything wasn't okay. They lost touch not long after college when JC went to Kuwait to serve her time in the Army ROTC. Bella went to Italy to write. There was never a long, drawn-out goodbye, simply time and distance making a friendship fade away. For JC, she considered it a lost love, but as far as she knew, Bella never saw what they had that way. The separation seemed amicable, but it wasn't impossible that JC had misinterpreted something so long ago. *Maybe I hurt her somehow*, she thought, feeling a prickle of anxiety. *What if she never wanted to see me again and here we are?* "*Is* everything okay?" she asked, looking harder into Bella's eyes, trying to read them.

"Yes," the other woman finally breathed. Lowering her hands, Bella shook her head. "Everything is definitely okay. I just can't believe it. JC, is it really you? After all this time?"

At those words, delight bloomed in JC's chest and all her worrying if it was really her Bella or if she had somehow offended her vanished. "It's really me," was all JC could muster before laughter bubbled up inside her. The impossibility of the situation, yet the wonderfulness of it too, seemed suddenly funny. After a beat, Bella started to giggle, then laughed harder. Before JC knew what she was doing, the two were hugging and laughing and crying all at once. In the magic of that moment, JC realized a piece of her had been missing all these years. By some miracle, on some random morning, what she had been lacking was back in her life, even if for only a moment. Not until Blake cleared his throat and caught her eye did JC reluctantly pull away. Her partner was grinning, looking confused as ever, but there was a touch of worry too. JC never normally acted so spontaneously and certainly never laughed and cried at eight o'clock in the morning over a guest. She was the serious side of the business, and he was the adventurous one.

His worry didn't matter to JC though. She would explain everything later, but in her mind, something special was happening, even though JC didn't know what bumping into Bella meant. She only knew that her long lost friend was on the trip with her. Even if the woman was married with three kids or was a criminal on the run, JC didn't care. All that mattered was having a chance to get to know her again.

3

With her mind spinning, Bella somehow managed to put on her life vest and learn how to hold the kayak's paddle correctly. She was also able to walk with the group to the broad, sandy beach where they would launch the kayaks, all while her thoughts raced over memories of JC. There were so many questions she wanted to ask her, but it was not the right time. *But will there be another opportunity?* she worried. JC was clearly as happy to see her as Bella was to see JC, and the hug had been tight. A warm glow lingered from where their bodies had touched. Reflecting on the magical moment, she had no doubt all the laughter and the tears were genuine.

Yet, when Blake interrupted, JC seemed to snap out of whatever was happening between them. Changing her focus to include all the group, she had switched into business mode and been the one to walk the group through the safety briefing. Bella tried to focus on the woman's words, especially since she was the one most likely to need to know what to do in an emergency. Yet, her eyes keep drifting down JC's sun kissed body. There was no other way to put it—she looked fantastic. The last fifteen years had been more than kind to her. Apparently being a kayaking guide suited JC because her broad shoulders, arms, and legs were all toned to perfection. *A very sexy perfection*, Bella thought and felt the warmth of a blush on her cheeks. It had been a long time since someone made her tingle like she was this morning.

Over the last fifteen years, she had three relationships. One whirlwind romance with a woman in Italy while Bella was there trying to find inspiration to write. That had been passionate but dramatic and looking back, thankfully short-lived. The next was back in the States with a woman sixteen years older than Bella. Because Bella was new to Los Angeles, the editor of the small magazine Bella worked for took the wide-eyed young woman under her wing. They went to galleries, museums, concerts, and the theater. The relationship was short, but there were no regrets on either side, and Bella was grateful for all she learned. Then came the habitually unfaithful Teresa. They were together for a decade before the last strings of their relationship were severed. The only good that came from it was that, after the painful separation, Bella turned to writing again for solace. Instead of lingering on all the sadness in her life, she wrote a passionate, romantic novel. A book that became a bestseller.

And somehow, all that led me here, she thought as she was left to wait on the beach with the honeymooners while JC and Blake carried the kayaks from the parking lot. *Here, where I have run into the only woman I think I have ever truly loved.* To her, the situation seemed like fate, but when JC and Blake returned, and the woman didn't even look at Bella, another thought came to mind. JC might not be as happy to see her as she first thought. Of course, first meeting after so long, considering how close they once were, would have made for a happy reunion. Hugging an old friend made sense. Unfortunately, JC seemed distracted afterward, and

Bella worried something she wasn't aware of stood between them.

For no real reason that Bella could remember, they hadn't kept in touch. Fifteen years was a long time, and back then, cell phones and text messaging weren't like today. A few emails and one awkward phone call were all they exchanged. Bella furrowed her brow. *And why was that?* she wondered because she had missed her friend. *Why did JC withdraw from me back then?* Bella worried, feeling a rush of sadness, that whatever happened then was what made JC act less interested that morning. Something was wrong between them, and Bella had no idea what it was or how to fix the problem.

USING ALL the willpower she could muster, JC somehow managed to get through the company's pre-launch routine. Seeing Bella after so much time had her thoughts and emotions in a tailspin. She became lost in the images of so many all-nighters spent studying and longing to get up the courage to confess how she felt. After so much time, all she wanted to do was take her old friend aside and talk to her. Find out about her life—where she had lived, where she worked, and especially who she loved. The realization of how much she missed Bella all these years was almost overwhelming. Unfortunately, that morning she had a job to do, and the only way to not act like a complete idiot was to get laser-focused on the tasks at hand. The enjoyment, and especially the safety, of her customers was foremost. Whenever her eyes drifted to look at Bella, to take in her familiar face, and to stare at the mouth she realized she very much longed to kiss, JC forced herself to look away.

Finally, after she helped Blake situate everything, all the customers were on the beach with their assigned kayaks, and the excursion could begin. Looking around to make sure they hadn't forgotten anything, JC had an idea. *Once we are out on the water past the surf break, maybe I can drift with Bella a bit and talk to her*, she thought, feeling a flutter of excitement in her stomach at the idea. If nothing else, she could be the one to help Bella get seated and comfortable on the kayak. Possibly she could ask a question or two. *Although blurting out 'are you married' might be a bit much.* She chuckled at the thought.

Before she could take a step, Blake was beside her. "What do you make of these waves?" he asked, once again bringing JC back to the present moment. Following his gaze, she wanted to kick herself for not paying more attention. Even though the weather was currently perfect, that didn't mean anything. The bright morning sun reflected off the vivid blues and greens of the Pacific, but there were significantly higher swells than normal. The storm out past the horizon was causing the ocean to roll with more intensity. She frowned. They sometimes took tours out with that kind of activity, but it was usually after the risks had passed. The waves were aftereffects and not in front of the storm like what was hitting the shore at the moment. JC faced a tough decision. She could call off the trip, but then Bella might disappear again without JC having a chance to talk to her. Unable to decide, she clenched her jaw in frustration. "Did you ask about the experience level of the honeymooners?"

He nodded. "Regular kayakers," he answered. "Although river mostly, but with some white-water trips. I have zero concern about them navigating out there." What he said was great news. They would be fine if things grew rougher on their return trip from the small offshore island. The question that remained was Bella and if she had ever kayaked before. JC let her eyes drift over. She hoped to see a confident, smiling woman, eager for adventure, but Bella was everything from that image. In fact, the woman was looking down at the sand, almost as if she were sad. *Defeated,* was the word that came immediately to JC's mind. She furrowed her brow, not liking what she saw. *Bella looks crushed*, she thought, not understanding why she would be feeling that way. *And like she doesn't even want to be here.*

For some reason, seeing Bella like that nearly broke JC's heart. She remembered the vibrant, funny, outgoing girl from college and wondered where that person might have gone. It was as if the old Bella was lost somewhere along the way between when they last hugged goodbye and that morning. "Let me talk to her," she said softly to Blake. "Find out what's going on and see if she even wants to go."

BECAUSE HER FOOTSTEPS were muffled by the sand, Bella didn't hear JC until she stood right beside her. Looking up, she saw a hint of worry on her face. "Hey, is something wrong?" JC asked in a gentle voice that spoke straight to Bella's soul. "You don't look like you want to do this."

All Bella could do was shake her head, tongue-tied yet again by the other woman's nearness. *How is she affecting me like this after so much time apart?* Bella wondered, but her heart knew the answer. The same feelings she had back in college may have been dormant for over a decade, yet seeing JC made them very much alive again. *I want her to touch me. To kiss me.* She bit her lip and tried not to stare at JC's mouth.

JC furrowed her brow. "You're sure?"

Bella knew she had to answer, or JC would think something was wrong with her brain. "Yes, of course," she said, trying to sound as casual as possible. "Why would something be wrong?" JC tilted her head and they looked into each other's eyes for a moment. Bella knew she could get lost in those blue depths too easily, so glanced away.

After another beat, JC cleared her throat. "The water's a

little rough this morning," she said. The all-business tone was back. "Have you kayaked before?"

Bella looked at the woman, trying to read JC's face. If she told the truth, she feared it would mean she couldn't go. Ironically, after all the wishing all morning that she could get out of it, suddenly the idea of not spending a few hours with JC was disappointing. *But she'll realize in a second I am lying once I get out on that thing*, she thought. With a sigh, she admitted the truth. "No."

JC nodded but Bella was sure she saw disappointment in her eyes. As she was about to speak, Bella interrupted. "But I still want to go. I'm a quick learner." The statement wasn't true, and she knew it, but she needed to say something. Losing JC again so soon would crush her. "Please?"

JC ran a hand over her face, clearly contemplating the options. Finally, she smiled. "Okay," she said before looking over her shoulder at her partner standing nearby. "Blake, hold up for another couple minutes. I'm taking this kayak back to the trailer."

Bella felt her heart fall. She was being sent home after all. "You got it, JC," he answered. "What's up?"

"I'm going to grab the tandem two-seater," she said, glancing back at Bella. "We'll be taking this adventure together." Before Bella could say a word, JC had the original kayak up on her shoulder and jogged like some sort of superhero up the trail toward the parking lot. The word 'together' lingered in her mind. *A tandem two-seater?* she thought, trying to visualize what that would mean. JC sitting behind her most likely so she could steer. *And provide all the power paddling with those amazing shoulders.* Bella flushed. So many times in college, she had rubbed her friend's muscles under the guise of helping her ease the tension of studying for hours while all the time aching to tell JC the truth.

Involuntarily clenching her hands with a longing to feel

JC's warm skin under her fingertips, Bella wondered as she waited, if there would ever be another opportunity like that again. *Which is ridiculous*, she thought, catching her runaway thoughts. Certainly, someone as wonderful and charming as JC would be in a relationship. Realizing there was no way JC was single, Bella felt the old familiar disappointments at her life trying to return. With a shake of her head, she willed her onrushing negative feelings away. *Not today. Today, I'm with an old friend. And like she said, we are taking this adventure together.* The two women crossing paths couldn't be random coincidence. Fate had brought them to the beach at the same moment, and there had to be a reason.

4

After her second trip from the beach to carry Bella's kayak and then her own, even JC was winded. The fact her heart raced at the thought she would be kayaking with her long-lost love didn't help. Unlocking the straps and then pulling them to loosen the tandem kayak hooked to the trailer behind the jeep, she tried to comprehend that in only a few minutes she would be out on the ocean with Bella Wood. Over the years, on occasional nights often brought on by one too many beers, thoughts of the woman rose to the surface. *Why hadn't I just told her how I felt? Especially right before we finished school,* she would think on those nights with a heart heavy with regret. *What was the worst that could have happened?* Bella's possible rejection and hurting their friendship was what stopped her, although upon graduation, they went their separate ways regardless. In the end, she had lost Bella.

But now I might have a second chance, she thought, unable to keep the grin off her face. *And this time will be different. I will find a way to make sure she knows how I felt in college.* Even if Bella laughed at such a crazy idea that JC used to have a massive crush on her, they could go back to their old lives and forget the day ever happened. Setting the kayak on the ground while she locked up the other two, JC prayed that wouldn't be the outcome. She had been attracted to Bella too long to not have her feelings somehow amount to something. From the very first moment she laid eyes on the woman, JC was hooked.

Lifting the kayak to her shoulder, she let her mind wander back to when that first moment happened so many years ago. It was day one of her freshman year at the university, and there was chaos as families tried to move their kids into the dorms. JC had arrived early on the scene and luckily had little to move in, especially since her family wasn't anywhere to be found. The minute JC turned eighteen, in the middle of her senior year of high school, her dad showed her the door. All summer she couch-surfed until the dorms opened at the start of September. Thankfully, her full-ride scholarship to play basketball for the university paid for housing.

With time to kill and no dorm room roommate in sight, she decided to try out the cafeteria. Using the elevator was out of the question with so much moving happening, so she headed for the stairs. It was four flights, but JC never shied away from extra exercise. In fact, she couldn't wait to try out the school's weight room. After a long and sometimes scary summer, life ahead looked great. In her excitement, JC took the stairs two at a time and burst through the stairwell door into the parking lot... and straight into Bella Wood carrying a fish tank full of water and two goldfish. Only JC's quick reflexes kept the entire apparatus from crashing to the pavement, but in the process of saving the glass, water splashed everywhere. Especially all over JC.

"My fish!" Bella said, and JC watched the young woman drop to her knees to scoop up two flopping fish.

Not knowing much about fish but well aware they needed to stay in water, JC lowered the tank. "Here," she said. "Put them back in."

There was almost nothing left in the fish tank, but Bella complied. "Now what?" she asked, but JC was already moving.

"Come on," she said over her shoulder. "What floor?"

Bella fell into step beside her. "Six," she said, and JC felt a strange moment of disappointment that they couldn't possibly be roommates. Then they were at the door to the stairs.

"Open it, and I'll run this up for you," she said.

Bella hesitated. "Six flights?"

JC shrugged, although her arms were already getting tired. Not that she would ever let it show. "The elevators are jammed with people moving in. I worry it will take too long for these two little guys," she said as Bella opened the door to let JC pass by. "And it's not that heavy."

As she hit the first set of stairs, JC heard Bella say the words that would capture her heart forever. "Thank you so much for helping me. You're my hero."

WATCHING JC jog back to the beach, Bella's heart beat faster. The woman was simply amazing to look at in her sleeveless and very fitted black and gold Oahu Paddle Adventures T-shirt and shorts—strong, tan, and gorgeous. The red tandem kayak appeared to be weightless on her broad shoulders. Plus, something about the confident way she moved looked so sexy. *She's got to have a partner,* Bella thought. *Maybe married with kids? No way she is single.* Not only because of how JC looked either, but because Bella remembered from college how kind and considerate her friend was to everyone. Whenever she saw someone in trouble, even a complete stranger, JC lent a hand. *Like the time she ran my fish tank up six flights of stairs to save my two goldfish.*

JC's strength and athleticism were even more impressive to Bella because she had absolutely zero talent in that department. They could not be more opposite. While JC's college scholarship came from her physical skills, Bella was there because of her grades. *And my ability to write a killer scholarship application essay*, she thought with a small smile. Writing had always been where she shined. *But JC helped with that too.* Her friend read anything and everything Bella wrote, providing constant praise and encouragement. Whenever Bella started to doubt herself and her abilities to create good stories, JC was there to pull her out of it. Although there were others in her life who gave her praise, Bella didn't remember anyone making her believe in herself more than JC Monroe. *How have I gotten by all these years without her in my life?*

Interrupting her ponderings, JC came with the kayak and set it on the sand. "Time to load up," she said with a confident smile. "You take the front." Bella appraised the narrow thing. It seemed impossible that the kayak could keep them both above water. Clearly seeing her hesitate, JC held out her hand. "Here, I'll help you. The nice thing about an ocean kayak like this is you ride in the seats atop it." Bella wasn't sure she agreed, but she took JC's hand anyway. The grip was warm and soft, while feeling strong too. Something in the touch comforted Bella while sending a sensual shiver through her. She was pretty sure she could hang onto JC's hand forever. The contact seemed to have impacted JC too, because Bella noticed color creep into the woman's cheeks that not even her deep tan could hide. *What does that mean?* Bella wondered, not sure if she should be embarrassed or encouraged by JC's reaction. She hoped there would be time to find out.

Trying to look as graceful as possible, but not quite pulling it off, Bella dropped into the seat in the first position on the kayak. "Like this?" she asked with a grimace, and JC nodded, seeming to hold her hand a moment longer than she needed although Bella couldn't be sure. If she wasn't so nervous about the adventure she was about to embark on, she would have analyzed things further. At the moment, she simply didn't want to fall over before they even got in the water.

"You're perfect," JC answered, her voice carrying a slightly husky tone as she stared at Bella. After a beat, Bella saw her swallow hard as JC handed her the paddle. "Remember, arms slightly wider than shoulder width apart, scoops outward. When we get in the water, I'll tell you when to start."

Bella nodded as she took the long, clumsy object in her hands. "Okay," she replied, doing her best to keep the unwieldy thing from smacking her in the head. "Scoops outward. Got it."

JC knelt beside her and put her hand gently over Bella's on the handle. "It's not a death grip. Firm, but flexible," she said softly, but Bella barely heard the words. The woman's touch felt more like a caress and warmth filled her body. Unlike before, now she was certain JC sucked in a small breath. *There's something there*, Bella thought. *A chemistry that she feels too. Different than when we were in college where I was too afraid to say anything. I can't be imagining it, can I?*

Nodding, Bella wished they were anywhere but on that beach about to embark on a trip with other people. "Thank you," she said. "I'm just..." She felt herself blush as the words she wanted to say wouldn't come and forced a little laugh. "I guess I'm really nervous."

"Don't be," JC said. "Just try to relax and have fun. I promise to take care of you." No words could make Bella happier.

5

Touching the soft skin of Bella's warm hand was like touching something electrified. A current of attraction sparked through JC's entire body. *How does she still have this effect on me?* she thought. *I haven't seen her in over a decade and suddenly it's like we are back in college again.* No matter how long they were friends, every time they casually touched even if incidentally, JC had to hide her reaction or else give away her feelings. *Just like right now.* Only the sound of her partner calling her name brought her back to the moment. "You ready to go, JC?" Blake asked from where he stood beside his kayak, and JC gave her head a shake to clear the hundreds of sensual memories threatening to creep in. Back massages, eating from the same plate, sharing a blanket on the couch. *Harmless to Bella, but such torture for me. But that was then. This is now and I'm not some lovesick college student anymore.*

Taking a deep breath to buy time to gather herself, JC finally nodded. "You bet," JC answered as she stood. "Let's get the show on the road. You guys go first."

Blake gave her a long look with a hint of concern clear on

his face. "Okay," he said, hesitating as if he might walk over to talk to her. *It's because I'm acting so weird over Bella,* she thought. *I need to get my head in the game.*

She put on her most confident smile. "Need a push or do you three got it?" she asked, and after a beat, he grinned back.

"Everything is set, and we are ready to hit the water," Blake said. "See you on the other beach."

JC watched the three of them get underway. "Bella," she said, glancing at the woman to see if she was paying attention. "Watch how they paddle hard through the surf break. That's the most challenging part, getting us underway." Bella bit her lip, looking a bit pale. "But I know we can do it."

"She knows we can do it," JC heard Bella murmur under her breath and wasn't sure if her words were a vote of confidence or the opposite. Peering closer, she realized it was the latter. *She looks scared to death*, JC thought, wondering why the woman signed up for something if it made her so uncomfortable. *There's more going on here than meets the eye.*

"Just listen to what I tell you," JC said as reassuringly as she could, moving to the back of the kayak to grab hold of a rope handle. Like she had hundreds of times, she would give them a hard push into the water, jump on, and paddle like hell. Before Bella could protest, she started to lift her end from where it was planted in the sand. "Hang on. We are going. One, two, three." Her timing was perfect, catching the lull in the waves, and she jumped into place with expert precision. In less than a second, JC paddled hard strokes to fight against the force of the ocean trying to push them back onto the beach. It was her favorite moment on every launch —the battle of wills against Mother Nature.

Apparently, Bella liked it less from the little yip of panic she made, but at least she started to paddle. A cresting wave approached. "Oh no," Bella said, her stroke changing to flailing.

Recognizing the start of panic, JC knew she had to rein Bella in, or she would end up capsizing them. "Bella. We are okay. Relax your stroke," she advised in a gentle but firm tone, putting all her strength into the powerful motion to propel them along. "Strong and precise is better than going too fast. Listen to me. Stroke, stroke, stroke." At the last moment, Bella fell into the groove, and together they cut through the biggest wave. Water splashed up the sides of the kayak around them, wetting them both with its spray, but then they were over to the other side and cruising through the water. "Great job! We did it."

"We did it? Already?" Bella asked with a shake of her head.

JC smiled at the tone of amazement in Bella's voice. "Yes, we are past the break. Like I said, that's the hard part," she said. "Congratulations, you are officially a kayaker." There was a pause, and JC wished she could see the face of the woman in front of her. *Is she okay?* JC wondered, but before she could ask, Bella raised her paddle over her head and let out a loud whoop followed by an excited laugh.

"We did it," Bella repeated, sitting up straighter. "I can't believe it. This never happens to me."

JC laughed too, loving the sound of Bella's excitement, and feeling herself getting caught up in Bella's energy. *She's acting like we climbed Mount Everest or something*, she thought, before a realization made her pause. *Maybe somehow, she has.*

FEELING the rise and fall of the kayak on the waves, Bella's heart raced with the exhilaration of being alive. *Not that I really worried I could die,* she thought. *Not entirely.*

"And now we only have to paddle ourselves over to that island," JC said, interrupting her thoughts. "Slow and steady, I'll keep us headed in the right direction."

Bella nodded. "Right," she said as another bit of laughter

bubbled up. "We still need to paddle." Starting to move the paddle again, she struggled for a moment to find purchase on the water. Waiting for JC to comment at any second on the pathetic attempts she made, when nothing came, she glanced over her shoulder. It was impossible to see JC entirely while they were seated, but out of the corner of her eye, Bella saw the even stroke of the woman's movement. *And maybe a glimpse of a proud smile?* she thought. *I forgot how patient she was in college. No matter how much I struggled with something, she never seemed frustrated. Just there for me.* Gathering confidence in the absence of pressure from anyone, Bella concentrated on what Blake and JC had taught her. After a few tries, Bella felt a rhythm to her strokes. The kayak started to move with a little more power. *I'm doing that,* she thought. *I'm actually helping us get there.*

"You're doing great, Bella," JC said as if to reassure her that what she thought was true. "I think you might be a natural kayaker."

Bella laughed. She felt far from anything natural when it came to athletic activities. "I'm not sure I quite believe that," she said. "But thank you." There was a minute as they paddled with only the sound of the ocean around them. Bella worried things were about to become awkward, her mind racing to think of something witty or clever to say. Anything to fill the void and not be boring.

JC interrupted her panic. "Bella, can I ask you a question?" JC asked before Bella could land on anything. "And you don't have to answer it, but I'm curious."

"Okay. What is your question?"

There was a pause, and Bella wondered if JC had changed her mind, but then she went ahead and asked. "Why did you come kayaking today?

It was Bella's turn to hesitate, both because of the actual question as well as why JC asked her. Clearly, Bella's discomfort with the situation was showing. "Uhm," she said. "I guess I wanted to try something new. Something completely different than anything else I've done. Why?"

"Don't take this wrong," JC said. "But you seem a little…" Her voice trailed off.

Bella smiled. "Terrified?" she said filling in the word for her. "I can't explain what motivated me other than I have horrible writer's block." She slowed her paddling. "I don't know. Maybe I thought a radical shock to my system would help."

"Ah, I see," JC said. "Well, I have to tell you, I am very impressed. Especially coming out here alone. Was that part of your test too? To try kayaking on your own?"

Not sure how best to explain why she was alone in paradise, Bella started back into a rhythmic stroke. "Something like that," she murmured, ready to change the subject. The last thing she wanted was for JC to know what a sad case she was—all alone in Hawaii, sitting inside her condo all day trying to write. *And failing at it miserably,* she thought with a sigh. *Time to get off this subject.* "And now I get to ask you a question."

"Okay, shoot," JC said, sounding as if there wasn't a question in the world that would catch her off guard.

Bella tried not to feel a little envious. Everything caught her off guard it seemed. "How did you end up working at a kayaking adventure company in Hawaii?" Bella asked. "You never talked about anything like it."

JC laughed. "Well for starters, I don't work for Oahu Paddle Adventures, I own it."

Bella's eyebrows went up. "JC, that's fantastic," she said. "But it still doesn't explain how it happened."

"That's kind of a funny story," JC said with a smile in her voice. "I came over here about three years after we graduated on vacation with my girlfriend." *Girlfriend?* Bella thought, hearing nothing else. A flame of hope she didn't realize she was holding died. *Of course, she has a girlfriend. She's fun, intelligent, great body, and has her own business in paradise.* "Bella? Are you okay?"

Bella snapped back into focus. "I'm sorry. What's wrong?"

"You stopped paddling," JC said. "What happened?"

"Oh," Bella said, starting to paddle again. "Just a little cramp. I'm okay."

"You're sure?"

Nodding, Bella simply wanted to move past the girlfriend reference and forget about her fantasy that JC was single. "I'm sure," she said. "I'm really proud of you, JC. You're as amazing as I always thought you would be."

6

As they paddled toward the small island to catch up with Blake and the others, JC wasn't happy with the increasing choppiness of the water. Although they rode easily enough over the waves in the kayak, her years of experience crossing to the island let her know things could quickly get rougher. Scanning the horizon, the sky was still cloudless, but there was definitely something beyond that was affecting the ocean. She no longer had any doubt that the weather forecast was accurate. *Let's hope the storm holds off until everyone enjoys their morning on the island*, she thought. She wanted to show Bella a few sites that made the location so special. Although there wasn't much to give her a sense Bella was into wildlife or outdoor activities, even she would have to be impressed with some of the views.

The option they always offered to customers was to swim in the lagoon on the west side of the island, but again, JC felt that might be a stretch for Bella. She seemed a little tentative around the ocean. Still, that didn't mean she didn't like swimming in general. Many people she encountered were fine in a manmade pool and could handle the lagoon but found the greater ocean daunting. All of which was totally unlike JC who couldn't get enough of the sea whether on it, in it, or under it.

Looking ahead, she watched as Blake and the other couple landed on the beach, making it look easy when they slid up on the sand. JC appreciated the experience the newlyweds brought to the kayaking excursion. It allowed her to focus on Bella, and she would be happier once they were on land. The lack of conversation from Bella for the last few minutes had her concerned. As if the woman wasn't feeling well. *Seasick?* she wondered. *That seems unlikely.* Even with the rougher water, getting sick on a kayak was unusual.

For some strange reason, JC was having a tough time keeping a conversation going with Bella. After JC's quick story about ending up with a business in Hawaii, Bella had gone quiet. Usually for JC, conversation came naturally with her clients. *But being around Bella makes me a little tongue-tied,* she thought. *I just don't want to screw anything up.* All she could do was hope things would come more easily once they were on the island taking in sights.

"Okay, Bella," JC said, maneuvering them near shore. "You can stop paddling and lift your oar, and I'll take us in from here."

"Do I only sit here?" Bella asked doubt in her voice. "Or do I jump out when we are on the beach?"

"All you need to do is relax and wait for Blake or me to help you stand and step off the kayak," JC said, steering with the oncoming wave. Then they were running up on the sand where Blake grabbed hold of the kayak with the rope tied on the front.

Blake grinned as he pulled them further up on shore. "Perfect landing," he said. As JC instructed, Bella didn't move to get out until Blake offered his hand to help. While Bella struggled to her feet, JC dismounted too. Even though they were off the water, the three stood on an incline, and when Bella took a step, she stumbled backward—heading straight for the water.

"Oh God," she said, waving her arms to try to get her balance back. In a flash, JC grabbed her around the waist and held her steady. The body-to-body contact was enough to take JC's breath away. The woman felt perfect in her arms. *I could hold her like this all day*, she thought but felt Bella rest a hand on her forearm.

"I'm okay," she whispered. "Thank you." JC immediately let go, causing Bella to sway, but before anyone could react, she took a step and righted herself. Clearly flustered, Bella looked around. "Do I need my bag?"

Blake pulled her drybag from the tiedown to hand it to her. "Head on over to join the others," he said. "And then we can get set for our hike." Without a word, Bella started across the sand, and JC couldn't shake the thought something was off. *Did I say something wrong out on the water?* she wondered. With a frustrated shake of her head, she forced herself to refocus on the more pressing issue at hand.

JC helped Blake pull the kayak higher onto the beach. "What do you think?" she said, nodding toward the ocean. "Rougher than normal."

Blake furrowed his brow. "Yeah," he said. "I did notice things are picking up. The couple is no problem. Naturals."

"I'm not worried about them," JC said, thinking of Bella's overall unease being on the kayak. "Let's keep an eye on the waves. I want us to enjoy our morning and not have to cancel midstream, but if the wind picks up, we might have to call it a day."

USING ALL her effort to walk across the beach without tripping over her own feet, Bella felt heat on her cheeks from what happened. After getting out of the kayak, she had stumbled, headed straight for the water, and then JC was there. *With her strong, sure arms around me,* she thought. *How long has it been since someone had their arms around me? Even by accident?* She shook her head. *Way too long considering my reaction.* The contact brought a wave of emotions of its own—a little embarrassment and a lot of desire. *I need to get a grip on this. It was an accident, for crying out loud.*

"Was that fabulous or what?" the bride of the newlywed couple said the minute Bella joined them. "I love the water. And the ocean! So majestic and magical. Doesn't it all just make you feel more alive?"

Bella blinked under the onslaught of enthusiasm. "Um," she said. "Yes?" She wasn't so sure the ocean made her feel more alive or if being on the beach made her simply feel glad she survived. Either way, she decided the woman deserved a smile at the least. Being so upbeat had to take a lot of energy. Before the conversation could continue, Blake and JC walked to them.

"Okay, everybody," Blake said, clapping his hands together with almost as much enthusiasm as the bride. *Am I the only one who isn't thrilled here?* she wondered, glancing at JC. The woman watched her, looking away when their eyes met. There was so much to be confused about there. Bella kept feeling that JC was attracted to her, but then she remembered there was a girlfriend to consider. JC wasn't available. Period. Ignoring the sinking feeling in her stomach, Bella refocused on Blake's spiel. "We're going to make a quick hike up and around the north end of the island until we get to one of the scenic overlooks. Is everybody ready?" The married couple nodded with their usual fervor, but Bella was stuck on the word 'up' in Blake's speech. When she signed on for the trip, there wasn't any mention of hiking anywhere, particularly not 'up.' As an author who sat at a desk all day, her cardio was crap, and she knew it. *Well, this will only continue to get embarrassing.* "Do you want to take the lead?" It took a beat for Bella to realize Blake had asked her the question.

She barked out a laugh. "Oh no," she said. "I might stay here and sit on that rock over there." Waving a hand in the direction of a smooth boulder in the sun, the idea grew on her by the second.

Blake laughed. "That wouldn't be any fun," he said, clearly not realizing Bella was entirely serious. Before she could explain her utter lack of interest in going anywhere, JC stepped right beside her. Their bodies were so close Bella swore she felt heat radiating off the woman's skin. It was extremely distracting, but in the best possible way.

The woman gave Blake a big smile. "I'll hang back with Bella," JC said. "And we will meet you three at the other side."

Blake gave her a little salute along with a smile in return. "You got it," he said before looking at the newlyweds. "Ready to go to the top?"

Before starting, the bride turned to Bella. "Are you sure you don't want to lead?" she asked, a considerate tone in her voice. "We aren't in a hurry, and I plan to take a lot of pictures along the way."

Although she appreciated the woman's thoughtful offer, Bella shook her head. "Really. It's fine," she said. "Go on without me and if it works out, I will meet you there."

"Okay," the bride said, back to her bubbly self as she looked at Blake. "Then let's do this."

Without another word, the three left at a pace aggressive enough to make Bella wince. *No way would I be able to do that,* she thought. *Nor do I want to.* "We can go at whatever pace you want," JC said as if reading her mind. "Or we can stay right here. It's up to you, but I promise some of the views along the trail are stellar."

"Are they?" Bella asked, focusing on JC's face, tempted for a moment to tell her the view was pretty stellar right there, but then she stifled a laugh. She would never in a million years say something so bold. Instead, she decided to be a good sport and not make JC wait with her on the beach. Besides, if she stayed there, she would simply wallow in the disappointment that JC had found someone else. Looking at the trail that wound away from the beach where they stood, she tried not to wince at the idea of climbing it and plastered a smile on her face. "Well, then I guess we better go see them."

7

JC held back as the other three in their tour group started on the dirt trail leading to the northern end of the island. There was no need to rush as few paths were available, and she knew where they would go if she took Bella that way. The routes were generally the same for every tour. Because the property was considered a national park, visitors were required to follow certain protocols. Staying on the marked routes was foremost among the rules to follow. "Bella, are you sure? I promise there is no pressure to make the hike," JC said when everyone else was well out of earshot. "Hanging out on the beach this morning is fine."

Bella looked JC up and down as if appraising how sincere her offer was under the circumstances. "Honestly? I just wasn't expecting to do much," she explained. "Other than surviving the kayaking, I mean. I'm not averse to hiking, don't think that I am not—"

JC held up her hands to slow the woman's rush of information. "It's really okay," JC said, unable to keep from smiling at the defensive rambling. "You're on vacation, and I get it."

"Well, that's the thing," Bella said with a frown. "I'm not on vacation."

JC's brow furrowed with confusion. "Wait. If you're not here on vacation, why are you in Hawaii?"

Throwing up her hands, Bella shook her head. "I keep asking myself that too. I thought coming here would be the glorious change I needed. To help me get my head on straight."

"And?" JC asked, more perplexed than ever. Their eyes met and held. "Nothing glorious so far?"

Bella looked on the verge of saying something but then let out a sigh, nodding in the direction of the trail. "Never mind. I'm ready to do this if you'll go slow."

Curious but not ready to press, JC started them on the trail at an easy pace. "I can do slow," she murmured. As they left the sandy beach behind, the sound of the waves faded, and the path narrowed with lush tropical foliage on both sides.

Multiple colors of green were sprinkled with bits of color from the variety of hibiscus flowers. "This is so beautiful," she heard Bella murmur from behind her and slowed to look back. "I mean, I knew it would be. This is Hawaii, but..." Her words trailed off. Again, JC had the impression Bella didn't spend enough time outdoors. Just then, a bird chirped in the distance. Bella stopped, her eyes searching the trees.

JC smiled at her reaction. "I'iwi," she said before Bella could ask. "Part of the endangered species here. Pretty sound, right?" A flicker of red gave away where the small bird perched on a branch. Cocking its head, it seemed to contemplate them for a moment before darting away. No matter how many times JC saw one of the little creatures, she found them inspiring. The last of their kind. She turned to

Bella. "I want you to know, that was special. Rare to see one anymore."

Bella's eyes widened. "Really?" she asked softly. "Everything about it was beautiful."

Watching the woman continue to scan the trees for another sighting, JC studied her. She remembered the long, dark hair and petite body, but the aura around her was different. *Less confident? Definitely,* she thought. *And much more closed off. Where did the carefree young woman set to change the literary world go?*

Stepping closer, JC leaned in. "You're lucky," JC said, making Bella turn toward her.

She stared. "Me?" she said with a shake of her head as if JC's words were impossible. "Why?"

JC smiled, wanting to find a way to break past the walls Bella had clearly built over the years. "Almost no one sees the I'iwi," she said. "I've led dozens of people, including devoted bird watchers, on tours here, and as much as they try to find it, the little bird doesn't show up."

Bella bit her lip and let her eyes roam back to the trees. "But that never happens for me," she whispered. "Why today?"

"Maybe you're in the right place at the right time," JC said softly, believing her words to be true for both of them. Although she didn't know precisely why Bella was on the island, she believed things rarely happened by accident. Her emotions toward the woman grew stronger by the minute. Everything she learned about Bella drew her closer. *And it's not only because we have a history as friends,* she thought. *Even if we first met, I think the chemistry would be there.* An urge to tell Bella what she felt was enough to make JC hold her breath. The last thing she wanted was to scare her away with some random statement about being attracted. *But before this day is over, I will find out why she is here in Hawaii.* JC wouldn't leave until the mystery of why Bella Wood was on the island was solved.

BASKING in the glow of not only hearing the song of but also seeing the bright red I'iwi, Bella followed JC's slow pace along the dirt trail. The woman had said Bella was lucky, and she wasn't sure what to make of the statement. There were times in her life she was fortunate, but those days seemed like distant memories. *Of course, I feel like today is something special*, she thought, looking at the back of her long-lost friend. Seeing solid shoulders and a fit body from kayaking, Bella couldn't help but appreciate the view. She guessed JC spent a lot of time outdoors from how she looked. *But then, who wouldn't here in paradise?* After being cooped up in her rented condo trying to write, the fresh air lightly scented with plumerias filled her, and the warm sunshine felt amazing on her face. For the first time since boarding the van that morning, Bella was truly happy she decided to be brave and come on the adventure.

"Penny for your thoughts?" JC said with a smile, looking back over her shoulder. "Or am I interrupting?"

Bella smiled back. "Not at all," she said. "I was thinking about how amazing it is here and that I'm so very glad I came today." She sighed with contentment. "This day was exactly what I needed to get my creative juices flowing."

JC turned until she was walking backward. It was obvious she knew the trail like the back of her hand. "Creative juices?" she asked with a tilt of her head. "That sort of talk sounds vaguely familiar from our days in the dorms." She grinned. "Does this trip have something to do with your writing?"

Shy for a reason she couldn't understand, Bella shrugged

a shoulder. "Yes, pretty much," she said. "I'm finding it hard to think of anything to say lately. I'm stuck."

"I see," JC said, nodding. "Is this still your memoir from college?"

Bella paused to think before answering, realizing JC had no idea what she had accomplished since they last saw each other. "Well," she started, in a way glad JC wasn't aware of her bestselling novel. The last thing she needed was for her to be like so many others expecting another book to appear. By not knowing, JC liked Bella for her and not the love story she wrote last year. *So, what do I tell her?* she wondered as they walked. *She's looking at me, and I need to say something.*

She shook her head. "No, I gave up on that," she gave a little laugh. "Why is it people at twenty-four think they have enough life experience to write such a thing anyway?"

JC laughed too and shook her head. "Good point," she said. "But what are you working on then?" Biting her lip, Bella walked a little further before making up her mind. The last thing she wanted was to deceive her friend after finally seeing her again after so long. *Especially since I can tell she is pretty special,* she thought. *And no doubt honest as the day is long.*

"Well," Bella started. "I write angst-filled sapphic romance novels."

"Sapphic?" JC asked.

Bella nodded. "Yes, women loving women predominantly," she answered. She looked away into the distance. "I actually wrote a bestseller."

JC stopped in the middle of the trail. "No kidding," she said a frown on her beautiful face. "How in the world did I not know that?"

Giving her head a little shake, Bella came to a stop barely a foot away from JC. "Do you read lesbian romance, JC?" she asked, not immune to the closeness between them. All she would have to do was reach out, and Bella could touch the woman's face. *How would she react?* she wondered before forcing herself to focus.

Clearing her throat, JC looked almost apologetic. "Well," JC said. "No, I don't. I'm kind of into thrillers. But still…" Her look softened and Bella could see nothing but tenderness in her eyes. "It's you." The two words could infer so much, Bella didn't know what to say. She met JC's eyes with her own. Suddenly, all the years lost between them were gone, and she was back in her dorm room, longing for JC to bridge the gap between them. To reach for her. To lean in. She bit her lip and watched JC swallow hard. "I can't wait to read your book." Her voice was husky, full of something Bella hoped was longing.

"You don't have to do that," Bella murmured, keeping up the small talk while her emotions whirled inside her. *If only I could say what I am feeling,* she thought but was afraid to ruin the little bit growing between them. "It's not a big deal."

JC shook her head but held her eyes. "It is to me."

8

Watching as a blush slowly crept up Bella's cheeks, JC couldn't understand why her friend would think for even a second that her writing any kind of a book wasn't special. Especially to JC. As if to underline her discomfort, Bella rubbed the toe of her sandal in the sandy dirt to dislodge a pebble, no longer meeting JC's eyes. "I'm glad you think so," she mumbled. "But it's really not a big deal. I think I was lucky." JC continued to study the woman's face. *Lucky? I don't believe that. Where is her confidence? What has happened to change her?* she found herself thinking again. *This is not the same person I knew in college. In school, she had every expectation of being a bestselling author. Why does she seem almost embarrassed by her achievement?*

"Bella," JC said. "I know it wasn't luck. You were an amazing writer in school, and I am sure that hasn't changed. I'm not surprised for a second people love what you create for them to read."

Bella gave her a small smile before looking up the trail, clearly not comfortable with the conversation. "We should probably get going, don't you think?" she asked. "To meet the others?"

JC fought back a sigh even though it was hard not to be a little disappointed Bella wouldn't talk to her. Although the woman was right, and they did need to start moving, her suggestion was clearly a way to deflect more questions and change the subject.

With a nod, JC prepared to go uphill again. "Yes," she agreed, but stayed in place until Bella moved. "We should move on, but that doesn't mean I want to stop talking." The pair started on the trail, and JC decided to take a little different approach to get her to open up. "So, tell me more about the process. You always wanted to be a writer. What is it like?" With the woman following behind her, JC couldn't see her face. Bella was quiet while they kept going another twenty feet and JC began to worry she pressed too hard.

She opened her mouth to apologize, but Bella beat her. "It's harder than I thought it would be," she finally said. "There's a lot more pressure."

"Pressure?" JC frowned. "Why?"

"Because I don't want to disappoint my readers," she answered with a wry laugh. "I worry about it so much that I can't seem to write anything else." JC heard her let out a long sigh. "I have such horrible writer's block, and like I said, I hope a change will snap me out of it."

JC processed what Bella said, thinking back over her earlier comments. *Is that why she's so down on herself?* she wondered. *Because she's worried and can't write?* JC glanced back, smiling at Bella. "Well, this place is magical," she said, wishing there was a way to help Bella remember how she once was. "You'll find your words here. I promise."

"Do you?"

"I do. And I'm sorry I can't help with ideas," she said with a laugh. "If you recall, I totally suck at creative stuff."

Bella surprised her with a sincere laugh in return. "Yes, actually I do recall," she said. "But you excelled at so many other things." She shook her head but kept smiling. "You were always so full of energy. You never seemed to stop moving."

"Still the case," JC admitted. Sitting still was never her strong suit. Even now, staying in one place doing the same thing for hours didn't appeal to her. "I think that's why I wanted to start the kayaking business. You know, to keep myself occupied." They rounded a bend in the trail, and the trees thinned, letting them enjoy a view of blue ocean. "Let's stop for another minute. This is a pretty spot."

Bella came to stand beside her. "You're right," she said. "This is a great view." JC barely heard what she said. Her eyes focused on the waves, and they were rougher than she liked. Even from where she and Bella stood, semi-protected by the trees, a warm, steady breeze blew in her face. *The ride back is going to be rough*, she thought, wanting to move faster to the island's crest and look further west out to sea. *I need to know what is on the horizon and see how far away the storm is.*

She realized Bella had asked her a question. "I'm sorry. What did you say? I was thinking about the waves."

A look of concern crossed Bella's face. "Is there a problem?" she asked, scanning the water herself. "You look worried."

JC kicked herself for not keeping a better poker face. The last thing she wanted to do was concern Bella, but she wouldn't lie to her. "It's getting a little rougher than normal. But nothing we can't handle," she answered, ready to steer the subject back to Bella. "Now, what was your question?"

Bella tilted her head as if not sure she was ready to let the conversation about the waves go but then repeated what she said. "I asked you if your girlfriend is as active as you are?"

JC's eyebrows shot up. "My girlfriend?" she said, completely confused. "What girlfriend?"

Bella didn't know what to make of the look on JC's face. Her friend was clearly puzzled by her question, which in turn confused Bella. While they were still on the kayak, she clearly heard JC say she started Oahu Paddle Adventures with her girlfriend. "Your girlfriend," Bella said. "Did you not say she helped you start your business?"

"Ohhh," JC said with a nod. "I see what happened there. And to answer your question—yes, I did start it with Chris, but we're not together anymore."

Letting the words sink in, Bella focused on keeping the excitement she felt over the new information off her face. *JC might be single?* she wondered. *Although, even if she broke up with that girlfriend doesn't mean she is alone.*

Gathering her nerve, something she rarely did anymore, Bella squared her shoulders. "I see. So, does that mean you're not in a relationship now?"

"With Chris?" JC asked with raised eyebrows, looking like she still wasn't tracking the conversation entirely. "No. I bought her out five years ago, when she moved back to the mainland." She shrugged. "We're still friends but don't do much more than email once or twice a year."

Bella shook her head, rushing her words before losing all her nerve. "That's not quite what I was asking…" she said, but then her confidence stalled. *There's no sense in making a complete ass of myself over this,* she thought and decided to change the subject, but JC spoke up first.

She met Bella's eyes. "What are you asking me, Bella?"

Unable to keep from glancing away, Bella looked at the ocean, and saw that whitecaps lined the rich blue color. "Well," she said with a bit of laugh at her situation. Amazingly, she found herself asking an old friend who was basically a stranger if she was alone and maybe available to consider a relationship. *And if she is?* Bella thought. *Then what? She hasn't asked about my status or anything either.* Knowing it was too late to turn back, Bella forged ahead. "I guess I was asking if you were, um… maybe single?" There was a pause, and after a beat, Bella stole a glance at JC, not sure what to expect. *Please don't let her laugh at me.* Bella feared being embarrassed most of all.

Instead, JC stepped closer. "Hey," she said. "Stop and look at me. You *guess* you're asking?" Letting her eyes roam JC's face, Bella saw no sign that her friend was about to laugh at her. Instead, there was a tenderness in her eyes. *Oh God,* she thought. *Not pity. That's worst of all.*

Looking away again, she waved her hands. "Never mind," she said. "Let's get going again."

JC reached for her, grasping one of her hands. "Don't do that," she said. "Let's talk about this." The physical contact was such a pleasant surprise, Bella froze. Heat radiated through her from where their hands clasped. "To answer your question, I'm not seeing anyone."

Trying to keep her voice steady while her heart raced, Bella could barely believe her ears. "But you're so amazing… why not?" she asked softly, and JC shook her head.

"Not for any reason other than I haven't been looking," she said, and pulled on Bella's hand until they were face to face. "I work a lot, but that's not really the reason. Mostly I haven't found anyone I feel special about." Bella watched her swallow hard before continuing. "No one special like you." A tingle of excitement ran over Bella at the beautiful words. She hadn't been special to someone for a long time. *Have I ever?* she thought. *Aside from when I was in college with JC. Was I special to her then?*

"I think you're special too," Bella said, wishing she could

call on her muse to come up with something more eloquent. They were like a couple of teenagers passing notes asking, "Do you like me?" with checkboxes for "yes or no." Then, a thought occurred to her. JC hadn't asked if she were single. *Does that mean she's not thinking like I am?* she worried. *Am I way off base here?*

As if reading her thoughts, JC glanced away in her own moment of shyness. "So…" she started. "Since I confessed…"

Feeling a wash of relief, Bella squeezed her hand. "I'm single too," she confessed. "Here all by myself on this beautiful island trying to figure out what to write." She laughed, feeling almost giddy as the reality of their situation set in. Both single. Both there. "I only came on this adventure on a whim after too many glasses of wine. And I'm so glad I did."

9

The woman's words were magic to JC's ears. *And I think they are to my heart too,* she thought, as crazy as that was considering they had only reconnected after fifteen years a couple of hours ago. *But the more time I spend with her, I am realizing my love never faded.* A part of JC wanted to pull the woman even closer to whisper exactly that into her ear, but she kept it all to herself. The last thing she wanted to do while standing there holding hands with a beautiful view of the ocean was overwhelm Bella. More than once that morning, the writer seemed skittish and shy. *And I can't have her running away from me because I very much want this to go on past today.* JC realized what she wanted was the opportunity to show Bella the most beautiful places that Oahu had to offer. *She deserves to see how magical life can be again.*

"If I promise you something amazing at the end of our hike, can we go a little faster?" JC asked, watching Bella's expression.

There was a shadow of skepticism, but it quickly faded.

"Maybe," Bella said with a hint of a playful smile that gave JC a glimmer of the woman she once knew. "Is it a secret?"

JC tilted her head and looked at the blue sky to ponder the question. "Sort of," she said after a beat. "Are you wearing a swimsuit under your clothes?" A light blush came to Bella's cheeks, and JC hesitated. She hadn't meant to put the woman on the spot and started to backpedal. "Hey, not that it matters. I mean, I asked because we recommend it in the brochure and—"

Bella laughed. "It's okay, JC. Yes, I am," she replied. "But don't expect to see it. I put it on in a very brave moment this morning, because I spent so much money on it yesterday. And it doesn't cover as much as I hoped."

It was JC's turn to blush as her mind tried to imagine Bella's body. Even though they spent nearly every waking hour together in college, they were both always modest. *Which was probably for the best, or I might have exploded,* she thought, forcing a little laugh. "Fair enough," she said. "The experience is still worth it. Let's go."

With that, she led them along the quickest route to the tiny lagoon on the other side of the small island. Usually, the tour would first take them to the summit, and she imagined that was where Blake and the newlyweds were at the moment. *Which could give us little privacy*, she thought before reminding herself that shouldn't be important. For all she knew, she was misreading the depth of every signal Bella was sending. Still, JC wanted as many memorable moments as she could get with Bella, so she couldn't help but hope Blake would hike slowly.

After fifteen minutes, JC stopped. Around the corner was a view of the lagoon fed by a small spring that came up from miles beneath the ocean's surface as part of the volcanic rock the island sat on. "We're almost there," she said, for the first time noticing how winded Bella was, and that there was a light sheen of sweat on her face.

"I'm sorry," the woman apologized after a deep breath. "I am completely out of shape."

JC mentally kicked herself for not being more observant. "You should have said something. I would have slowed down."

Bella held up a hand to stop her apologies. "No," she said. "It was obvious you wanted to get here quickly." She looked around, but there was nothing much to see but trees. "Is this it?"

Smiling, JC shook her head. "Not at all. Cover your eyes." Bella surprised JC by responding without hesitation. *Because she trusts me,* she realized, touched by the thought. *I need to make sure I never do anything to lose that.* Taking her by the elbow, JC walked them around the last bend in the trail. Ahead was an exquisite view of turquoise waters that made up the calm pool. "Okay." JC slid her hand to the middle of Bella's back to steady her and heard Bella suck in a breath at the contact. *Is that from my touch?* The idea caused a warmth to spread through JC, and she did not back away. "You can look."

Slowly Bella lowered her hands, and her mouth opened, but she didn't say a word for a moment as she stared at what JC knew was a breathtaking sight below. "JC, it's magical," Bella finally said, and JC smiled.

"I take it that means you like it?" she asked.

Bella slowly nodded. "I do," she said. "I honestly think it's one of the most incredible views I've ever seen."

STANDING at the top of the hill, looking down at the lagoon, Bella felt like she was in the middle of one of the romance novels she loved to read. The water looked inviting as it glimmered blue against the golden sandy beach. A few green palm trees swayed at the edge, throwing shade over one corner, and at the base of the black lava rock wall, she could see where the tiniest bit of a waterfall sprang from the rocks. *If I didn't know better, I would think I was dreaming*, Bella thought. *It's just so perfect.* Glancing over, she found JC watching her. *Yes, perfect.* There she was in paradise standing beside a woman she had somehow lost track of but was slowly realizing she had never really forgotten.

"Shall we go down?" JC asked. "The water will be warm and perfect for a swim."

Although not sure about the swimming part, Bella nodded. At the least, she could wade. "Absolutely," Bella said. "I'll follow you."

JC led the way down a short, but steep trail of switchbacks until they were on the narrow strip of beach. As soon as she hit the sand, the woman grabbed the hem of her tank top and stripped down to her bikini top before tossing the shirt onto the rocks. "I think it's time for a quick dip," she said as she kicked off her sandals. Bella watched with her mouth open in surprise as she took in the sight of the goddess jogging a few steps before taking a shallow dive into the pristine water. *Yep, like right out of a romance novel*, Bella thought. *Only I don't think I fit the mold of the leading lady.* She was suddenly self-conscious of her body under the oversized T-shirt that she wore. She hadn't lied when she said she was wearing a swimsuit underneath and that she had spent too much money on it the day before. She also hadn't lied that the small pieces of bright red fabric didn't cover as much as she hoped. When JC surfaced, she shook her head to clear the water out of her eyes and looked at Bella. "You should try it." She was smiling ear to ear. "It's bathwater warm."

Bella bit her lip. It looked so inviting. *What do I have to lose?* she wondered. *I'm well past old enough to stop worrying about impressing people.* Somehow she knew that JC would never judge her. A few extra pounds around her middle would be nothing in the eyes of her long-lost friend. *And let's be honest, I am hoping she will in some way be more than that when this is all said and done.* Taking a deep breath, Bella slipped the baggy shirt over her head and quickly waded into the water. JC's description of the temperature wasn't wrong. It was bathwater warm and absolutely exquisite. Once she submerged to her shoulders, Bella let out a little laugh, thrilled with the sense of freedom and adventure. "I can't believe I'm actually doing this," she said. "What an incredible day."

"Are you happy?" she heard JC ask and turned to look at her. A serious expression was on her friend's face and their eyes held over the calm blue water.

Bella nodded. "More than I can ever express," she whispered, feeling the chemistry crackling between them. Slowly, JC swam in her direction, closing the distance between them. *If this were one of my novels, then she would be about to kiss me*, Bella thought, waiting with anticipation to see if it would come true. It had been a long time since she was kissed and never in such a romantic setting. She bit her lip and saw the desire in JC's eyes. *I think she truly wants me.* The realization made her catch her breath. Every part of her body was alive, yearning for JC's embrace.

When they were only a foot apart, Bella's hopes were dashed when she heard Blake calling to them.

"Hello," he said. "You must've taken the shortcut."

All the frustration Bella felt at the moment reflected in JC's face. Filled with a sense of utter disappointment, Bella closed her eyes, knowing there could never possibly be another moment as magical as the one she almost shared with JC. *Please don't let this be the end of everything*, she thought before opening her eyes to turn in the direction of the beach.

Blake stepped onto the sand with the newlywed couple behind him.

"Oh, this is so beautiful," the bride gushed as she moved to the water's edge. "And is that a waterfall?" Bella watched her turn to her husband. "Baby, come on, I want to swim over there." Then she paused as if only just noticing Bella was already in the water. A sincere smile of pleasure crossed her face. "Now aren't you glad you decided to hike a little?"

Even though the timing of the woman's arrival was horrible, Bella couldn't help but return the smile. "I am. Very much," she answered and could not mean it more.

10

JC's employee and partner was one of her favorite people in the world. She and Blake more than worked together but were good friends and often hung out on Friday nights. The guy had a wonderful girlfriend named Heather, who was as friendly and fun as he was. Because JC had no other relatives on the island, they often treated her like family for holidays and special events. *So, I'm going to miss him*, she thought as she watched him pull off his T-shirt before diving into the water. *Because after his horribly timed interruption, I'm going to kill him.*

Although she didn't mean it literally, the frustration she felt over his interruption was genuine. If the three others from their tour group hadn't descended on them when they did, she was certain Bella would have let JC kiss her. A look in the woman's dark eyes, the way her lips had slightly parted, and how she had paused as JC drew nearer—every sign was a green light that she wanted the same thing JC did. *And then, bam, here comes Blake*, she thought, holding back a groan. *And everybody jumped in the water.* She wasn't surprised the newlyweds were excited to swim in the lagoon though and certainly couldn't blame anyone for the intrusion. It was simply a case of miscommunication and bad timing.

Looking at Bella, her old friend had turned away to move her hands casually back and forth through the warm water as she walked deeper into the lagoon. If she was frustrated too, JC couldn't see it. *But she's definitely not interested in interacting with me in front of the others,* she thought with a pang of disappointment. *I'll simply have to be patient.*

Hearing splashing, JC turned to see Blake swimming toward her while the newlyweds went to check out the small waterfall. "Hey, there," he said, clearing his throat before dropping his voice to a whisper. "I think I kinda, well, did I interrupt something?"

JC sighed. "Not exactly," she answered, keeping her voice low too. "But if you were two minutes later, you might have seen me kiss her."

"No way," Blake said, eyes wide and starting to grin. "That's awesome."

Waving a hand, JC shushed him before Bella could overhear. Sound carried easily over the water's surface. "Don't get excited," she said. "Like I said, you *might* have. I'm not sure what she's thinking about me."

Blake nodded. "Okay, okay," he said. "Well, something to look forward to after we get back to the shore? Maybe you can go out on a date?"

Maybe, JC thought, not sure how to proceed. "I don't know," she said and decided it was time to change the subject. "Did you three get to the summit?"

"Yeah," he said his face growing serious. "Ocean was getting choppier."

Nodding, JC ran through their options in her mind. "Probably should cut this trip short," she finally said, although usually the tour included a simple lunch of deli sandwiches and soda or water that Blake carried in a dry bag on his kayak. "I can offer them all a refund or credit toward a redo."

"Okay," Blake said, looking a little more relieved than JC had expected. *Am I letting my desire to spend more time with Bella cloud my judgment?* she wondered, not happy that it was even a question in her mind. Her client's safety was the number one priority, and there should never be an exception.

JC watched the newlyweds splashing water at each other at the base of the falls. "Let's give them another few minutes but go tell them know we need to leave soon," she said to Blake. "I'll break the news to Bella."

The trick would be not frightening the woman while still being honest about why they were leaving early. Considering Bella's concerns with kayaking to the island in the first place, a rougher ride back would not be popular. *Maybe I shouldn't have brought her over,* JC thought, again feeling a pang of unease at her possible lack of good judgment. All she could do was hope the storm kept sitting offshore a little longer. Swimming toward Bella, JC also hoped the woman would forgive her if things got too scary.

"Hi," she said, and Bella turned around, a gentle smile on her face. Encouraged, JC moved closer until they were only an arm's length apart. "I wanted to let you know we will be heading back to the kayaks soon."

Bella furrowed her brow. "Already? That doesn't sound particularly reassuring," she said, pausing for a second to apparently process the change. Then she looked hard at JC. "Is it because of what you saw at the overlook before? The bigger waves?"

"Yes," JC replied, seeing no reason to try and hide the facts. "An early summer storm is coming our way, and I don't want to chance it."

"Chance what exactly?"

"Well," JC said. "Mainly being stuck on the island until it passes."

Bella blinked at JC, not able to tell by the look on the woman's face if she was serious or not. *It seems like an unlikely thing to joke about being trapped,* she thought. *But I remember she was funny in college. Still, not in a way to make a person worry.* "Could that actually happen?" she finally asked. "Us being stuck here in a storm?"

"Yes, it could happen in a worst-case scenario," she answered, motioning toward the beach. Realizing JC wanted them to get out of the lagoon immediately, Bella followed the woman as she started walking through the water toward the shore. "But we won't let it because we are going to take off before the storm gets here."

Feeling a tiny bit more assured, Bella hurried to her pile of things the moment they stepped on the beach. Grabbing her baggy T-shirt, she quickly shook the sand off it, ready to put it on. There was no sense letting JC see her love handles even if they were in a hurry to get back on the trail to the other beach. While she pulled it over her head, the newly-weds and Blake swam up and climbed out of the water. "Sorry about this," JC said once everyone gathered around. "I didn't anticipate the storm coming in early enough to have to cancel, but I can give refunds or credits toward another later trip."

"I was wondering about that storm forecast," the usually quiet husband said. "Things looked to be getting choppy from what I could see from the summit." He put his arm around his wife's waist. "Leaving seems the smart thing to do."

"And we can take a credit toward another trip," the

woman said, her perpetual cheerfulness not wavering. "I love it here, and we will definitely be back soon."

Not sure what to say, Bella certainly didn't want JC to have to issue her a refund but was very unlikely she would ever kayak again. Once seemed enough, and she dreaded the trip back over the water as it was. "We can work something out," she mumbled, then caught herself as the thought her statement could be taken as an innuendo made her blush. "I mean, I am sure a refund or a redo will work."

JC grinned. "I appreciate that from all of you," she said. "Everybody got their stuff?" Grabbing her bag and putting it over her shoulder, Bella nodded. The others did likewise, and then they were off up the trail the way they had come. If Bella thought she had hiked fast with JC before, it was nothing compared to the pace Blake set to get back to the kayaks. Winded in only a few minutes of navigating the rocky trail, she started to slow her steps. JC was behind her and put a gentle hand on her back. "Blake," she called up the line. "Let's slow down a little."

"No," Bella said, shaking her head, while she drew in a deep breath. "I can keep up, and I don't want to cause us trouble getting off the island."

JC nodded. "I understand that," she said, still assisting Bella in a way that was both helpful and distracting. "But we are not in a race, and I want us all to stay together right now." Not wanting to waste any breath arguing the point, Bella kept climbing. *At least we will be going downhill soon,* she thought. *I only hope I will have the strength to paddle once we get there.*

Before long they approached the spot where she and JC had stopped to appreciate the view. A glance as they passed let Bella know they weren't kidding that the ocean looked rougher. The amount of white lines on the water made her worry they were too late.

Clearly seeing Bella's worried expression, JC leaned closer. "Don't get overly anxious about this, Bella," she said. "We will go together, just like before. And well…"

"Well, what?" Bella gasped, not sure what she expected, but if JC believed she wasn't going to be anxious, she didn't remember her as well as Bella thought. When JC didn't finish her sentence right away, Bella glanced at her only to see the woman studying her face even as they walked. "Should I be worried about what you're going to say?"

JC shook her head. "You should not," she said. "I was only going to tell you I won't let anything happen to you."

"Oh," Bella said between gasps. "Thank you." Even through the pain in her legs from hiking fast, she felt a tug of tenderness in her chest knowing JC cared so much. The kindness and consideration were something she did remember from college—JC always watching out for her and keeping her safe. *Just another thing I didn't realize I missed so much,* she thought. *Until now.* As she reflected on that reality while putting one foot in front of the other, she had to admit that no one had ever treated her a special as JC.

11

Watching a wave crash and then run up the beach, JC was even happier they decided to leave. The surf had raised considerably, and a strong wind threatened worse weather to come. *This is going to be a rough ride back,* she thought and glanced at Blake. Their eyes met, and it was clear from the concern on his face that he felt the same. "Okay," JC said as she moved to help tie everyone's bags onto the front and back of his kayak. "Lifejackets on. Make sure the straps are pulled tight. We're going to make a quick trip of this."

Knowing without even having to look that Bella would be even more anxious than the rest, she picked up Bella's life vest from the pile and took it to her. "Thank you," Bella said, reaching for the vest. JC's guess was right, the woman was pale, and her eyes were wide. Without another word, she dressed and clipped the fasteners together to secure the vest around her.

JC moved closer. "Here," she said, reaching for the top strap on the life vest. "Let me help with these." With expert fingers, she pulled on the black nylon until the device was more secure. "How does that feel?"

When Bella didn't answer, she looked at her face. Bella stared hard at JC. "Be honest with me," she said. "We're going to tip over, aren't we. I'm going to have to swim." It wasn't a question, and the resignation in her voice would have been almost humorous to JC if the woman wasn't so utterly serious. Unlike JC who was always comfortable in the water, going in the ocean, especially with it so rough, was possibly Bella's worst-case scenario.

Knowing she had to be honest, JC nodded. "There's a possibility, but it is small. Remember, I've navigated this stretch of water hundreds of times in all kinds of weather," she said. "What I want is for you to stay in your seat and not let go of the paddle. But keep it out of the water until I tell you when to start rowing." She smiled, hoping to look as reassuring as possible. "Then we will go like hell." When Bella didn't smile back or even reply, JC went on instinct and took her hand. "Bella, you can do this. No matter what you're thinking, you will handle it because you're brave and resourceful, and I will be with you. We will do this together."

The message seemed to get through because Bella grasped JC's hand, nodding, slight at first, but then with more confidence. "You're right," she said. "I can be brave, and we will do this."

"Exactly," JC said, and knowing to capitalize on Bella's moment of confidence, she led her to their kayak. Blake had already unfastened it from the rope that kept it safely ashore during their hike. Standing close to hold the craft steady, he waited for JC to help Bella into her spot at the front. "Remember, focus on staying in your seat. We will rock some, but not tip over," she gave Bella's shoulder a reassuring squeeze before letting go. "I promise."

Not wasting a second, JC moved to the back of the kayak

while Blake handed Bella her paddle. "JC's the best kayaker on Oahu," he said to her. "So have some fun with it." Then, he moved to JC, handing her the other paddle. "Ready?"

"Are you three okay launching on your own?" JC asked, knowing she was responsible for the entire party. Bella was important to her, and her highest priority if she was honest with herself, but so was the safety of everyone else.

Blake nodded. "Yes," he said. "We will be right behind you if you need anything."

Reassured, JC held her paddle in one hand, took ahold of the kayak with the other, and started watching the waves come in to get her timing. "Meet you over there," she said before looking to her passenger. "Here we go, Bella." The woman nodded, and as if on a cue, JC and Blake started to push. After three steps, she leaped onto the kayak while he gave them a final heave. The minute her butt hit the seat, she threw all her focus into paddling with rapid, strong strokes. The kayak plowed through the oncoming wave, but the ones behind it were not so easy. Three waves back, she could see a bit of a monster building and knew that staying upright would be difficult if it crested before they were past it. Worst case scenario, if it did roll before she was over, she could spin the kayak to go with the flow and keep them vertical. But the choice would mean riding the wave back ashore to the little island where they started. Relaunching would only get more challenging as time passed and the storm closed in. Truly the clock worked against them, and she sliced the kayak through the water with a strength built over years on the ocean. The race was on.

BELLA STARED STRAIGHT AHEAD, doing exactly what JC instructed and focusing on staying in her seat. It wasn't going to be easy though, and she knew it. There was a wave coming that could not miss knocking them over. White had already formed along a knife's edge in the turquoise blue water. As crazy as it was, because JC surely would already be aware of the oncoming threat, Bella wanted to call out a warning. But when she opened her mouth to yell, only a croak came out of her dry throat. Impulsively, she wanted to paddle or do something to avoid the collision, but JC hadn't told her to start. *And my flailing about would only make our progress worse*, she thought, instinctively knowing bad paddling was worse than no paddling. *And we are moving fast.* She eyed the wave growing as the kayak bore down on it. *But so is the wave.*

"Hang on, Bella!" JC yelled, sounding a little out of breath. "Don't panic and stay in your seat." Then, they met the wave head-on the moment the water started to curl toward them. The kayak bucked, and Bella grasped her paddle in one hand and the rope tied in loops along the side with the other. As the nose lifted, it seemed impossible they wouldn't tip. A million backup plans for after they rolled ran through Bella's mind in the blink of an eye—hang on to the paddle, grab a water bottle in case they needed it to survive later, try to float on her back… all of which were probably worthless, but her reasoning mind had to grasp at something. Just when tipping over and going into the water seemed inevitable, they were through the top of the wave and racing down the other side. JC let out a whoop of victory, and Bella was sure she heard her laugh before getting back to business. "Now paddle Bella. One, two. One, two."

Not wasting a second, Bella obeyed because, in her opinion, they weren't out of the forest yet. *Or, in this case, out of the water,* she thought. *I don't care how fun JC thinks this is, I see plenty more waves coming.* They did make easier headway though, and before long, they were riding with the current forcing them toward the other shore. The already strong wind started to blow harder and pushed at their backs. On their final run to the beach, Bella felt the first heavy drops of rain hit her face. The predicted storm had arrived in full force. *And we beat it.* If she was being honest with herself, Bella felt a sense of accomplishment for having survived the day, even with JC's reassurances.

As she watched, Blake and the others caught up to them. Once again, they made landing look easy but at least it meant Blake could wait for them knee-deep in the water as JC steered to shore. The man grabbed the front tie and started to drag them onto the sand as Bella felt JC step off the kayak. Between the two of them, they moved the seated Bella all the way out of the water.

Once clear, JC held out her hand. "We have arrived," she said with a smile. It was more relaxed than before, letting Bella know the woman had been more worried about the trip across than she initially let on. "Follow the others to the van, and Blake and I will bring up the stuff." Bella took the offering, loving the warmth that radiated from contact with JC's strong hand.

Standing, she didn't think she was ever happier to be on solid ground. "Thank you," she said, looking into JC's eyes. "For getting us back safely. I know it wasn't as easy as you made it seem."

JC shrugged, still holding Bella's hand. "That first big wave made me wonder," she said with a smile. "But the rest was a piece of cake. And you helped too."

With a scoff, Bella was about to dispute the claim when the newlyweds joined them. "Wasn't that a trip?" the bride asked, absolutely beaming from the excitement of the endeavor. "I think I like ocean kayaking more than white water now." Bella didn't know how to comment. There was little chance she would ever agree to do either again, so which was better was irrelevant.

Slowly, JC let go of Bella's hand, clearly not wanting to

call attention to the fact she held a customer's hand. "They both have their advantages and challenges," JC said. "But the lack of rocks to bash against gives ocean kayaking the win with me."

The bride laughed. "Good point," she said. "We will so be back for another run soon."

"We'd love to have you," JC said. "Once everyone is loaded up, I will hand out some gift cards that will cover another visit." She looked at Bella. "Hopefully, you'll consider going again soon too."

Before she flat out refused the offer as insanity, Bella paused. *What if that's the only way I'll be able to see JC again?* she wondered. *If that is the case, then I might have to.* "We'll see," was all she said and hoped there was another way.

12

As Blake helped JC load the kayaks onto the trailer behind her jeep, she couldn't keep her mind from racing through possible ways to get Bella alone for even a few minutes. As slowly as she moved, time slipped by far faster than she wanted. To get out of the approaching stormy weather, the group quickly loaded into the passenger van Blake would use to deposit them back at their respective hotels. *Assuming I get her alone, then I have to make the most of those minutes and ask Bella out to dinner or something*, she thought, trying to swallow the lump in her dry throat. Out on the water, she was confident and able to navigate the rising waves to get Bella safely to the shore, but in the parking lot, with rain coming down heavier by the second, her nerves were out of control. Thinking Bella might ride out of her life forever had her in knots. *I can't let that happen. It's time to do something, but what? In front of everyone?*

"JC," Blake said as they strapped the last kayak to the rack. "Since we're done for the day, I was wondering if I could take off a little early once everyone's dropped off." JC shrugged. Since she had already made the few quick calls to cancel the afternoon tour, there was no reason she needed Blake to hang around.

She could unload the trailer herself and close the office. "Sure," she said. "Everything okay?"

"Oh yeah," Blake said. "Nothing big. I only wanted to run a couple of errands I've been putting off. But I thought if you could maybe take Bella with you?" The idea seemed too good to be true, and JC glanced at him, but he wouldn't meet her eye as he fiddled with the last tie. "If I only had to make a single stop at the newlyweds hotel near the shop, I could drop the van off quickly and be on my way."

Slowly, JC nodded, pretty sure her friend made up the excuse of errands but being smart enough to take advantage of what he offered. "I would be more than happy to do that for you," JC said, a wide smile crossing her face. "Thanks, Blake."

He finally turned to her, a smile of his own on his handsome face. "Seemed like the best option all around," he said. "Let me go tell everyone the new plan."

Before JC could say another word, the man walked toward the van. The opportunity of being alone with Bella for the twenty-minute drive was more than enough time to talk to her, but her heart raced too. She wasn't a hundred percent sure how Bella might take being asked on a date. *A romantic date*, JC thought, wanting to make sure there was no mistaking her intention. Not that JC didn't want to spend time getting to know Bella again, but she wouldn't make the same mistakes as in college. No more pretending she was only Bella's friend. There were no expectations the woman felt the same, but she needed Bella to know she had JC's heart ever since college. *We are adults this time, and no more excuses.*

Feeling a new resolve, she looked toward the van only to see Bella coming across the parking lot, her bag over her shoulder. Even though the rain poured down on her, her steps were slow and calculated. If JC wasn't mistaken, a light blush bloomed on her cheeks, and when their eyes met, the lump in JC's throat came back in a blink. *What if she rejects me, and all that I've built up in my mind is my imagination?* she wondered but took a deep breath and smiled. "Are you okay with not going with the others?" JC asked when Bella reached her.

Bella nodded. "I am," she said. "When Blake explained…" The light blush turned a little deeper. "I have to admit I jumped at the idea." A little laugh. "Maybe a little too obviously."

Raising an eyebrow, hoping she understood Bella's meaning, JC considered asking what she meant, but then let it go. *Maybe I'll run with my assumption she likes me too and stop over-analyzing everything*, she thought, moving to open the passenger door for Bella. "Well, your chariot awaits," she said. "And for what it's worth, I really hoped you'd say yes."

As confident as JC was in the water, she was as much so behind the wheel of her jeep. Comfortable in the passenger seat, it was all Bella could do not to stare at the woman's hands on the steering wheel as she navigated through the rain. Traffic wasn't handling the lousy weather well and going was slow. Bella's hotel in the tight streets of Waikiki would be a pain to get to, and she wished she had an excuse not to go there yet. Then, they hit an unavoidable pothole on the highway, and when it rattled, she remembered the trailer of kayaks was behind them.

"If it's not more trouble, would you like to take the kayaks back to wherever you store them first?" she asked, hoping JC was as eager as she was to spend more time together.

"You're sure?" JC asked, and when Bella nodded, she hit

the blinker to take the next exit. JC blew out a breath once they were clear of the mess and back on surface streets. "Thanks. That wasn't any fun."

Bella smiled. "No, it wasn't," she said. "Although I wasn't worried. You're an excellent driver."

JC glanced at her, a smile on her face too. "Thank you," she said. "I do my best to be alert about everything around me. Although I will admit, you're a little distracting."

A rush of heat ran up Bella's body as she took in JC's words. "I hope you mean that in a good way," she said barely above a whisper, and JC glanced over again. An intensity was in her eye that made the heat inside Bella even hotter.

"In the very best way," JC replied. She paused, and Bella watched her bite her lip. Letting JC take her time but anxious to hear what the woman would say next, Bella held her breath. Finally, after driving them through a busy intersection, JC nodded. "If you're okay waiting while I rinse these off really quickly and stow them, I'd like to take you out for a bite to eat. I mean, it's lunchtime and—"

Bella laughed, unable to hold in her happiness at the invite. "You don't have to explain anything else," she said. "I will even help if I can."

A wide grin crossed JC's face as she looked out the windshield where the wipers swished back and forth on high. "I appreciate your offer. It really won't be more than thirty minutes to take care of it and shut up the office."

Instinctively, Bella reached out and squeezed JC's forearm. "It's fine," she said. "Really." She saw JC stiffen at the contact, and her muscle flexed under Bella's hand. *Good response? Or bad?* she wondered. After all their interactions over the morning, the awkward yet heated touches, the shared moment in the lagoon, all of it added up. Her gut told her JC felt the same way she did—one hundred percent attracted to each other. The chemistry could not be denied any longer. Deciding to be brave yet again that day, Bella ran her hand along the woman's arm. "I want to spend time with you. No matter what we are doing."

JC nodded slowly. "I feel exactly the same," she murmured. "As crazy as today has been, I have loved every minute." When they stopped at a light, she glanced over. "Meeting you again has changed my life in the blink of an eye, and I won't let you slip out of my life again without telling you how I feel."

Her stomach tightening at JC's words, Bella didn't know how to react. If JC truly meant what she said, Bella's life would have changed entirely too. *Oh, don't get carried away,* Bella scolded herself. *For all we know, this could simply turn out to be lunch.* Yet, somehow she believed it was more. Bigger and more important.

Forcing a little laugh, Bella pulled her hand back. "I think I might need a little wine with that confession," she said. "For a writer, I suck at telling people how I feel."

JC laughed too, dispelling the slowly building hint of awkwardness in the air. "Well, if it's all the same to you," she said. "I'll have a beer. And then let's find a place we can sit and talk. I have a lot to say."

Bella nodded because she did too.

MAKING record time unloading the kayaks and rinsing the saltwater off them, JC couldn't stop smiling. Inside the small Oahu Paddle Adventures office, Bella waited with a cup of coffee from a fresh pot JC made her. She had offered again to help, but JC declined considering the weather and task. "Would it be a hassle if I borrowed some paper and a pen?" Bella asked after they arranged her on a stool at the counter. "I have some ideas to write down."

"For your book?" JC asked, excited to hear Bella might be

feeling creative after their morning. "I have a legal pad you can have. No problem."

Bella smiled. "That's exactly what I need and, yes, for a book. I think my current work in progress suddenly needs to be set in Hawaii," she said, warm light in her eyes.

JC liked hearing that. "Well, if I get to have any input, I hope it's a romance with a happy ending," she said, a tightening in her chest at the idea she was being so bold. The insinuation could not be clearer.

With a slight smile on her lips, Bella nodded. "I only write happy endings, JC," she said. "Now go do what you need to do. I want to write down these words before they slip away."

Not needing to be told twice, JC did precisely that, and when she made it back to the office, Bella was busily writing. Being as quiet as possible, JC slipped inside deciding to pour herself a cup of coffee and wait. Not as stealthy as she thought she was, Bella looked up from the notepad and smiled. "I hear you," she said. "But thank you. You always were super respectful when I was in the rhythm of writing."

"I want to make sure you don't forget an idea or something," JC replied. "With zero creative skills myself, I consider the whole thing magic anyway."

Setting her pen on the notepad, Bella turned her full attention to JC, and although her face was soft, she was serious too. "JC, I think you might be my muse," she said. "All through college, I could write and write. A hundred ideas were in my head all the time."

Nothing Bella could have said would have made JC feel more special. There were a lot of times in college when JC brought Bella food because her friend was in the middle of a writing fest. Supporting Bella and her craft meant so much to her then.

And now, JC thought. *I feel exactly the same.* "Well, as your muse, I say keep going with your flow, and I'll go grab us lunch. There's a great teriyaki truck two blocks over, and the two-scoop rice lunch special is fabulous."

She watched as Bella bit her lip until finally shaking her head. "No," she said. "I have what I need to get started." Tearing off the sheets she used from the pad, Bella slipped from the stool. "But teriyaki sounds delicious. I didn't realize it, but I'm starving."

Her statement made sense to JC considering everything physical they had done already. "Are you thinking rowing for your life made you hungry?" she said with a laugh, but when Bella's eyes widened, she stopped. "What?"

"It wasn't really that close, was it?" Bella whispered, making JC regret her joke. She should have known better. Her friend had been honestly terrified out on the water.

Going on instinct, JC moved the few steps between them and put her hands gently on the woman's shoulders. "No," she said. "Never. I shouldn't have made a joke." Her voice softened. "I said I would never let anything happen to you, and I meant it." JC watched Bella search her face for the second time that day, and again she wondered what happened to her to make her so wary. *She needs to learn to trust me like she did once,* JC thought, vowing to be more patient than ever in her life.

Standing there, like so many times before, the desire to kiss Bella was strong. After another moment, their eyes met, and JC explored the depths of Bella's gaze trying to unravel the mystery of what she thought. Before JC said anything else, Bella stepped closer, slipped her arms tightly around JC's waist, and put her head on her shoulder. "Thank you for coming back into my life," Bella said in nothing more than a whisper. "I missed you." Hugging her tighter, JC felt exactly the same.

13

*B*eing less than impressive after all the hype, the storm blew past the island without much rain, but the next three days were no less of a whirlwind for Bella. While JC took more tourists out on kayak adventures, Bella went back to writing in her condo. Slowly at first and then it became an avalanche as the words flowed out of her fingertips and onto the page, filling the screen of her laptop. She hadn't been so inspired to write since her days in college, and she knew it was all because of her reunion with JC.

The last three evenings had been extremely special. Once JC's workday was over, they would meet for dinner at some fantastic restaurant only the Oahu locals knew about and afterward go for long walks on different beaches. Nothing could be more romantic than the sunset over the Pacific, especially after the first night when JC got up the courage to take Bella's hand. An unspoken bond grew between them, accelerated perhaps because of their history. All the time they spent together in school was the perfect foundation. As if those days of longing counted toward what they were doing now. Although she was afraid to analyze it too closely, Bella couldn't think of a time she had been happier.

After wrapping up another great day of writing, she sat at her desk looking at the clock and counting down the minutes until she could see JC again. While she impatiently waited, she opened her email and scrolled down the dozens of messages. Some from fans, which she responded to with a short but heartfelt thank you, a lot were junk mail on gimmicky ways to best market her books, but one was from her editor. Skimming it, the message was clear—when might her next book be ready, and how long did she plan to stay in Hawaii? *That's an excellent question*, Bella thought as she stared at the screen. *How long am I staying in Hawaii?* Her ticket home was open-ended, yet in her mind, she had always thought a month to six weeks might be enough to kickstart her writing. That time was coming to an end, but she saw no reason to go back just yet. Her sister was looking after Bella's little house in Portland, Oregon. She didn't even have a pet to worry about. *I definitely want to stay a little longer.*

Knowing her editor and friend, Joanie, deserved an answer with more than she could explain in an email, Bella picked up her phone to call her. Joanie answered on the first ring. "Tell me you have a wonderful tan," the woman said without even a hello. "I'm so jealous you're in Hawaii."

"Not too much of a tan actually," Bella said. "But I am having the time of my life."

"Really?" Joanie asked, clearly unable to hide the surprise in her tone.

Bella laughed, and it felt good to be so happy. "Really," Bella said. "So much so, I don't know when I'll be back to the mainland."

There was a pause as her editor seemed to take in the information. "So, you've fallen in love with Hawaii?"

A warmth radiated through Bella's body. "Well, I don't

want to jinx it, but I think I may be falling in love," she said with a smile on her face. "But not necessarily with Hawaii."

"What are you saying?" her editor asked, the hint of a squeal in her tone making Bella think of girls in high school talking about a new crush. "Are you telling me what I think you are telling me?"

"I think so," Bella confessed. "I met someone. A wonderful woman who I went to college with. It's crazy, but we reconnected in a way I never imagined."

"That is music to my ears! I'm so happy for you," Joanie said, then hesitated before dropping into a more serious tone. "How is that impacting your writing?"

Bella shook her head at her editor's never ending focus on business, but the smile was still on her face. "It's all about the writing with you. But this old friend... she's been my muse. In fact, she has been since college. And I think you will love this new book."

"Oh Bella, that makes me so happy," the editor said. "I can't wait to read it. So, you're staying for now to keep things going with your old flame?"

Bella paused because that was a good question. "I'm simply not sure what my plan is," Bella said. "But I want to explore what's growing between us a little more, and I'm not in a rush."

"Well, as long as she's inspiring you to write, then take all the time you need," Joanie said with a laugh. "You deserve to be happy, Bella."

Do I? she wondered as the old whisper of doubt arose in her mind. *Damnit, I do.* "I'll keep you posted," she said. "But for right now, I am going to keep things very simple." *And focus on falling in love.*

. . .

Humming the words to a classic love song playing on the radio, JC filed the day's liability release forms into the cabinet at the office. The day was a good one. Both the morning group and the afternoon one were filled with enthusiastic, experienced kayakers. With perfect weather, the trip across to the Moku island and back was so easy to be almost boring. Everyone enjoyed the lagoon, including JC. She had taken a quick swim to the waterfall, wondering if Bella would ever see the beautiful sight up close. *Probably not*, she thought with a bit of laugh. *I might get her to hike to a few beautiful places, but her kayaking days are probably over.* JC didn't mind. She believed opposites attract, and her outdoorsy side complimented Bella's preference for the indoors or a simple day by the pool. *Or a walk on the beach.* They shared one every night, and it was the highlight of JC's whole day.

"You are in a super good mood," Blake said as he came in the office's back door. He had a wide grin on his face. "But then that's been the case for a few days now. Ever since…" The young man paused, and JC looked at him.

"Ever since when?" she asked, but playfully because she already knew the answer.

Blake shrugged. "Well, ever since you ran into Bella."

Closing the cabinet door, JC smiled wide. "What can I say? Life is good."

Blake nodded. "It sure is. I'm guessing you're taking her out again tonight."

"Actually…" JC hesitated, not sure of her decision over an idea that had been on her mind all day.

"What?" Blake asked.

JC rubbed her cheek. "Well, I thought I would call her and ask if she wanted to come to my house and let me cook for her."

The young man let out a low whistle. "Wow, JC, you're

getting serious," Blake said, walking to the counter to put the key to the kayak's storage area on the top. "But I think it's an awesome idea. Do you think she'll go for it?"

Picking up the key, JC stalled as she put the thing away on its hook. *Will she go for it?* she wondered. *That's the question.* The last thing JC wanted to do was screw anything up. She hadn't been kidding when she said life was good. With Bella back in her world, she had never been happier. *And if I'm asking her to move forward too soon, she might back away.* But the last few nights felt terrific, and their reconnection solid. They could talk about anything for hours—memories from college, what they did since, hopes for the future, and everything in between. All were reasons JC believed Bella would be receptive to her offer. "I think so," JC finally answered. "And I guess I won't know until I ask."

Blake smiled. "Exactly," he said, turning to leave for the rest of the day while JC closed things up. "And I think she's a very lucky lady. Saying no would be crazy."

With a laugh, JC waved as he opened the door to leave. "Thanks, Blake. We'll see."

Alone again and with nothing left to do, JC stared at her phone on the desk. She would normally call Bella and discuss where they wanted to eat and then pick a place to go. *Only this time is different*, she thought and, taking a deep breath, scooped up the cellphone and dialed.

"Hi," Bella said after the first ring. "I was just thinking about you."

JC smiled, loving the sound of that answer. "And what were you thinking?" she asked.

There was a pause on the phone, followed by a bit of laugh. "I'm not going to say," Bella said, causing a flash of heat to fill JC's body. *Did that mean what I think it means?* she wondered, because it wasn't like she hadn't thought of Bella in a sexy way plenty of times in the last seventy-two hours. "Maybe we should talk about dinner instead."

Swallowing hard, JC tried not to be distracted by the sexual tension and instead focused on what she wanted to propose. "About dinner," she said. "I had an idea. Maybe try something a little bit different."

"Okay," Bella said, a hint of curiosity in her voice. "Do you have some new place to try?"

"Sort of," JC said, working on the best way to deliver her next line. There seemed nothing to do but blurt it out before she lost her nerve. "I thought you could come over to my house." Suddenly sure she had made a horrible mistake, JC rambled on. "I mean, nothing serious, I'll cook up some chicken breasts on the grill. Maybe put some broccoli in the oven and—"

There was a delighted laugh over the phone. "Stop, JC," Bella said. "You don't have to convince me. I would love to see your house."

14

Admiring JC's home set along the maze of canals in Hawaii Kai, Bella couldn't miss noticing the care the woman had put in to making the simple yet spacious house beautiful. The dark wood floors complemented perfectly with the cream walls and tan accents she used throughout. Large windows let in light from all parts of the house, with nine-foot high folding glass doors that led to a gorgeous patio. Beyond was a small swimming pool and then a peek-a-boo view of the water. The outdoor space was incredibly private with tall, lush, tropical greenery flanking both sides, dotted with local flowers, and only the blue water of the canal behind them. Everything reflected a sense of serene yet functional design. Bella loved every inch of it.

"JC, your house is unbelievable," she said when they finished their tour in the modern kitchen decorated in olive green and a soft gray. "Did you do everything yourself?"

Smiling, JC took a tray of raw chicken and vegetable kabobs from the wide, French door, stainless steel refrigerator. "I did," she said. "The house was a total fixer-upper and needed a complete remodel." She laughed. "No one touched anything since the 1970s. But I didn't mind because that way I could do what I wanted to with it."

"Well, you've worked wonders," Bella said, looking around to take everything in. The kitchen's glass cabinets, granite counters, and high-end appliances almost made Bella want to cook something. Considering she was only so-so at it, that impulse was a surprise to her.

JC nodded at the fridge as she started toward the patio doors. "I'm going to get these on the grill. There's white wine in there for you if you want," she said. "Or some local beer."

A cool drink sounded fabulous. "I'll have the wine," Bella said. "You?"

"I'll join you," she said. "You can find glasses in the cupboard to the left of the sink." Then she was gone outside. Finding what she needed exactly where JC described, Bella followed only to pause when she stepped onto the patio. The smell of plumerias caught her nose, and the sounds of birds in the trees made her think she was in a movie. While the house was welcoming, the patio and backyard were an absolute oasis.

JC stood at the edge of the patio at the built-in grill putting their dinner on to cook. *She's another part of all that is amazing about this place,* Bella thought, watching her work with confidence. *How can she always look so in control all the time?*

As if sensing her gaze, JC looked up from what she was doing at the grill to catch her eye. "Twelve minutes for these to cook," she said, with a smile Bella was learning to love looking at already. It lit up the woman's tanned face, making her blue eyes twinkle. "Do you want to pour the wine? I opened it for us earlier."

Bella cocked her head. "How did you know I'd want it?" she asked, and JC shrugged, but there was a playfulness to it.

"You've had some type of white wine every night we've gone out," she said. "So, I played the odds."

Laughing at the woman's clever intuition, Bella poured for each of them before settling into the flowery red and gold cushions of the comfortable patio loveseat. "You think of everything, don't you," she said, not asking a question but making an observation. "I always feel so special around you." The words came out before Bella had a chance to censor them, and she felt a blush start on her cheeks.

Their eyes met across the space. "That's because you are special to me," JC said before Bella could take her statement back. Her look had a sudden intensity to it, and even feeling a hint shy, Bella couldn't look away. JC set down the tongs she held but never broke their gaze. "I'm happy you can tell. I want that." There was a pause while the chemistry between the two women seemed to crackle in the air. For Bella, being at JC's house letting her make them dinner felt like a pivotal moment in their relationship. *But a part of me knew that before I agreed to come here,* Bella thought. *And I came because I don't want this specialness between us to end.*

A question came to her, something she had never considered before but realized she should have. "And what about you?" she asked. "Do I make you feel special?"

As an answer, JC moved across the patio to sit on the loveseat beside her. She gently took her wine glass from Bella's hand to set it on the end table, getting Bella's full attention. "Yes, you do make me feel special," JC replied, taking Bella's face in her hands. "Like no one ever has." Then JC did what Bella hoped so much that she would. She kissed her.

THE SENSATION of finally having Bella's warm lips on hers was nearly indescribable. JC had kissed a few women throughout her life, some of whom were special to her, but no one compared to the emotions she felt toward Bella. JC's entire body reacted to the temperature building between them from the simple contact. When the woman didn't pull away, JC took the kiss deeper, relishing every second. In response, JC heard a slight hum of pleasure but didn't know if it came from her or Bella. With the birds singing in the tropical oasis around them and the perfume of flowers in the air, the moment could not be more perfect. As the embrace lingered, she was sure she could sit on the loveseat and kiss Bella all night.

Then, another scent caught her attention. "Oh crap," she said, pulling back in a hurry. Bella's eyes widened, clearly surprised by the sudden change of direction. JC jumped from the cushions and rushed to the grill. "I forgot about the chicken."

"Oh, no," Bella said, starting to get up as if to come to investigate. "Is it bad?"

JC lifted the lid and let out a breath of relief. "No," she said. "We're okay." Dinner wasn't charcoal, and the food looked fabulous as she turned the kabobs. "I'll turn the flame down a little, though."

Settling back among the cushions, Bella reclaimed her glass of wine. "That's good," she said. "I'd hate to be the reason dinner burned."

JC laughed. "I can't think of a better reason, actually," she said, closing the grill's lid. "I don't know about you, but I liked how it felt to kiss you."

When Bella didn't respond, JC looked at her only to see an unexpected uncertainty filled her face. A little confused, she returned to the loveseat, and took Bella's free hand. She wanted to build their physical connection again. "What are you thinking about? Did I do something wrong?"

Bella shook her head. "Never," she said. "And I'm thinking

about a few million things." She hesitated for a beat, but then leaned closer. "But I agree that kiss was amazing... you are amazing. JC, I'm so happy here, it scares me a little." Before JC could respond, the woman gave a little laugh. "But now I'm being melodramatic. What I'm trying to say is thank you for inviting me tonight."

Liking what she heard but a little unsure about what Bella was worrying about, JC held the woman's hand a little tighter. "Thank you for saying yes," she said. "And not only for tonight, but the last few too." She smiled. "I know how busy you are writing your next book."

"I'm never too busy to spend time with you," Bella said. "But thank you for always being so respectful."

"Of course," JC said, meaning it wholeheartedly. Protecting Bella's writing time was important to her. "And is the process going better now?"

Nodding as she took a sip of her wine, Bella's face lit up. "So much better," she said, all hints of her moment of uneasiness gone with the change of subject. "I've been hitting my word count goals and beyond every day." She laughed. "My editor is thrilled."

"I'm not surprised," JC said. "Another book from you will make everyone excited."

Bella sighed. "We'll see," she murmured.

JC considered digging into why Bella seemed apprehensive about her next book, but she hesitated. With the chicken on the grill needing another turn in a minute and setting up for dinner, she couldn't give the topic the time and attention it warranted. *And another glass of wine might be just what is needed to help us talk about what's bothering her later tonight,* she thought, resolving to come back to the subject until they could work through Bella's fears.

JC gave Bella a gentle kiss before leaning back to study her face. "I know you're a fantastic writer, and it will all work out. Now, are you hungry?" she asked, standing to go back to the grill. "I think this chicken is probably about ready to plate. Do you want to sit outside or—"

"My editor asked me when I'm coming back," Bella interrupted, catching JC by surprise. She paused for a half step, then finished walking to the grill.

Lifting the lid, she didn't meet Bella's eyes. "And what did you tell her?" she said, bracing herself for any possible answer. JC always knew the conversation would come up at some point. Unlike JC, Bella didn't live on the island. Somewhere she had a home and a whole different life. JC had tried to reconcile that fact in her mind often over the last three days, but whenever she did, the possible outcomes were never pleasant. At some point, Bella would have to leave Oahu.

When Bella hesitated, JC thought the worse but worked to keep her face neutral. "I told her I wasn't sure," the woman finally answered. "Because I'm not."

15

Watching JC work the grill and turning the kebabs, Bella couldn't miss the change in her body language. Clearly Bella's answer that she wasn't sure when she would leave Hawaii affected her. One second ago, she was relaxed and carefree, but suddenly was tense and even a little distracted. *Because she doesn't want me to go yet?* Bella wondered, hoping that was the case. *Why else would she react so much?*

Nodding, JC kept looking at the grill. "Okay," she said. "But you must have had a plan in mind when you started." She hesitated before going on. "Be honest with me. Am I messing things up for you?"

"What?" Bella said, caught by surprise at the insinuation JC could mess anything up. "No, absolutely not. Why would you think that?"

The woman shrugged, finally looking away from the food to meet Bella's eyes. "I imagine you have lots of things back home you miss. Family? Friends?"

Shaking her head, Bella wanted to be clear about her next statement. "No, JC. Or at least not anything or anyone urgently missing me. Not really," she said. "I have family back in Portland, but they support what I'm doing here. One hundred percent. I can stay as long as I need to get back in the writing flow." *But the words are flowing,* she thought. *So, haven't I accomplished what I came for? Is that my signal to go home?* The idea of leaving made her chest tighten. She was slowly getting her confidence back, and JC had to be the reason.

JC nodded, a small, slightly sad smile on her face. "I see. Well, it sounds like the plan worked," she said before changing the subject. "Now, about dinner. Eat inside or outside?"

Although the shift was abrupt, Bella went along with it. "Outside would be nice, I think," Bella said, letting the topic of her leaving go for the moment. Her indecision made the conversation difficult, and the last thing she wanted was to mess up their dinner. "Your patio is lovely, and the night is perfect."

"I agree," JC said, moving toward the patio doors. "Let me grab plates, and we can eat."

Bella started to stand. "I can help."

"No need," JC said. "Stay where you are and enjoy the wine. Setting the table will take two minutes."

Settling back against the cushions after JC disappeared into the house, Bella sighed. "You're spoiling me," she whispered. "And that only makes me more confused about what to do." At some point, she would have to return to Portland and pick up her life there. Although she told JC things could wait, and they absolutely could, she had a house, a car, clothes, and all her things. The seven outfits she brought with her to Hawaii were tired. Pretty soon, JC would see every shirt she had with her. *But I could buy more at the mall if I stayed longer,* she thought. *And my sister will keep checking on my place.*

JC returned with arms full of plates, flatware, and a big bowl of green salad. "I think this is everything," she said. "Unless you are ready for more wine."

"Not yet," Bella said, standing to go help. "Let me set the table, and you grab the food on the grill." Taking the plates from JC's hand, their fingers brushed, and Bella warmed at the contact. Mixed with the effect the kissing had on her, Bella started to crave more. A vision of JC's arms wrapped around her made her stomach flutter. With slightly shaking hands, she began to set the table while JC placed the rest of her load down. She touched Bella's arm gently as she passed to go to the grill.

"Thank you for helping," she said, and Bella held in a gasp. Her entire body reacted, and she started to think about more than only kissing. *Okay, calm down,* she thought. *Just because we are here at her house doesn't mean anything. It's only dinner.* Finished with her task, Bella grabbed their wine and slipped into a chair at the same time JC set a tray full of delicious food on the table. "That looks and smells fantastic."

"It does, right?" JC said with a wide smile. "Even though we almost burned them." The woman reddened a little at the statement, and Bella guessed she immediately thought about their kissing too. JC's lips on hers had felt like magic, and Bella realized she wanted more of them. A lot more.

After JC sat, Bella looked at her over the table. "JC," she said, and the woman focused on her. "I've made up my mind."

"About staying longer?" JC asked, and Bella nodded.

"Yes, and I'm going to tell my editor I'm not leaving right away," she said, watching JC smile. "I'm not ready to go home."

. . .

With her heart racing a little, JC raised her wine, unable to keep the broad grin off her face at Bella's announcement. "I'll toast to that," she said, and Bella laughed.

"Absolutely," she said, lifting her glass. "I'm relieved you are so happy with my decision."

Shaking her head, JC clinked the glasses together. "You're crazy if you thought I would have any other reaction," she said. JC was so happy she had to restrain herself from jumping over the table and kissing Bella. The feeling was the best she'd had in a long time. *Maybe since I realized it was her waiting with the other kayakers less than a week ago,* she thought. *What an incredible change it has made in my life.* All of it helped her decide on the spot to say what she had been thinking. "I hope you already know I want a chance to get to know you better, but maybe I've not been as clear as I should have been. I love having you back in my life. So, thank you."

Bella blushed, but there was a twinkle in her eye. "I love it too," she murmured, acting flustered as she set the wine down. "And this food smells too good to let it get cold."

Not precisely sure what brought on the change in conversation, JC considered asking but then waited. She would continue to be patient with Bella. *And now thankfully there isn't as much of a rush,* she thought. *She didn't say how long she would be staying, but I plan to make every moment last.*

Picking up her knife and fork to start on the first kabob, JC nodded. "It does smell good," she agreed, taking a bite. After chewing for a beat, letting the blend of spices on the juicy chicken fill her mouth, she nodded and swallowed. "And if I can say so myself, it tastes good too."

Following suit, Bella ate a bite and then sighed. "You're amazing, JC," she said. "Don't be surprised if I start inviting myself over to dinner regularly."

JC raised an eyebrow. "Really?" she said, knowing Bella's

statement was intended to be a compliment but really liking the sound of her words. "Well, you're always welcome here."

Pointing her fork in JC's direction, Bella smiled. "Be careful what you say," she said. "I'm sick of the place I'm in, and your home is fantastic." She waved in the direction of the pool. "The outdoor space is amazing. I can't imagine how much time you spend out here on the veranda, but if I lived here, you'd hardly find me inside."

Bella's words hung in the air as both seemed to register what she said. "Is it that bad there in Waikiki?" JC finally asked, feeling her pulse pick up at the possibility Bella liked her home so much more. "Is the condo not what you were looking for?"

Clearly trying to backpedal from her suggestive statement, Bella waved a hand. "Oh, it's not that horrible," she said. "I tend to exaggerate. But I won't lie, it is noisy and crowded with all the tourists. I don't know what I was thinking, letting my editor talk me into staying there."

"Which would make it hard to focus and write," JC said, taking a moment to process what Bella said. *She doesn't have a good writing environment in Waikiki,* she thought. *And my home makes her feel good.* Realizing the opportunity before her might not come again, JC swallowed hard to steady her voice. "Move in here."

Again, there was a long pause between them while Bella picked up her wine, studying the contents for a second. "That's crazy," she said just above a whisper, not looking at JC. "You need your space." There was something in her tone that wasn't entirely convincing. In fact, JC was sure her words were a touch wishful.

JC shook her head. "Don't think that. There is plenty of room here for two people," she said. "A master suite at both ends of the house." Working to not get her hopes too high but feeling her breath coming quicker with anticipation, she leaned forward until Bella looked at her again. "It has a separate entrance on the side of the house. There is access to both the street and the pool. When I remodeled the place, I kept in mind I might need to put the room up as an Airbnb vacation rental if my kayaking business ever got slow."

Her eyes widening with everything JC told her, Bella looked as if she couldn't believe it. "That does sound perfect," she said slowly. JC stayed quiet, letting the woman process the opportunity until finally Bella started to nod. "If that's the case... I insist you let me pay you rent."

The moment held as Bella's comment made it sound like she accepted the offer. JC needed to be sure. "So, you'll move in?" JC asked softly, and Bella slowly nodded.

"I will," she said, and at the woman's perfect answer, JC realized what had started out to be a simple dinner had turned into a possibly monumental night.

With a slightly shaking hand, she lifted her wine glass. "I know we already toasted tonight, but I think this warrants a second one," she said, and Bella laughed, sounding more carefree than she had all evening.

"To roommates?" she asked, and JC smiled wide.

"To roommates."

16

As Bella watched JC pick up the last of her suitcases and load them into the back of the jeep, she couldn't believe how excited she felt. Although everything was happening fast, amazingly she didn't mind. Normally, rapid change made her feel overwhelmed, but not this time. As unbelievable as it sounded, even to her own ears, she was about to live with JC in her fantastic house on the canals. *Such a beautiful space, filled with so much light, so much positive energy,* she thought. *It's going to be perfect for my writing.* Bella felt the words bubbling inside her, ready to spill out through her fingers onto the keyboard.

When JC first suggested she move in, Bella's immediate concern wasn't if she would like to live with her friend. She already knew she would because the woman was thoughtful and generous and, from what Bella saw of the house, neat and tidy too. Instead, her worry was what if JC saw something in Bella she didn't like. Their relationship was new and, until last night, always out in public places. Nothing like what actually living with someone felt like. *And then there was the kissing,* she thought. There was plenty of that after dinner the night before. She smiled. *We were like a couple of teenagers.*

"Well, I like that smile," JC said, shutting the jeep's tailgate. "What are you thinking about?"

Caught thinking of her friend in a less than innocent way, Bella felt her cheeks get hot. Not quite ready to express all her feelings, she shrugged instead. "Just that I am so glad we decided to do this," she said. "I hope you don't regret it."

JC laughed, and it was the usual warm, carefree sound Bella loved since college. "I am confident I won't regret anything," she said with a wink. "Are you interested in stopping for lunch somewhere or heading straight back to the house?"

Thinking about her answer, Bella climbed into the jeep and put on her seatbelt. "I'm not sure," she said, biting her lip. A part of her really wanted to start settling in. "I think I'd rather go straight back if you don't mind. And unload my stuff?"

JC started the engine. "What about this," she said. "We swing by the food truck on the way and take lunch home to eat on the patio?"

"Love it," Bella said, impulsively grabbing JC's hand. Although they held hands at times while walking on the beach, and the relationship had evolved to passionate kissing, the intimate feeling from the touch caught her by surprise. *Like we've always done this,* she thought, and when JC intertwined their fingers, warmth radiated through her. Not sexual, although there were plenty of those moments, but comfortable. Happy. *Like she always makes me feel.*

Riding in silence, Bella simply closed her eyes and savored the moment. JC was an excellent driver, and she trusted her completely. Everything was perfect when they took the offramp to swing by the food truck and grab lunch. Then, JC jerked her hand away as she slammed on the brakes. Cars honked behind them, and Bella braced for impact at any second while they came to a quick stop. After a beat, JC put on her flashers but did not move the jeep out of the line of traffic.

"What's happening?" Bella asked as JC quickly unfastened her seatbelt. "Where are you going?"

"There's a dog in the road," she said. "It looks like someone hit it."

Eyes wide, Bella watched as her friend jumped out of the jeep and ran down the offramp toward something black and white on the ground. "What the hell are you doing?" she heard someone bellow from behind them. "Move your car." Not entirely sure what JC's plan was, but knowing she was only trying to help, Bella wasn't about to let someone yell at her. Getting out of the jeep, she walked toward the man's open car window. He was leaning out and glaring at her as she approached.

"Hey," Bella said.

"What?"

"I am only asking you to be patient," she said. "There's an animal or something in the road further down the ramp."

The man shook his head. "Well then kick it to the side and let's go," he said in a tone that Bella found extremely offensive. "I have an appointment."

Putting her hands on her hips, Bella returned his glare. "You're just going to have to be late," she said. "Because no one is moving until JC says it is okay."

ONE MINUTE, everything was perfect as JC drove on the highway with Bella relaxing beside her. The feeling of their hands clasped together was wonderful. A glance over, and she noticed the woman's eyes were closed. Seeing her so content and trusting brought a smile to JC's face. There was no way to know where their relationship would end up, but for the moment, she liked where it was headed.

Then, refocusing on the road as she took the offramp that would take them to the neighborhood with the food truck, she saw movement to the right. Something black and white, making her blink to see what was on the shoulder. She realized it was an animal, possibly a dog by the size. *Too big for a cat*, she thought. *And it's hurt.* Slowing the jeep, JC watched as the thing collapsed. *Shit, that's not good.* Without giving it a second thought, she hit the brakes and pushed the hazard light button, blocking traffic in case the dog crawled into the traffic lane.

"What's happening?" Bella asked as JC quickly unfastened her seatbelt. "Where are you going?"

"There's a dog in the road," she said. "It looks like someone hit it." Without another word, she climbed out and jogged down the onramp. She heard an angry motorist yell after her, but everyone could wait a minute while she checked the situation. If something was hurt, they couldn't leave it. Approaching the crouched dog, the first thing she noticed was its rapid panting and a hint of blood on its muzzle. The second was how unkept and underfed it looked. "Hey there," JC murmured using her gentlest tone. "Looks like you're hurting."

The dog fixed her with its dark-brown eyes but didn't get up to run. Seeing that as a good sign, JC crept closer, keeping her stance as relaxed and unthreatening as possible. "We need to get you out of traffic. It's not safe for you to stay here," she said, noting there was no collar. Leading the medium-sized dog away from danger wasn't an option. *I'll have to pick it up*, she thought, knowing to do so would be risky. The last thing she wanted was a dog bite from some stray. *But I'm kind of committed now.* Taking a deep breath, JC slid closer before crouching slightly out of reach. Watching her every move, the dog didn't try to stand and run, and she wondered if it could. In the distance, more cars had started honking. *Time to do this.* "I'm going to pick you up and take you with me, okay?" When the dog gave a bit of a whine, JC slowly nodded. *I'll take that as my cue.*

Moving in, JC held out her hand palm up and let the dog sniff her fingers before gently petting it on the neck. There were no growling or other signs of panic other than another whine. "You're okay," JC said. "I'm going to get you all fixed up. Let's go." She slid her hands under the animal as gently as she could and lifted it into her arms. Cradling the dog, she moved up the ramp to her jeep. Bella appeared to be trying to appease a gathering group of angry drivers, and JC appreciated what she did, knowing the task wasn't easy. Thankfully, it bought her the time she needed to not run with the dog. The last thing she wanted was to jostle it if there was an internal injury.

JC watched Bella notice her and start in her direction. "Is it bad?" she asked, and JC shook her head.

"I'm not sure," she replied. "But I need you to drive. We need to go to a vet. I'm pretty sure there's one near the food truck."

Thankfully, Bella only hesitated for a second before nodding. "I can do that," she said, helping JC into the jeep before climbing into the driver's seat.

Cooing to the animal on her lap while she buckled in, JC was relieved it remained calm with no hint of aggression. *Hopefully, being in a moving car won't upset it,* she thought as Bella started driving. The start was a little jerky, and the dog let out a slight whine.

"Sorry," Bella grimaced. "It's been a long time since I drove a stick shift."

"You're doing great," JC said, impressed Bella agreed to drive if she wasn't confident driving with a manual transmission. *Not that I gave her much choice,* she thought with a frown. "I'm sorry if I came across as bossy."

Bella shifted, much smoother that time, and grinned. "Under the circumstances, having me drive was the only thing that made sense," she said with a glance at the dog. "And you're very brave."

JC tenderly patted the dog's furry neck. "Honestly, I was reacting on instinct," she said. "I saw something in trouble and, well, I couldn't just drive past."

When Bella didn't respond, JC looked to see a smile on her face as she drove them down the street. "Of course you couldn't," the woman said. "Because you're good and kind. And I am extremely lucky to have you in my life."

17

Getting to the vet clinic took longer than Bella expected as she worked the jeep's clutch and gears. Thankfully her dad taught her how to drive a stick shift when she got her driver's license. Even though her first car was an automatic, he insisted. "It's a skill everyone should know," he had said, beyond patient as Bella killed the engine over and over again. So far, that hadn't happened, but it wasn't exactly a smooth ride. Every time she jerked the jeep forward, the dog let out a small whine, and Bella cringed. "I'm sorry," she said to JC and the animal, but JC proved to be as patient as Bella's father.

"You're doing fine," she said. "You're only out of practice."

"Well, the last time I drove a stick was when I was sixteen," Bella said. "So, yes, way out of practice."

"Then I'm even more impressed," JC said, nodding to the right. "That's the clinic up there."

Pulling into the lot, Bella managed to find a spot near the door and park without further problems. With JC right behind her, carrying the dog in her arms, Bella rushed into the vet clinic. There were two other people in the small, sterile-feeling waiting room—one with a cat carrier with a meowing pet inside, and the other wringing her hands looking anxious. Guessing they were already checked in, Bella went directly to the window at the front counter. "Excuse me. We have a dog who I think has been hit by a car," she said before the receptionist even said a word. "It's whining a little, and there is blood in the mouth, but we don't know what happened."

"Okay, let's slow down and find out what's wrong," the receptionist said in a comforting tone that helped Bella relax immediately. She wasn't sure what she expected, but the calm voice of the plump, middle-aged woman at the counter who radiated a soothing demeanor was perfect for her job. After setting a clipboard holding a form and a pen on the counter, the receptionist picked up the handset on the desk phone. "I will need that filled out in a minute, but first let me get a technician to come to help us."

Bella nodded. "Thank you," she said, taking the clipboard.

"You're welcome," the woman said before speaking into the phone and asking for someone to come to the front. After hanging up, she settled in at her keyboard. "Now, let's get a few basics. What's the name of your dog?"

Bella glanced at JC who held the dog and was unsure if saying it wasn't their dog would matter. "I think it's a stray," JC answered for her after a second. "We found it hurt on the side of the road, but I'll pay whatever charges there are to help it."

Nodding, Bella refocused on the receptionist. "We both will," Bella added without hesitation.

The woman smiled, and her eyes were gentle. "You are good people," she said. "Have a seat, fill out the form, and someone will be right out."

Moving to sit next to JC where she sat with the dog on her lap, Bella studied the hurt animal. It was panting and looked anxious, but not like it was ready to bite. Normally, she was not a pet person. There weren't any in her household growing up, although she wished for a kitten at times. Meeting a strange dog was outside her comfort zone, but if JC stayed relaxed, she would trust her instinct. *I've been doing all kinds of things out of my comfort zone lately,* she thought. *And all of it has been good.* Wanting to let the animal know her a little, but being wary too, Bella slowly put out her hand so the dog could sniff her. After a pause, the dog gave her fingers a gentle lick.

"That means she trusts you," JC said.

Bella's heart melted a little. She gently caressed the dog's face. "We're going to get you all taken care of, okay?" she said as a door to the waiting room opened, and a young man in green scrubs entered.

Like the receptionist, he radiated reassurance. "Hi, I'm Justin," he said. "Let me take her into the back for an x-ray and run some tests." He slowly took the dog from JC. "Are you going to wait? Or Teresa can call you. It will be a while."

Uncertain, Bella looked at JC. "What do you want to do?" she asked.

"Let's go get a cup of coffee," JC said, and Bella nodded, knowing JC was making the best choice. Bella wanted to know the dog's prognosis right away but sitting in the waiting room for an hour or longer would be nerve-wracking. "We won't go far."

"Good," the vet technician said. "Make sure you have your contact number on the form when you give it to Teresa, and we will call as soon as we know something."

AFTER USING an app on her phone to find a coffee shop a few blocks away, JC found them a table near a big plate glass window with a hint of an ocean view in the distance. "What can I get you?" JC asked Bella as the woman slipped into her chair.

Bella shifted in her seat. "I don't know if I should have anything with lots of caffeine right now," she answered. "I'm so anxious about our dog. So, maybe a green tea on ice would be best."

Our dog? JC thought, a little surprised at Bella's statement, but not unhappy. Anything that could be classified as theirs felt good. Still, she worried Bella would be devastated if the animal were truly hurt. Anything could be wrong internally from being hit by a car. JC hoped the injuries were minor. *And then there is the likelihood the dog has a microchip, and an owner is looking for it. It's not like we can take it with us.*

"That sounds refreshing," JC said with a reassuring smile. "Green tea it is." Before she made her way to the counter, Bella grabbed her hand. Turning back to her, JC saw a heartfelt look in the woman's eyes and paused. "What is it, Bella?"

"You're amazing. I hope you know that," Bella said. "Going after that poor animal and then willing to take responsibility for it at the vet..." She shook her head, and JC saw the glimmer of tears. "Well, you're special. Thank you."

Without thinking, JC leaned down to brush her lips against Bella's. "So are you," she murmured, giving Bella's hand a soft squeeze. "I'll be right back." As she went to get in line to order, JC reflected over the last week. *My life has made such a radical change in such a short time,* she thought. *And has become so wonderful.* Even though she wanted to appreciate all the goodness, she could not stop wondering what the future held. *I can't go on ignoring what has to happen at some point.* Even the thought of Bella leaving made her chest tighten. Luckily, before she could sink into the worrisome thoughts, it was her turn at the counter. Happy to distract herself, she ordered their green teas, took a number on a metal sign, and returned to the table.

Bella was looking out the window, clearly lost in her own world as JC approached. "Penny for your thoughts," JC asked, joining her.

Turning from the view, Bella gave her a small smile. "Lots of things," she said. "But mostly about that poor dog. Do you think it is a stray?"

Glancing through the big window, JC focused on the horizon for a second and thought about the question, picturing the skinny animal with matted fur and how it had acted since they found it. "I don't know," she said. "There isn't any collar, so no tags to identify an owner." She pursed her lips. "But there weren't any signs of aggression, and I'm not sure a stray would be so trusting."

When Bella didn't comment, JC shifted her gaze and caught the woman looking intensely at her. "You don't see it, do you," Bella said, but it didn't sound like a question. "Of course, the animal was trusting."

A little confused, JC raised her eyebrows. "I don't understand."

"How you are," she answered. "So confident, at the same time warm and friendly. Anyone and anything would trust you in a second. I did."

JC felt a blush rising on her cheeks at the unexpected compliments. "Well, I am not sure—"

Bella shook her head. "I'm not kidding," she said. "It's why your business is such a success. Everyone knows from the second they meet you that, even though they are going on an adventure, things will go okay. Including that poor dog." She laughed. "And me, as nervous as I was with those scary waves. Deep down, I stayed calm because I trusted you entirely." Not sure what to say, JC reached for Bella's hand and held it for a moment. JC didn't know how things would turn out with the dog, with Bella, with any of it, but she did know three things for certain—Bella could trust her with anything, that she would never hurt her, and most of all, she loved her.

Squeezing Bella's hand tighter, JC prepared to tell her exactly that when the woman from behind the counter approached the table. "Two iced green teas?" she asked, making JC pause.

"Yes," Bella answered, taking her drink. "Thank you." As JC took hers too, she was unsure if she was glad or disappointed about the interruption. *Maybe this isn't the time or place,* she thought. *But once we settle things with the dog and get home, I think it's time I tell her how I really feel.*

18

After waiting anxiously in the coffee shop for what felt like forever, Bella's phone finally rattled on the tabletop. "It's the vet clinic," Bella said when she looked at the screen, with a flutter of nerves in her stomach. She picked up before it buzzed again. "Hello?"

It was Teresa with news about the dog. Luckily, the prognosis was good. Tests showed two broken ribs, but no damage to the lungs. Still, she needed to speak with them as soon as they could get back. "Unless you want to handle things over the phone," Teresa said, making Bella frown.

"What? No," she said. "We are on our way."

Hanging up, Bella explained everything to JC. "Finish your drink and let's go," the woman said. Ten minutes later, Bella led JC into the waiting room and went straight to the counter.

"Hi," Bella said, her stomach fluttering with nervousness. Even though the woman had sounded upbeat on the call, Bella sensed an urgency in her voice when she asked them to come back soon. "We're back about the black and white dog."

"Of course," Teresa said with a smile. "Thank you for coming back."

Bella furrowed her brow. "Why wouldn't we?"

"Well, since she is a stray and not yours, you could have settled the bill over the phone," the receptionist explained. "Or even worse, skipped out altogether. Unfortunately, we have a protocol for that." *Is she kidding?* Bella thought, feeling strangely irritated by the comment. *And does she really think we would abandon the dog here?* Then she realized how crazy she was thinking. In many ways, releasing the animal to the vet clinic made sense. *But what exactly is that protocol?*

As if reading her mind, JC took Bella's hand before focusing on the receptionist. "What does that mean?" she asked, and Teresa reached for a form on her desk. She had partially completed it, and Bella guessed the woman had started it, expecting them to leave the dog behind.

She slid it across the counter. "When an animal is brought in with no collar and unfortunately no microchip to identify them, we have an arrangement with the county humane society," she explained. "After we fix them up the best we can, a volunteer from the agency picks up the dog or cat."

Not liking that plan at all, Bella started shaking her head. "That must be so scary for them," she said. "To have been hurt and then put in a cage." When she pictured it, tears came to her eyes—the sweet dog who had licked her hand and been so good all the way in the car. *No way,* she thought, looking at JC, who was already looking at her. "JC, I know this is asking a lot, but…"

Her voice trailed off as she watched JC study her face. "Bella, are you sure about this?" JC finally asked. "I don't want to leave her behind either, but we have to be realistic. I have a full schedule with tours for the next two days. It would fall to you to take care of her during the day."

A hint of panic threatened at the idea she would be alone

with a strange animal, but Bella pushed it down. "I can do it," she said. "We can make a bed for her next to the table where I'll be writing." Teresa had stayed silent throughout the exchange, but when Bella and JC turned to her at the same time and said "we want the dog," she laughed.

Taking the form back, there was a twinkle in her eyes. "I had a good feeling about you two," she said. "You have made this sweet dog a very lucky girl today." She turned to her computer. "First things first, you'll need to give her a name. It doesn't have to be permanent, but I must have something in my records."

Again, Bella looked at JC, already having a name in mind. It came from their days in college and too many nights at the karaoke bar a little off campus. *But I've already pushed for a lot,* she thought. "What do you think?" she asked, and JC gave her a wide smile.

"You're the creative one, and I think you have something in mind," she said. "I can see it in your eyes."

Bella laughed. "I love how you always seem able to read me," she said. "But I was thinking of a name you will remember too. From college and karaoke."

Pursing her lips in thought, JC tilted her head. "A name I will remember too..." she said, and then her smile returned. "Wait. This has nothing to do with my horrible singing voice, does it?"

"Oh yes, it does," Bella said. "One of my favorite memories. Is that okay? A tribute, sort of."

JC shook her head, but she was smiling. "In that case, yes," she said, and Bella turned back to Teresa.

"Her name is Roxanne," she said, loving the idea more every second. The name was perfect because it was associated with so many beautiful memories. "But we will call her Roxie for short."

. . .

With a very drowsy Roxie in the backseat on a beach blanket and with Bella beside her, JC drove them home. Looking in the rearview mirror, JC saw her gently petting the animal. "Just rest, Roxie," the woman murmured. "JC and I will take good care of you." The scene warmed JC's heart and they made a quick stop at a pet store where JC ran in to buy the essentials—bed, collar, dry food and water dishes, plus some wet food and treats. As she shopped, she felt that the situation seemed a little surreal. Suddenly, not only did Bella live with her, but they had Roxie to care for.

Grinning, she remembered the karaoke bar. *I sang that song so badly,* she thought. *But Bella could always talk me into it after a couple of beers.* Apparently, she could still talk JC into anything, including bringing home a recovering dog. She hoped the hasty decision was the right one. Taking time off from her business was impossible for the next few days. The situation left Bella to do all the work during the day, and she worried the woman didn't realize what that would entail. Not that JC thought she wouldn't be able to do it. *But it could certainly derail her writing if Roxie needs to be taken outside.* Only time would tell if their willingness to take Roxie in was the right choice.

Once they arrived at the house, JC carried Roxie inside while Bella handled putting the bed in the living room near what they would use as her writing area. "Okay," Bella said, stepping back, but JC noticed she bit her lip, clearly appraising the setup. "Do you think she will be okay out here when we go to bed? I worry she will be scared when the drugs wear off."

JC nodded. "That's a good point," she said. "I can sleep on the couch out here tonight."

"That's not fair to you," Bella said, shaking her head. "Especially since you have to get up so early for your job."

Appreciating Bella's consideration about everything, JC

smiled. "I don't mind," she said. "I promise to wake you up when I am ready to leave in the morning."

Frowning, Bella didn't look entirely convinced but nodded. "Okay," she said. "I guess that will work, as long as you come to get me if you need help in the night."

Without hesitating, JC put her arms around Bella's waist. "You're a wonderful person, Bella," she said, and the woman met her eyes. A tenderness filled them. *But is there a hint of something more?* JC wondered, not sure how to interpret what she saw.

As if in answer, Bella leaned closer, surprising JC with a kiss on the lips. "Not half as good as you," she murmured without pulling back. Encouraged, JC kissed her again, with more intensity this time. In response, Bella slid her hands up JC's arms to put them around her shoulders. Their contact started a fire in JC, making her want more from the woman than only a kiss. The only thing that kept her from pulling Bella closer was the responsibility of taking care of Roxie. The basics, if nothing else, were in order.

Pausing, she studied Bella's face. "Can we put this on hold for five minutes?" she asked. "Maybe get water for Roxie while I unload your bags?"

"Okay," Bella responded, desire in her eyes, but understanding too. "You're right. But only five minutes. I really like kissing you." Liking the sound of that, JC moved into action and before long, all the suitcases were tucked away in the bedroom Bella would use. Returning to the living room, she found Bella sitting on the floor next to Roxie. The dog slowly took a drink from the bowl Bella had filled for her.

As JC walked closer, Roxie shifted her eyes to watch her every movement. *Starting to wake up from the drugs a little more,* JC thought. *And probably realizing everything has changed. Hopefully she understands it's for the better.* From the beginning, every instinct told JC the dog would not bite. She had yet to even raise a lip to show her teeth. *So, how did such a gentle animal show up on the street?* Although she hated the idea, tomorrow evening after work, they would have to put up flyers in the neighborhood where they found her. Someone was probably looking for Roxie and finding the owner before they grew even more attached would be the best thing to do. Still, for tonight, she would enjoy the specialness of sharing time with Bella and Roxie.

19

Settling onto the comfortable leather couch beside JC, Bella loved the familiar way the woman slipped her arm over Bella's shoulders to pull her closer. The warmth of JC's firm body pressed beside her was both comforting and thrilling at the same time. Thinking of the kisses only a few minutes ago and how much she enjoyed them, Bella wasn't sure what to do next. *Should I make a move?* she wondered, feeling a strange time warp from when they were in college. So many times when she was close to JC, wanting more, but unsure what to do about it.

For the moment, JC seemed content to relax and watch Roxie fall asleep, but Bella wasn't sure she could let the evening slip by and then go to sleep if she didn't get at least a little more of the woman. *But what does JC need out of this? Am I expecting too much?* The last thing Bella wanted was for JC to think she moved in with an agenda. *Although we made out last night and were kissing again tonight.* Things felt so confusing. As if in answer to Bella's subliminal messages, JC turned her face to kiss Bella on the forehead. "You are quiet," she said. "Do you want a glass of wine or something?"

Bella bit her lip, knowing her best chance to say how she felt was right now. "Well," she said, hesitating as her mind ran through a million scenarios—unfortunately including JC turning her down if she made the wrong proposition. She couldn't do it. "Wine would be nice."

JC didn't get up right away, as if sensing something in Bella's tone, but then sighed and stood. "I'll be right back."

Before she could take a step, Bella bravely grabbed her hand. "Wait," she said. "I don't want wine yet." She took a deep breath. "I want you to kiss me."

Sinking onto the couch, JC smiled. "That I can do," she said, taking Bella's face into her hands. "As much as you want."

"I want a lot," Bella murmured an instant before she felt JC's lips on hers. Like all the times before, the contact made heat radiate through her body, only this time, the kiss seemed to hold more promise. Definitely more passion. Each taking the kiss deeper, their tongues teased, and someone moaned, but Bella wasn't sure who it came from. It was good, so good, yet as exciting as the kissing was, including last night, the hunger inside of Bella wanted more. An ache throbbed low in her body, and she needed to feel JCs hands on her, but so far, the woman's hands hadn't left Bella's face.

Breaking the kiss, JC rested her forehead against Bella's. "What are you thinking?" she whispered. "I can almost feel something circling in your head." She hesitated before asking, "Is this all too much?"

"No, it's not," Bella breathed. "It's just… well…" *Oh screw it, I can't take this anymore*, she thought and pressed her hands against JC's shoulders to push her away.

Acting surprised, JC pulled back, a look of apology on her beautiful face. "Bella," she said clearly not understanding. "I'm sorry. I thought—"

"Stop talking, JC," Bella said, continuing to push until the woman's back was pressed against the cushions, and in a brave moment, Bella slid a leg over the woman's legs until she straddled JC's lap. A flicker of arousal showed in JC's eyes, but she sat as if frozen and afraid to do the wrong thing. Not to be dissuaded, Bella took one of the woman's hands and placed it on her ass, only to do the same thing with the other. Satisfied for the moment, Bella wrapped her arms around JC's neck and leaned in. "Now. Kiss me some more."

A smile broke out on JC's face, and the fever of excitement shined in her eyes. "That I can do," she repeated, but before she could act, Bella took over, covering JC's mouth with her own. Unlike the interactions before, this time Bella was in complete control of the passion happening between them. Also, unlike before, the intensity of their kisses rapidly grew into a raging fire. After a few moments, they were both breathing heavy, and JC's strong hands pulled her in tighter. Bella couldn't remember the last time she was so turned on and flirted with the idea of suggesting they go to JC's bedroom. *But can we leave Roxie alone out here?* she thought with a groan. *One of us was going to sleep on the couch tonight.* As JC nuzzled Bella's neck, she realized they definitely had a dilemma.

WITH BELLA across her lap and her head spinning from the long, passionate kisses, JC didn't think she had ever been more excited. Her whole body ached at the idea Bella wanted to sleep with her, and under normal circumstances, JC would know precisely what to do. But they had one, small catch. A four-legged, furry one actually. JC moaned with frustration, and Bella pulled back to look at her.

"Is this too much?" she asked, and JC could not shake her head fast enough.

The kissing and everything Bella did was definitely not too much. "No," she answered. "It's not that. Trust me. I want more. Just…" JC nodded at the sleeping form of the dog in one of the cushioned beds they bought for her.

Bella sighed but stayed in place with her arms around JCs neck. "I know," she said. "I was thinking that too. If she wakes up and we are busy…" Bella's face blushed red. "Oh no, I didn't mean that as it sounded." She laughed, sounding a little self-conscious. "Well, kind of I did."

Slowly, the woman started to move from JC's lap, but JC held her tight and kissed her lips. "I like how that sounded and I want you too," she murmured. "My whole body is on fire." She hesitated, feeling not entirely sure how honest she should be with Bella. Coming on too strong might be a mistake. *Although she did straddle my lap without much prompting,* she thought. *And I'm pretty sure she's as turned on as I am.* She swallowed and forged ahead. "Bella, every part of me wants to pick you up and take you to my bedroom. I've wanted it for a long time, but I always wanted you to be ready."

A tender look mixed with the desire in Bella's eyes. "Thank you for that," she said, touching JC's cheek. "But tonight, I am ready, I promise."

Whatever arousal JC felt before tripled at Bella's confession, but it didn't solve their dilemma. "And Roxie?" she asked, for a fleeting second considering laying Bella back on the couch and making love to her there, but that scenario wasn't what she wanted. The first time they came together needed to be special, and she wanted to take her time pleasing the woman she cared so much about. *And having Roxie right there would feel a little awkward too,* she thought. *I don't see a way around this.* She sighed. "I don't know what to do."

"I feel the same way," Bella said, sliding off her lap enough to rest her head on JC's shoulder. JC felt the moment cooling as the passion turned to cuddling, and she felt a moment of frustration but then set it aside. Considering their history, another night of wanting Bella wouldn't be unusual. They took on the responsibility of Roxie and leaving her alone the first night in a strange house wouldn't be fair. *And now I finally know Bella feels the same,* she thought with a small smile. *Everything will happen between us, and then we may break the bed.* Sitting together, snuggled on the couch but not talking, JC watched Roxie rest. The night wasn't red hot monkey sex like she hoped, and her body craved, but the moment was still special. As if the animal could sense they looked at her, Roxie half-opened her eyes.

For a second, she didn't react, but then she thumped the floor a couple of times with her tail. "Did you see that?" JC asked, feeling a tenderness in her chest that wasn't related to how turned on Bella made her.

"Yes," Bella answered, lifting her head from JC's shoulder. "Hey there, Roxie. How are you?" Sighing, the dog closed her eyes, and JC saw Bella frown. "Do you think we should try to get her to drink some water or something?"

JC considered the question for a moment. "No," she said. "Sleep is probably the best for her right now. Let her body heal." JC's stomach growled, and with her other senses calming, she realized they pretty much hadn't eaten all day. "Are you hungry?"

"That's a loaded question," Bella said with a laugh. "But yes, starving."

"Then let me see what I can rustle up," JC said, but when she started to get up, Bella laid a hand on JC's chest.

"Let's do pizza delivery if that's okay," she said. "You've done more than enough, and trust me, letting me try to cook something, especially on the spot, would be a mistake."

Resting against the cushions again, JC smiled. "I can go for that," she said. "And maybe a movie?"

Bella returned her smile. "I would love it," she said, and as JC reached for her phone to call in an order, she let out a slow breath of contentment. Maybe they didn't get to sleep together tonight, but there would be other nights, and Bella was worth the wait.

20

The words flowed. Bella wrote on her work in progress for the next three days with a freshness she hadn't felt in years. Everything came together perfectly in her mind, and she almost couldn't type fast enough. Roxie rested in her fluffy bed on the floor beside the table where Bella worked. Although the dog was asleep pretty much all the time, Bella found comfort in having her around. Even though they were still getting to know her, she and JC agreed that Roxie was a gentle soul.

Because she was so well behaved and trained to let people know when she needed to go outside to do her business, it seemed impossible there wasn't someone looking for her. Although Roxie didn't have a microchip to reveal an owner, that didn't stop JC and Bella from posting flyers about her in the neighborhood where they found Roxie. After taking a picture of Roxie's sweet black and white face, JC used her printer at work to make flyers that they stapled on posts and tacked to bulletin boards everywhere. There was no way to know how far Roxie traveled before they found her, so they also posted on the local lost and found pets pages on the internet. So far, no one had called JC's cell phone number. She was beginning to think something had happened to Roxie's previous owners, or perhaps they had moved off the island.

Before starting a new chapter on her laptop, Bella glanced at the time. JC had sent a text half an hour before that she was caught in traffic, and Bella hoped she wasn't stuck. Pursing her lips, she tried to decide what to do next. "Hmmm," she murmured, and Roxie raised her head. Noticing, Bella smiled. "What do you think, Roxie? Should I make an attempt at fixing all of us dinner?" It wasn't that she minded putting something together for them, but the kitchen still felt unfamiliar. Plus, they hadn't been shopping so she didn't know what ingredients were available. Roxie raised her eyebrows but otherwise didn't comment. With a laugh, Bella leaned closer to run a hand over the dog's head. "Well, I can at least figure out something for you."

As she stood, there was a knock at the front door. *Did JC call ahead and order takeout?* she wondered as she walked to the entranceway. *That would be just like her since she is stuck.* Smiling at the idea, she opened the door. Instead of a delivery person, a pretty blonde woman stood on the walkup. "Oh," the woman said, clearly surprised to see Bella. "I'm sorry. I was looking for JC." The familiar way the stranger said JC's name made it clear she knew the woman, and Bella wasn't sure what to make of it. It seemed bizarre to be instantly jealous, but she couldn't help it.

Bella shook her head at her silliness and forced a smile. "She's not here," she said. "Can I take a message for her?" The woman tilted her head, looking Bella up and down. There didn't seem to be any malice in it but simply curiosity.

She smiled in return. "I can call her cell," she said. "I was hoping to surprise her, is all."

"I see," was all Bella could think to say. Her feeling of jealousy only seemed to be getting stronger, and it made no sense. Bella didn't like her reaction, especially since the stranger came across as nice enough. "Well, she's stuck in traffic but should be home soon if you want to wait here for her."

Raising an eyebrow, the woman clearly ran the scenario through her mind. "I don't think I will," she said. "But thank you."

She turned to go, but Bella took a step closer. "Can I at least give her a name? To let her know you came by?"

"Chris," she said. "I'm actually JC's ex-business partner."

Her ex? Bella thought, her mind working to connect the dots. "I see," she heard herself say again, aware she was probably coming across as awkward. Still, it didn't take her long to realize ex-business partner equaled ex-girlfriend. Before she could say more, she felt something beside her leg and looked to see Roxie standing with her in the doorway. Although the dog wasn't doing anything aggressive, something about her stance came across as protective to Bella. It warmed Bella's heart.

The stranger's eyes landed on Roxie, and she shook her head. "And a dog too," she murmured, though it wasn't a question.

"This is Roxie," Bella said, not bothering to explain that the dog wasn't really theirs. In fact, she liked the idea Roxie was theirs.

Chris started back down the walkup. "Hi, Roxie," she said. "Nice to meet you both." She gave a little wave and headed toward a car parked along the street. Bella couldn't help feeling glad to see her go.

FINALLY TAKING the exit toward her house, JC was ready to get home. She missed Bella, wanted to check on Roxie, and have a cold beer by the pool. Although she loved her job, knowing she was fortunate enough to do something she enjoyed every day, once in a while, there would be a batch of tourists who were challenging. She and Blake had their hands full with a large group, most of whom were inexperienced on the water, and one couple spoke very little English. That wasn't necessarily a bad thing but made the adventure a little more complicated. As always seemed the case after a long day, traffic would not cooperate as she tried to navigate the way home. By the time all the kayaks were hosed down and stored, JC was late getting on the freeway, which was always bad news. Throw in a fender-bender blocking one lane, and circumstances tested even JC's infinite patience. Luckily, she had finally driven into her neighborhood and would be where she wanted in less than five minutes.

Smiling at the thought, she considered what to do about dinner when her cellphone buzzed in its holder on the dash. The Bluetooth announced the caller, surprising JC enough to make her glance over. Chris Thornback. *Well, that is a heck of a surprise*, she thought, unsure what to do with the call. She didn't like to talk while she drove but would rather not have a call interrupt her evening at home either if Chris tried again. At the last second, she pressed connect from a button on the steering wheel. "Hello."

"Hi," came a voice JC hadn't heard in years. "I know you're driving and probably still hate to talk on the phone, so thanks for answering."

JC furrowed her brow. "How do you know I'm driving?"

"Well," Chris said, pausing as if trying to find the right words. "I stopped by your house a few minutes ago. And your..." She hesitated, making JC frown. "Your friend said you weren't home, so I made a guess."

JC shook her head, trying to keep up with the conversation that came out of left field and somehow involved her ex-business partner, who was also her ex-girlfriend, meeting Bella. "You were at my house?" she asked. "Why?"

Another pause. "I'm sorry, JC," Chris answered, sounding a touch hurt. "I didn't mean to upset you or anything. My plan was only to say hi."

JC grimaced, knowing she was being a little abrupt. "Hey," she said in a softer tone. "That came out wrong. I'm just surprised. I mean, it has been a while."

"You're right," Chris said. "That was silly of me to drop by without warning. I shouldn't have assumed… well… I should have called first."

Using her turn signal before making the last left before her house, JC wished she had let the call go to voicemail rather than end on an awkward note. Still, she wanted to hang up before pulling into the driveway. "It's okay," she said. "Maybe we can talk tomorrow sometime." Then, she realized there might be a more serious reason Chris called wanting to catch up. "Chris, are you okay? Is your family all right?"

"Yes. Absolutely," Chris answered in a rush. "I'm not calling with bad news, I promise. Honestly, I simply wanted to see you."

See me? JC thought, even more surprised than before. *What is going on?* It wasn't as if she and Chris broke up on bad terms or anything, but the woman had elected to return to the mainland without much input from JC. Considering they had a business together and what JC thought was a solid, long-term relationship, the decision was hard to take. When Chris explained she wanted to go to graduate school, JC had no problem with it, even when she learned the program was in Chicago. A long-distance relationship was never fun, but the separation wouldn't be forever. But that was not what Chris wanted, and in what felt like the blink of an eye, the woman severed ties and left Hawaii. JC could count on one hand the number of times they spoke afterward. *And suddenly she wants to see me?* "I'm not sure—" she started, but Chris cut her off before she could say much.

"I know you have someone new in your life," she said. "Hell, you even have a sweet-faced dog. But I hope we can catch up."

JC pulled into her driveway, not sure if explaining the situation about Bella or Roxie made sense to share, plus there wasn't time. "Let's talk tomorrow," JC said. "I'm home now, and it was a long day."

"Okay," Chris said. "You go relax. But you promise to call me back tomorrow?"

Not seeing an easy way out of the situation, JC nodded as she reached to shut off the Jeep. "I promise."

21

When the front door of JC's house opened, Bella took a deep breath to calm her nerves. She was in the kitchen with Roxie lying on the floor but out of the way, once again showing Bella the dog was owned by someone who took the time to train her. It felt nice to have her company, because she decided at the last minute to make a salad with whatever she could find in the fridge. JC would likely be hungry and tired after such a long day and rough commute. *Plus, I want to be helpful,* she thought. *And make her happy I'm sticking around.* It was the least JC deserved. *And let's be honest, the visit by JC's ex-girlfriend sort of motivated me too.* Bella wished she had thought to start the task of preparing food earlier.

"Anybody home?" JC asked with a playful tone, and Roxie left her post at the sound of the woman's voice. "Well, hello, Roxie." A warmth to JC's voice made Bella smile as she sliced the bright, red tomato while standing at the kitchen counter. "What did you do with Bella?"

"In here," Bella called. "Can I get you a beer?" After a

moment, she heard JC's footsteps on the tile and glanced over her shoulder. "Or I can open a new bottle of wine."

"Hmm," JC murmured through pursed lips as she crouched to pet Roxie. "A cold beer sounds magical, actually," she answered. "What are you making?"

Bella wiped her hands on a kitchen towel. "Only a salad," she said, moving to the refrigerator. "But it needs a protein I think."

As she took a cold beer from the shelf, she felt JC come up behind her and put a hand on her lower back. "You didn't have to get it for me," JC said softly, close enough Bella felt her breath on her neck. "But thank you." The contact made an unexpected but very pleasant shiver roll through Bella. Everything about the touch warmed her body. Wanting more, she spun in place until they faced each other with only JC's cold beer between them. Their eyes met, and a craving to kiss JC was too much to resist. Leaning in, their lips met, gentle at first but then with more heat. A low growl of pleasure came from JC's throat before she broke the kiss. A smile danced on her lips. "Now that is a hello to come home to," she said, taking the beer from Bella's hands before stepping away. Going to the drawer, she took out a bottle opener to pop the cap.

Bella blinked with surprise, unsure what had happened and confused by the abrupt end to the kissing. "Well, okay, I'm glad you think so," she said to JC's comment. "And to be honest I'd like to have more."

JC finished opening her beer with a sigh and took a long swallow. "We need to talk for a minute," she said, and Bella felt her stomach twist with unease. That had to mean she talked to her ex-girlfriend. Planning to tell JC about the whole encounter with Chris over dinner, Bella hadn't considered the woman would reach out to her so quickly. *I hoped I had until tomorrow*, she thought, although she was unsure why. The topic might be simple and mean nothing.

Seeing JC's body language though made her worry the conversation would be far from simple. "I think I know what you have on your mind," Bella said, moving back to the cutting board to pick up a mushroom to slice. She needed something to hide her trembling hands. "A woman named Chris stopped by looking for you."

"Yes, she said that she did," JC replied. "Sorry about that."

Pausing what she was doing, Bella didn't understand why they both were taking the sudden appearance of JC's ex so seriously. In reality, Bella and JC hardly knew each other again, and it certainly wasn't like they were officially a couple. *And eventually, I will go home*, she thought, feeling more and more removed from the situation with the ex-girlfriend. "Why are you sorry?" Bella asked. "It's not a big deal. She seemed nice." She shrugged. "Am I right?"

There was a pause, making Bella glance over. "You're right," JC said, relief in her voice. "I am blowing this out of proportion. There's nothing wrong with you meeting my ex." Giving a little laugh, JC took another drink of her beer. "I wish she hadn't dropped in uninvited though."

Bella scooped up the vegetables she cut and put them in with the mixed greens already in the large bowl. "Everything is fine," she said. "You can tell me more about her over dinner."

Rarely drinking on evenings when she had to get up early for work the next day, JC decided tonight was an exception. The first beer went down fast as she processed the random phone call from her ex-girlfriend while at the same time trying to read Bella's body language. Bella's words sounded surprisingly indifferent, as if the entire event of Chris's unexpected visit didn't faze her at all. Unfortunately, her attitude was only more confusing because JC's first impression when she brought the subject up was that Bella was anxious about it. *But that reaction doesn't make much sense to me either*, JC thought as she rinsed out the beer bottle before setting it aside for recycling. The temptation to grab another made her pause. *And why am I in the mood to get a buzz on?*

"Do you want to eat on the patio again tonight?" Bella asked as she tossed the salad. "It's not the grandest of dinners, I'm afraid."

"Actually," JC said, moving to the refrigerator. "Let me put some shrimp in a skillet to add to the top. There's a dozen I was defrosting to make into something tonight."

Bella turned from the counter, smiling. "Of course, you were," she said. "You're always thinking ahead." Opening the door, JC wondered if that was why Chris's call had her so out of sorts. She liked things planned and could admit one of her flaws was a lack of spontaneity. Not that she wasn't romantic or original, but JC preferred to operate on a schedule. She liked to have a plan. The funny thing was that Chris knew that about her, and they had at times discussed JC's inability to let things simply happen. *She had to know that showing up at my house would not go well*, she thought. *Whether I was home or not.*

With the raw shrimp and a second beer in hand, JC nudged the refrigerator door closed with her elbow and moved to the stove. "Mind if I add a little heat to these?" she asked, thinking some Cajun seasoning might be a nice twist tonight. When Bella didn't answer immediately, JC glanced at her. The woman leaned against the counter studying JC, but her face was impossible to read. JC paused what she was doing. "What are you thinking, Bella?"

Bella tilted her head. "Only that I'm extremely lucky," she said. "That I picked the brochure for your kayaking adventure company from the dozens of other activities." She shook her head. "And that I went through with it and got on the van. I tried to chicken out a half dozen times before seeing you."

Appreciating the change to a lighter mood, JC grinned as she dumped the shrimp into a frypan. "You never told me that part," she said but didn't have any trouble imagining Bella wavering. She could easily remember Bella's face full of concern when JC explained the plan to paddle to the island. "But I think I am the lucky one."

"Hmm..." Bella murmured as she slipped closer until she against the cupboards beside the stove. "We will see. But seriously, JC, you are amazing. Kind, sexy, a wonderful cook..." She paused, looking at the floor as if trying to make up her mind. Finally, she sighed. "You don't have to answer if it's not my business, but why did you and Chris not work out?"

After adding a few shakes of seasoning and turning the heat down on the shrimp, JC faced Bella. "It's not a secret," she said. "And I want you to feel like you can ask me anything." She took the woman's hands in hers. "But the problem came down to her wanting to go to school on the mainland."

Bella slowly nodded. "I see," she said softly. "And, of course, you wanted to stay here." Neither said a word as the reality of the situation between them seemed to fill the room. At some point and not too far away, Bella would leave for the mainland too. Before JC could comment, Bella leaned in to give her a quick peck on the lips. "But you've had a long day, and we don't have to talk about any of this tonight."

For a moment, JC thought about resisting Bella's deflection, but she was right that her day was long and there was nothing urgent that needed to be discussed. "Thank you," she said. "Let me turn these shrimp a couple of times and then we can enjoy some dinner."

"Perfect," Bella said with a smile, as she moved to the cupboard that held the dinner plates. "Let me set the table, and then we can eat and relax."

JC liked the sound of that, especially as she realized she was more tired than she first thought. "Would you be up for taking it easy with a movie after dinner?" she asked.

Bella walked by her with plates and silverware on the way to the patio. "That sounds nice," she said over her shoulder. "I'm happy with whatever you want to do."

JC watched the woman go out the door for a moment. Even though Bella appeared to be normal, something felt off. *It has to be over Chris*, she thought with a sigh. *But tonight, I think I'll let that go.* She simply didn't have the desire to talk about the past, or even more, about the future.

22

Coffee cup in hand, Bella leaned back in her chair to study the screen for a moment. She had gotten up when she heard JC in the kitchen, filled with a new idea for her book. After a quick but very nice breakfast and goodbye kiss with her new roommate, she had settled down to write. Finally, the chapter was finished, and she let her eyes scan what she wrote. Then, with a fist pump at her accomplishment, Bella let out a loud "yes." When Roxie moved on her bed beside the table, Bella leaned to look at her. Her head raised, the dog's warm eyes held a quizzical expression. Bella smiled. "Sorry, but I'm excited about this one. Big plot twist to end act two."

After a beat, Roxie yawned, lowering her muzzle back to her paws. With a laugh, Bella stood. "Oh, I see. Well, you're new to this, so I forgive you," she said, picking up the small bag of chewy dog snacks from the corner of the table. "I bet you will get excited if I offer you a treat though." Roxie's head popped back up, her eyes bright. "That's what I thought."

She fished a nugget from the bag while Roxie sat up and

studied her. Bella continued to be impressed. There was no hint of begging or other antics trying to convince her to pass over the treat. Bella had an idea, and she held the snack higher. "Can you catch?" she asked, and Roxie's eyes didn't waver. Not sure if all dogs could catch or not, Bella tossed a soft lob in the dog's direction. Moving only her head, Roxie snapped the treat out of the air, chewed for a moment, swallowed with a gulp, and then refocused on Bella. "Well, you made that look easy." Bella tilted her head. "I wonder how many tricks you know." She picked out another treat. "Lay down?"

Roxie gently lowered her body, her focus never wavering. Impressed, Bella gave her the reward before running a hand over the animal's soft, furry head. "When you're feeling one hundred percent better, I think the three of us need to find a place outside and check out your other talents." She guessed JC would have some fun ideas to try, and thinking of the woman, she thought back to the evening before. Although lacking the passion of their other evenings so far, the night had been sweet as they wrapped up in a blanket on the couch and watched most of a movie together. JC had surprised her by falling asleep partway through the film and the woman had apologized profusely over it, but Bella took it as a good sign. She liked knowing that JC was comfortable around her.

Setting down the treats, Bella was about to go to the kitchen when her cellphone rang. Seeing Joanie, her editor's name, on the screen, she scooped it up before making her way to grab another cup of coffee. "I've had the best writing morning," she answered without even a hello. "You're going to love it."

"Well, I won't say no to that," Joanie said with a laugh. "And aloha to you too."

Bella laughed too. "Sorry," she said, opening the refrigerator and finding the creamer. "I'm excited. My writing has never been better."

After a beat, Joanie cleared her throat. "About that," she said. "What is your plan, Bella?"

Bella bit her lip. She knew things couldn't go on like they were forever, and understood she needed to figure out a plan. But that was easier said than done. "I am not sure," she finally answered. "But I'm not ready to leave yet." Then, JC's ex-girlfriend's face came to mind, and she was even more sure she wasn't ready to go. Not until she learned about what the woman wanted from JC. "I promise, I will come up with a timeline soon."

"That's the thing," Joanie said. "You're scheduled to speak at a literary conference in Albuquerque at the end of the month."

Pausing mid-pour, Bella realized she had forgotten all about the summer literary conference. "Oh no!" she said. "That slipped my mind. When exactly is that?" she asked, wondering if getting out of it was possible.

"It's too late for you to cancel on them," Joanie said as if reading her mind. "And if you fly straight there, you have ten days."

But that's way too soon, Bella thought, filling the rest of her mug. *There's not only JC, but now Roxie. I have to take care of her.* Still, Bella was not the type of person who walked away from commitments. The organizer of the conference counted on her, and her readers would be disappointed. "Crap," was all she could get out, a surprising burn of tears in her eyes. The fantasy life she had been living was about to end.

AFTER HELPING the last pair of kayaks launch from the small Moku island, JC pushed off her own kayak and hopped in. She caught up to the others in a few quick strokes, and the group glided over the ocean water toward home. The weather was perfect, the waves gentle, and overall, a beautiful day. Only she couldn't stop thinking about Bella and the strangeness in the kitchen last night, followed by her falling asleep on the couch. The short conversation about JC's ex-girlfriend seemed to lead to a sort of resignation in Bella as if she recognized their time was short and accepted it. Accepting it was not something JC wanted. Not by a longshot.

When she had said Chris left for the mainland while JC stayed, and that was why they split, she never guessed Bella would take the statement to heart. Their situation was different, but JC hadn't wanted to take on the tough topic last night and in hindsight kicked herself a little. What the two of them were going to do needed to be addressed soon. Instead, they had stuck to light topics. Like Roxie, for example. *What a good dog,* she thought, paddling through the small waves. *She's so calm.* JC knew from experience most dogs weren't. She would have expected Roxie to be nervous or restless at least, but instead, she rested on her bed beside Bella's work table. It could have been the drugs, but those would have worn off long ago. *Maybe she's been different today.* A hint of worry tickled at JC. The last thing she wanted was for Bella to be stuck at the house with an unruly dog.

As they slipped onto the sand at the other shore, JC quickly disembarked. Her phone was in her dry bag lashed to the tip of her kayak, but she couldn't dig it out until all her clients were safely standing on the sand. While she was helping each of them along, Blake came up beside her. "Everything okay?" he said under his breath, making JC pause. A look around, and she realized her movements had been rushed and even bordering on unfriendly.

With a sigh, she nodded. "Sorry," she said. "Yes, everything is fine. Just eager to check in with Bella."

Blake grinned. "And that's what I wanted you to say," he said. "She makes you happy, so I get it."

Unable to resist his smile, JC returned it. "She really does," she said, feeling a sense of longing to be near Bella again. "All I want is to be with her."

"Well, I don't think she was much into kayaking," Blake said. "So maybe you need to take a couple of extra days off." JC started to protest, but Blake waved it away. "The new guy Shaun has been looking for some extra time on the water, and the groups are small the next few days." What Blake said was true. Considering the time of year, the bookings were slower than usual. Normally, JC would be concerned, but she welcomed the opportunity to take some extra time under the circumstances. Even though neither said it the evening before, Bella's nights in Oahu were numbered. If they had to separate soon, JC wanted to make the most of the time they had left.

JC nodded. "Thank you, Blake," she said. "I will take you up on that offer."

Clapping JC on the back, Blake smiled ear to ear. "Good," he said. "What will you do?"

Thinking about his question, JC thought of a few things she would like to do with Bella, but those only made her feel a blush coming on. Instead, she focused on the more tangible. "Maybe a drive around the island," she said. "We could take Roxie in the jeep and spend the day exploring." The idea grew on JC by the second. "I don't think Bella has seen the North Shore or anything beyond the South Coast."

Blake scoffed. "Then that's a no-brainer," he said. "Turtle Bay, Waimea Valley..." He laughed. "Giovanni's Shrimp Truck!"

JC laughed with him. The man was spot on. Taking Bella, and of course, Roxie too, to more remote and more beautiful places than Waikiki and Hawaii Kai seemed almost mandatory. *Especially if she is leaving soon*, she thought, but then pushed it away. Her goal would be to enjoy every minute they had left. Bella had yet to mention what her plans were, and for the moment, JC would hope for a lot more time together.

23

Relaxing on one of the loungers beside JC's pool, Bella tried to resolve the many questions swirling around in her mind. When and how she would tell JC her predicament was foremost. She could not deny the literary conference was coming up. Bella knew her editor was right and that she must go, but now nine days to get ready for the event was not a long time. Although she would rather swing home to Portland and pick up some fresh clothes, that would shorten her time in Hawaii with JC and Roxie even more. *But am I overreacting?* she wondered. *Just because I have to go back to the mainland for a while doesn't mean we are over. Lots of people have long-distance relationships.* Still, a part of her worried. Especially with the sudden addition of Chris, JC's ex, to the equation. Although they steered clear of serious topics the night before, tonight looked like it would need to be different. It seemed such a shame for what looked to be another beautiful evening in paradise.

Closing her eyes to soak up the last bit of late afternoon sun, Bella was surprised to hear the sliding doors from the house open. Even Roxie let out a little "woof" at the unexpected visitor. Sitting up to look, Bella saw JC coming out onto the patio, and she carried a glass of white wine and a beer. "Hey there," she said. "Didn't mean to spook you two but Blake sent me home early."

Bella smiled, trying desperately not to feel self-conscious that she was in a small two-piece swimsuit. "It's a great surprise," she said and couldn't help but scoop up her beach towel on the lounger beside her and rest it across her midsection. "I wasn't expecting you home for another hour at least."

JC joined her, handing over the glass of white wine before settling in the lounger beside Bella. "I know," she said with a shrug. "And I should have sent a text, but I kind of wanted to surprise you a little." She smiled playfully, but Bella noticed a bit of heat too. "Maybe catch you sunbathing, just like this."

Fighting off her self-consciousness, Bella tossed her head, feeling a blush come on but liking JC's line of thinking. "Oh really?" she asked. "And why is that?"

"Because you're sexy as hell," JC replied without hesitation before taking a sip of her beer. "And I can't stop thinking about you." This time, Bella couldn't hold back the blush or the tingle that ran through her body at the woman's words.

Daring to be bold, she held JC's gaze. "So here I am," she said. "What are you going to do about it?"

Just then, JC's cellphone rang in her pocket. "Shit," JC muttered, fishing it out. "Sorry." Bella watched her look at the screen and frown. "Seriously, Bella, I am so sorry. But it's Blake, and I need to take this."

Disappointed at the bad timing but knowing it wasn't JC's fault, Bella nodded. "Of course," she said. "I hope everyone is okay."

JC answered the call. "Hey, Blake," she said. "What's going on?" The woman listened for a minute. "Oh, okay, hold on." She stood and started toward the house. "I have that on my laptop here." She glanced at Bella. "Two minutes," she mouthed and then was gone. Bella sighed but knew JC was worth the wait and looked at the still blue water of the pool. The evening was warm, and JC's comments only made her feel warmer. The water seemed to call to her suddenly.

She looked at Roxie. "I think I need to cool off," she said to the dog, and Roxie raised her eyebrows but otherwise didn't respond. Bella laughed as she stood. "And you stay right there."

Bravely leaving the towel behind, Bella walked to the steps leading into the pool. In a moment, she descended into the cool water. It felt good against her hot skin, and she sighed. Having a swimming pool was a perk she truly appreciated. JC had made a good choice picking the little house where she lived, and although Bella didn't know what the place looked like before the renovation, she loved the house now. It was the best environment she had for writing in a long time, if not forever. Leaving, even if temporarily, would be hard.

Easing through the water, Bella heard the patio doors open again and looked to see JC walking toward her. "That looks fantastic," JC said, stripping off her tank top to show the bikini she always wore for work and her fantastic body. "Mind if I join you?"

Bella took in the sight of the sexy woman who for some reason truly seemed to desire her. "I don't mind at all," she said. "I would love it."

NOT SURE IF it was the warmth of the evening, the heady smell of plumerias filling her backyard, or seeing Bella in a bikini in the pool, but suddenly JC wanted the woman more than ever. They had been flirting with having sex for what felt like forever, and she wasn't sure she could hold back any longer. The shared kisses on the couch, the heated looks over dinner... they all added up to an ache inside JC that would not subside.

Tossing her shirt aside, JC moved to the edge of the pool and made a shallow dive into the water, gliding under the surface until she reached Bella. Coming up for air beside her, they were face to face. Looking into Bella's face, the woman was biting her lip, and JC saw the same desire she felt reflected in her eyes. "Hi there," JC breathed as the cool water dripped down her face, unsure what to do next.

A sultry smile crossed Bella's face. "Hi," she said. "Did I mention I'm glad you're home early?"

"Mmm hmm," JC replied, moving a little closer while holding Bella's eyes. "You did."

"And did I tell you how sexy I think you look in only that bikini top and swim shorts?" Bella asked, making JC raise an eyebrow.

"I don't think you did," JC murmured, closing the gap between their mouths even more. "But I'm glad you do." She put her hands on Bella's hips and pulled their bodies closer until they bumped under the water. The contact sent a charge of excitement through JC. Clearly feeling it too, Bella gasped. Unable to stand the tension much longer, JC licked her lips. "I want you."

"I want you too," Bella whispered, letting JC know there was no reason to wait any longer to follow her instincts. Pulling Bella tighter against her, JC closed the distance completely and kissed her. Like all the kisses before, the touch was enough to make JC's heart skip a beat, but this time there was more hunger between them. As if both knew the time had come to follow their desires and take things further.

Feeling Bella open her lips to invite the kiss to go deeper, JC didn't hesitate, conquering the woman's mouth. The intensity of feeling their tongues dance forced a growl from deep in JC's throat. Bella slipped her arms around JC's neck and kissed back harder in response. They stood in the pool, lost in each other's kiss for a long moment, but it wasn't enough. JC wanted more and slowly started to push Bella backward toward the pool's edge.

When they gently bumped the tile, Bella broke the kiss. JC could feel her breath coming fast, and before she knew what was happening, Bella wrapped her legs around JC's hips. Relishing the feel of being enveloped in the woman, JC pressed forward against Bella's center. The touch blazed hot through the fabric between them, and all she wanted was to get Bella naked so she could feel their skin on skin.

Instinctively knowing Bella would be shy, JC set the example by quickly untying her own top and letting it slip free into the water. "Oh God," Bella moaned as her eyes ran over JC's body. "Your breasts are fantastic."

In answer to the compliment, JC kissed her again and slipped her hands to the ties of Bella's top. For a moment, the woman stiffened and then, with a shiver, relaxed. "Is this okay?" JC murmured against her mouth.

"Yes," Bella breathed and let JC continue. With nimble fingers, she removed the clothing, freeing Bella's larger breasts. Not giving the woman time to react, JC kissed her again while massaging Bella's skin and running a thumb over one of her tight nipples. She was rewarded with a sharp cry of passion from Bella, and again the woman broke the kiss. "You're making me crazy." She hesitated for only a second. "I want more."

Encouraged, JC lowered her head to kiss the skin above the water but was teased by the nipple barely under the surface. She had two choices: keep going and take Bella in the backyard working around the water or coax the woman inside where they had more privacy and a bed. The hunger of the moment made it hard to slow down, but the chance to have the woman laid out beside her in the sheets was a strong motivation. Making up her mind, she kissed Bella hard again before trailing her mouth around to the woman's ear. "I want more too," she whispered. "Will you come inside with me?"

"Yes," Bella replied, her voice husky with passion. "Oh, definitely yes."

24

Even though she was turned on beyond anything she ever remembered, Bella grabbed for her beach towel as soon as she slipped from the water. It was as much to dry off as to hide herself a little. Although JC repeatedly made it clear she found Bella sexy in her swimsuit, the anxiety was still there that the woman might not like Bella's body. As if reading her mind, JC came up behind her and wrapped her arms around Bella's waist, pulling her close. "Are you sure you want this?" JC asked in a husky voice.

"More than I can express," Bella said quickly to make sure she wasn't sending the wrong signal by covering up. "Let's go in the house." Without another word JC took her hand and led Bella through the patio doors.

As always Roxie was right on their heels, and JC paused looking at the dog. "Go get in your bed Roxie," she said in a gentle tone. Roxie tilted her head, clearly appraising them but then as if understanding she went to her cushion, turning in a circle once before lying down with the little huff.

Bella could not help but give a little laugh at the dog's dramatics. "She really is special," she said before turning to

JC, unable to miss the smoldering passion in her face. "And so are you."

"Then, let me show you how attracted to you I am," JC said pulling Bella's hand again and leading her to the hallway that connected to JC's room. Once inside the bedroom, Bella's nerves kicked into high gear. As much as she had craved the moment, the reality of it actually happening after all these years felt almost crazy.

Apparently, her hesitation showed because JC wrapped her arms around Bella's waist again. "What's in your head?" JC asked.

"I'm sorry," Bella said. "It's just that..." She wasn't even sure how to explain, and JC kissed her gently.

"I want you," she said against Bella's lips and those three words made her brave. She truly did feel desired. Slowly, she let the towel slip until it was on the floor, and she stood in nothing but her bikini bottoms. After a beat, she removed them too.

JC sucked in a breath. "Thank you," she said, removing her own swim trunks in a flash before kissing her again so deep and passionate that Bella felt herself melt a little. Slowly, JC's hands slid up Bella's back, sending a delightful shiver through her. The skin on skin contact felt amazing and made Bella want more. Pushing gently, she backed JC toward the large bed in the center of the room, never breaking the kiss. The woman did not resist and in a moment fell back when she came to the edge, pulling Bella down on top of her.

As they intertwined their bodies, Bella's thigh slipped between JC's legs, and she felt heat at the woman's center. At the contact, JC moaned and lifted her hips a little to intensify the pressure. Her hands moved to Bella's waist, and JC held them tightly together as she slipped her tongue into Bella's mouth just enough to tease her. Heat flashed through Bella at the touches, making her body throb in response. Slowly, she rocked her hips, moving her thigh enough to start friction between them. A growl of excitement came from JC's throat and after a moment, she broke the kiss with a gasp.

"Bella, if you keep doing that, I'm going to come already," JC said, making Bella feel a thrill of pleasure in knowing she could please the woman so easily. She picked up her pace, rubbing them together with more intensity while JC closed her eyes.

Moving her mouth to JC's ear, Bella whispered words she had longed to say forever. "That's what I want," she said. "To finally make you come."

Pulling Bella in harder, JC responded by thrusting her hips in perfect rhythm to Bella's movement. "You're going to get what you want," JC groaned. "I have wanted you for so long, and this is so good."

Feeling another throb low in her body, Bella wondered for a second if she would come too. It wasn't something that normally happened from grinding, but taking JC was so exciting that passion rippled through her body. Every part of her was on fire, and an ache began that Bella knew could only be fulfilled by one thing—she needed to feel JC inside her. But first, she wanted JC to come, and she kissed and nipped at the hot flesh of the woman's neck. JC gasped, starting to squirm under her. "Yes, more of that," she said, and excited by JC's request, Bella sucked and teased with her tongue. "Yes, oh God. Don't stop." In the next moment, JC cried out in pure pleasure and Bella felt satisfaction fill her knowing she had tipped the beautiful, sexy, wonderful woman over the edge.

LYING on her back with her eyes closed, JC relished Bella's weight on top of her while she tried to slow her pounding heart. Her body tingled in the aftereffects of the incredible orgasm she just had. What Bella had done to her had felt beyond good and she loved basking in the glow. "Bella?" JC asked. "Do you know how amazing you are?"

Bella gave a little laugh. "You sound very satisfied," she replied, and JC chuckled.

"You're right," she said before opening her eyes and turning to nuzzle Bella's hair. When the woman lifted her head so they were face to face, JC kissed her on the lips, quickly taking the kiss deeper, letting Bella know that no matter how fulfilled she felt, JC was not through. When Bella hummed with pleasure, JC took it as a good sign and easily flipped them until she was on top of her. Bella gave a little cry of excitement at the sudden move making JC smile. "You didn't think we were done did you?" She ran her mouth along Bella's chin and then onto her neck. "What we did rocked my world, but I hope it was only the tip of the iceberg."

"Mmmm," Bella hummed as she gently raked her fingernails up JC's back. "I like the sound of that." Shivering under the sensation of Bella's hands on her, JC slipped lower until she was kissing the woman's collarbone. She moved her hand up Bella's body and began to caress her breast, loving the tight nipple she found. Bella gasped. "That feels good." Taking that as a sign to keep going, she slid lower until she found the other breast and without hesitation pulled the nipple into her mouth. Sucking and tugging on it, she loved the way Bella arched her back wanting more. Teasing gently, she continued to caress the other breast with her fingers. After a minute Bella started to squirm. "You're teasing me." Again, JC smiled. She loved every minute of the anticipation she knew she was building.

Sliding lower, JC trailed kisses down Bella's stomach, moving her body between the woman's legs while spreading them wider. "I have dreamt of this so many nights," she said as she kissed Bella's inner thighs. "A part of me can't believe it is actually happening."

"Oh, it's all happening," Bella said reaching down and putting her hands in JC's hair. "Soon, I hope. You have me so turned on."

No longer able to resist, JC dipped her head and ran her tongue between Bella's wet and swollen lips to find her hard clit. Circling it before giving it a gentle suck, she was rewarded with a little cry of pleasure from Bella. Caught up in the moment, she started to move her mouth faster and after a minute she heard Bella's breath starting to hitch. Knowing she gave Bella so much pleasure only made JC want more. She wanted to feel all of her but wasn't sure how Bella would respond. Hoping she wasn't going too far, JC slid her hand along Bella's thigh until she positioned her fingers at the woman's wet opening. She felt Bella's hands in her hair clench with excitement. "Yes," Bella breathed. "I want to feel you inside me."

Needing to please, with her own body on fire with the passion of the moment, JC slid a finger inside her, relishing the warmth she found there. Slowly she slipped in and out while continuing to suck and tease Bella's clit with her mouth. "More," Bella said in a gasp and JC used a second finger inside her, feeling the tightness and immediately Bella responded by starting to move her hips and grind against JC. While the woman rode her hand, JC never relented her contact with Bella's clit until finally the woman was panting with pleasure. "Yes, oh yes." The words were everything JC could hope for, and she held on with her other arm around Bella's leg as the woman bucked, grabbing at the bedspread, and shook as she came.

When Bella started to still, JC moved up her body to rest

her head on Bella's chest. She could hear the woman's heart racing. "I can't believe we waited so long to do this," JC said.

"I know," Bella said, caressing JC's face. "I'm so glad we finally figured this out."

"Me too," JC said as her body relaxed. "Me too."

25

Humming a happy song with a name she couldn't remember, Bella finished making the morning coffee in JC's bright and cheery kitchen. She could not think of a time she felt more content. The night before was everything she imagined it would be, and as she thought of a particularly sexy moment, Bella felt a blush heat her cheeks as a small smile crossed her lips. It was a fantastic night indeed. "Well now," she heard JC say as she came through the patio doors off the attached dining room. "I might need to know what's making you smile like that." Turning to look, Bella loved the sight of the remarkable woman with Roxie walking into the house beside her.

"I imagine it isn't hard to guess," she replied with a toss of her dark hair. "But if you want me to show you later…"

Meeting her at the counter, JC was all smiles. "I will be cashing in on that," she said, picking a pair of blue ceramic coffee mugs from the cabinet. "Thank you for making coffee."

Bella pecked JC on the cheek. "And thank you for taking Roxie out," she murmured before leaning against the counter to look at the dog lying near the glass doors in the sun. "She's doing so well."

Nodding, JC poured the coffee. "I agree," she said. "Actually, I remembered an idea I had while she and I were outside." She handed one of the mugs to Bella. "And tell me no if you need to spend the day focusing on writing, but what if the three of us took a drive around the island?"

Not even needing to think twice, Bella nodded because the idea of spending the day exploring with JC and Roxie sounded like heaven. "I would love that," she answered. "I've never even seen the North Shore."

JC grinned. "Then let's do it," she said. "Let me grab the cooler, and we can pack a few drinks and maybe sandwiches for lunch. Some of the beaches are pretty isolated."

"What can I do to help?" Bella asked, feeling more excited by the minute.

A sexy look crossed JC's face. "Pack that bikini from last night?"

Feeling a tingle of arousal run through her, Bella wondered how isolated those beaches might be. Sex on the beach was certainly a fantasy of hers. *But about as far out of my normal comfort zone as I can get,* she thought. *Still, JC makes me courageous.* "I will go put it on under my clothes right now," she replied, her voice huskier than she expected. JC set her coffee mug on the counter before taking Bella's to do the same.

She put her hands on Bella's hips and pulled her closer. "That would entail you removing your clothing then?" JC murmured.

Bella licked her lips. "That's generally how it works," she said, moving her face closer until their mouths were an inch apart. "Does that interest you for some reason?"

"Mmmm hmmm," JC whispered against Bella's lips. "Interests me very much."

Loving the way warmth enveloped her simply by being close to JC, Bella kissed the woman. At first tenderly, as JC teased her mouth, but it quickly grew hotter, and Bella wrapped her arms around JC's shoulders to pull them even tighter together. As their tongues touched, every bit of excitement she felt the night before built in her, but the feelings were even more intense this time. After the hours wrapped up together in JC's bed after those first kisses in the pool, Bella knew how amazing being with the woman would feel. JC was every bit the lover she imagined, and the idea there would be a repeat performance happening soon made her knees a little weak.

Pulling back to try and catch her breath as her heart raced with excitement, Bella gathered her courage, knowing in her heart JC would never reject her. "Take me to bed," she finally said. "And do what you did to me last night."

Surprising her with the swiftness of her movement, JC swept Bella up in her arms, turning them in the direction of the bedroom. "Thank you, Bella," she said, her voice low and filled with desire. "I thought you would never ask."

STILL BASKING in the glow from their quick but very satisfying lovemaking, JC put a few towels, a boogie board, and a backpack filled with sunscreen and other essentials into the jeep. All JC needed to add was the cooler Bella was packing. Excited about the day ahead, JC had a spring in her step as she headed to the house.

"The cooler is ready, and I can't think of anything else I need to bring," Bella said when JC walked in the door.

JC went to give her a peck on the lips, but then lingered. The spark from their trip to the bedroom not more than thirty minutes ago still pulled at her. "Thank you," she murmured against Bella's lips and the woman laughed, although it was deep and throaty.

"But you better stop it or we will never drive anywhere today," she said, and it was JC's turn to chuckle.

"You're right," she said, giving her one more quick kiss before turning to grab the cooler. "Let me load this, and then we can see about Roxie." Afraid that the dog might be skittish about riding in the jeep after her accident, JC had a short leash and treats at the ready. With Roxie's ribs still tender, a regular harness would be uncomfortable for her, so JC fitted her with a thin nylon vest. She had wondered how Roxie would take to wearing it, but like most things, the dog accepted it without much coaxing. Although it seemed clear she never wore a vest, she seemed to be okay after sniffing the cloth before JC put it on her and then turning in a circle a dozen times as if to shake the thing off.

Leading Roxie outside, she put the cooler in its place, while Bella buckled into the passenger seat. JC stopped at the backdoor with Roxie beside her. "Want to go for a ride?" she asked the dog who had followed along patiently so far, apparently not fazed by the attached leash. *People must really be missing this dog,* JC thought, once again impressed at her training. *At some point, someone walked her on a lead, that's for sure.*

Opening the backdoor, JC pulled a treat from her pocket and held it inside the jeep. "Can you jump in?" she asked, ready to scoop up the dog if she faltered. There was no reason to worry.

In the blink of an eye, Roxie bounded inside, turning quickly toward JC to receive her reward. "Good, girl," Bella said from the front seat while JC ran a hand over Roxie's head.

"Yes, she is," JC added, including a quick scratch behind

the dog's ear. Then, Roxie settled onto the blanket without being asked. "Roxie, you are amazing."

"She really is," Bella added as JC secured Roxie's leash to ensure the dog didn't jump out. Although it seemed unlikely considering how she acted, JC didn't want to risk her seeing something on the side of the road that made her excited. The idea of Roxie jumping out of a car and getting lost again crossed JC's mind a few times. It was possibly the way she escaped before.

Finally ready, JC took the driver's seat. "I thought we would go counterclockwise around the island," she said, pulling a simple island map from the glovebox. "We will bypass the more touristy beaches for now by taking the H3 through the Koolau mountains." She traced a line on the map. "That is a beautiful drive and drops us near Kailua."

Bella's smile beamed. "I am open to going and doing whatever your heart desires," she said, making JC feel a little heat flare in her body. Their brief but passionate detour through the bedroom seemed like not enough. Even in the moment, only the promise of much more got JC and Bella out of bed to start their adventure. Although exploring the island would be fun, she felt her pulse jump at the idea of exploring Bella's body again later.

Catching Bella's eye and holding the gaze for a beat, JC ensured her look conveyed her thoughts. "Then let's get started," she said, her voice pitched low.

This time it was Bella's turn to blush, and she squirmed a little in her seat. "JC, I warned you… if you talk to me in that voice again, we aren't going to be leaving anytime soon."

Considering her options for one more second, JC finally let her sultry look turn to a playful smile. "Roxie might be a little disappointed if we bail now," she said, glancing at the dog's happy face in the back seat. "I think she's used to road trips, and I promise this will be a good one."

26

While the warm summer wind whipped through Bella's long, dark hair as they drove north along the Oahu's coast, she held her sunhat on her head and couldn't keep the huge smile off her face. As alternative rock played through the jeep's speakers and the salty smell of the ocean filled the air around her, Bella couldn't believe the turn her life had taken. Not much more than two weeks before she was horribly depressed, lonely, and unsure of what to do with herself in her little condo studio in Waikiki. She had been desperate to try to find words to fill the pages of a novel she realized that at the time she didn't want to write. Her entire future looked bleak. Then, in what seemed the blink of an eye, she found herself riding in the passenger seat across from a fantastic woman who was gorgeous and sexy while sweet and considerate too.

I don't know what I did to deserve this, she thought. *But I promise to be grateful every day if it can keep going.* That would be the trick as she had yet to find a way to explain to JC her commitment to leave the island for the writer's conference. Even though she couldn't quite see a clear path forward for them from there, she wanted to do everything possible to reassure JC they would work the details out. *But I won't bring it up yet. There's plenty of time today, and this is too perfect.*

As if reading her thoughts as to the day's perfection, JC reached to take her hand. "Thank you for being open to exploring today," she said, making Bella shake her head.

"Are you kidding?" she said. "I can't imagine a more perfect way to spend the afternoon than here with you." Glancing into the backseat to see the sleeping dog, she smiled. "And Roxie too."

Lifting their hands, JC kissed the back of Bella's. "I agree," she said. "And just ahead is a nice little beach. It's public but small so usually pretty quiet, and I think you will like it."

Although not a fan of the ocean, nor did she think she ever would be, the idea of laying on a blanket on the warm sand beside her sexy lover sounded very welcoming. "Let's stop then," she said. "We're not in a rush, right?"

"Not at all," JC said, putting on her blinker as Bella saw the small, brown sign along the side of the road. It had an arrow pointing toward the ocean with a promise of parking and restrooms. In a few minutes they parked under the shade of a tall Eucalyptus tree and unloaded the jeep. After being a perfect passenger the entire ride, when it was time and JC motioned for her to go ahead, Roxie hopped out of the vehicle with what appeared practiced ease.

"You're such a good, sweet girl, Roxie," Bella said while JC attached the lead to the dog's jacket and handed the end to her.

JC grinned while walking to the back of the jeep and opening the tailgate to gather the things they would need. "I can't wait to see how she reacts to the water," she said. "I have the strangest suspicion she will love it."

After learning of Roxie's many other talents, Bella was curious too and led the way along the short gravel path to the sand where she was even more impressed with the beach than she imagined. Only one other couple plus a small family shared the space with them, and they were all far enough away that everyone had plenty of room. The turquoise color Bella had become so accustomed to in the waters around the island seemed exceptionally bright. "Oh, JC," she said, stopping at what appeared to be a perfect spot. "How can it always be so beautiful here?"

Letting the bag of towels and blanket slip from her shoulder, JC nodded. "This is a magical place," she said. "I'm glad you see it too."

Watching the woman she was so attracted to roll out the blanket, Bella thought there was more than only water and sunlight that was magical in Oahu. JC was one of a kind, and for Bella, it seemed impossible that she could ever leave her behind, even if temporarily. Life was unpredictable, and Bella was wise enough to know that sometimes things could be too good to be true. She prayed JC wasn't one of them.

As SHE LET the warm water splash over her feet, JC smiled. The ocean was precisely like she hoped it would be—calm and with small waves. Of course, the size of the waves would make any boogie-boarding she might want to do nearly impossible, but she didn't mind. Bella, and possibly Roxie, would fare better in the gentler water. "Is it warm?" Bella called from where she sat on the blanket farther from the water. Roxie sat beside her, watching JC's every move with rapt attention. Loving the sight, JC went to rejoin them.

"Like bathwater here this time of year," she said with a smile, and Bella returned it but shook her head.

"Not my bath, I assure you," she said. "That would make it a hot tub, and no one would want to swim in it."

Sitting on the edge of the blanket, JC ran a hand over

Roxie's head. "Fair enough. But still very pleasant. I'm going to go for a quick swim. Are you okay staying here with her?"

"Of course," Bella replied, pulling her floppy sunhat from the bag. "I brought my Kindle and have the latest novel by Jae all loaded and ready to read. Part of her shapeshifter series, and I can't wait."

As Bella put on her hat, JC leaned closer. "I won't be gone very long," she said as Bella responded to her movement and met her halfway. Their lips met, lingering for a moment, and JC couldn't help but feel both a thrill of excitement as well as a warmth from the tenderness. "Be right back."

"We'll be here," Bella said, breathiness to her voice that let JC know the kiss affected her too. JC stood, stripping off her shirt to reveal a bikini top. She noticed Bella staring at her. "I will never get enough of watching you do that," Bella said. "Never ever."

JC grinned. "Then I'll be sure to keep doing it in front of you," she said a moment before she started jogging toward the shimmering blue water. Before she was even halfway, she heard Roxie barking. Alarmed, she turned to see Bella trying to hold back the excited dog. Seeing her tail wagging, JC relaxed. There wasn't something bad upsetting her. *She wants to run to the water with me,* JC thought, surprisingly pleased to see the dog's desire to play in the ocean. Looking up and down the beach, the family had left, and the other couple was a reasonable distance away. "Do you want to come with me, Roxie?"

"Are you sure, JC?" Bella asked. "She's still learning her name."

Walking back to where the other two waited, JC considered her question. *We definitely don't want her to get lost again,* she thought, starting to nod. "You're right," she said. "Probably better to keep her on the lead, and we can wade in together."

JC watched Bella hesitate, but after a moment, she stood with Roxie's leash in her hand. "I'll come too," she said, a sliver of doubt in her tone but determination too. "Then you can still swim."

"You're sure?" JC asked, proud of her for being brave but not wanting to make her do something she didn't want to do only for her.

Starting to walk to the water's edge, Bella nodded. "I know I'm safe with you," she said, and JC agreed. Nothing on earth would keep JC from trying to keep Bella safe. Reaching the edge of the waves, JC waded out, and Roxie started into the water too until she was lightly pulling on the lead. As if not understanding why they stopped, the dog looked back at Bella, who was barely in the waves. "She wants to keep going."

Even more curious, JC turned back to take the end of the leash from Bella's hand. "Well, let's see what she wants to do," she said, and as soon as she had the handle, Roxie headed further out. *It's a good thing I had a firm hold on it,* she thought, trotting deeper into the waves. After a moment, they were past the wave break and waist deep, making Roxie paddle in place. Looking at the dog, JC would swear she saw a smile on Roxie's face. It was clear she was not only familiar with the water but loved to be in the ocean. *She has to have grown up on the island.* With a shake of her head, JC simply didn't understand. *So then where are her owners?*

27

Sitting on the blanket, Bella watched JC playing with Roxie in the water. Both looked to be having the best time ever as they splashed, swam, and rode the short waves. Once it was clear Roxie liked the ocean, JC had run back up the beach to grab her boogieboard from the jeep while Bella held the dog's leash. When she came back and started to ride the shallow waves with Roxie splashing along beside her, barking the whole time, Bella left them to their fun. She knew without a doubt that Roxie wouldn't be running off as long as she was playing with JC, and so had returned to her Kindle. The story was good, as she expected it would be, and she was completely into the life of the characters when Roxie ran up to her. Her tongue wagged, and water dripped from her fur. JC was close behind. "Watch out," she called. "I think you're about to get sprayed." At the last possible second, Bella tucked the e-reader under a towel as Roxie shook her body from head to tail.

Water went everywhere, and as unpleasant as the cold water was on her skin, the playfulness of the scene made her laugh. "Roxie," she protested between giggles. "Stop."

JC grabbed another towel from the bag and started to dry off. "I love that you're laughing," she said, squeezing some water from her hair. "You're still sure you don't want me to show you how to boogieboard?"

"I'm sure," she said, picking up her own towel to wipe her face. "But you two did make it look like a lot of fun."

Plopping onto the sand beside Bella, JC nodded. "That dog sure does like the water," she said. "I imagine someone taught her to swim in the ocean from when she was a pup. I've never seen anything like it." She reached for the cooler at her feet. "Thirsty? Hungry?"

"A bottle of water would be great. Are you having a sandwich?" Bella asked a moment before JC pulled one out.

"Yep," she said, starting to unwrap it. "Want half? I don't want to fill up yet. Not until we get further north." She grinned. "Then we'll stop at the shrimp truck and get stuffed."

Bella held out her hand to accept a share. "This shrimp truck must be quite some place," she said. "I've seen ads for it in every tourist brochure, and you're very excited."

"It is," JC said, leaning in for a kiss. "Just wait and see."

Liking the tiny tingles she felt knowing JC wanted to kiss her, Bella met the woman halfway and touched her lips with her own. "I'm sure it will be wonderful. Everything's been perfect," she murmured against JC's mouth and wished the beach was empty. A make-out session on the blanket sounded incredibly erotic. Getting ready to tell JC precisely that, a buzzing phone interrupted the moment. It took her a second to realize it was JC's making the noise.

JC frowned as she dug in the bag for her phone. "I hope everything is okay with Blake," she said before fishing the thing out. Bella watched her glance at the screen and then grit her teeth.

Not sure what to think about the reaction, Bella touched

JC's shoulder. "Is something wrong?" she asked, and JC sighed as she silenced the call.

"Not exactly," she said, facing Bella to look into her eyes. "It was Chris again."

Bella blinked. "Again?" she asked, not liking the idea the woman called JC often. "As in she calls you a lot?"

Shaking her head, JC looked away to put her phone back. "Once a day," she said. "And I let them go to voicemail. At some point I need to call her back."

"What does she want?" Bella blurted, not liking the hint of anxiety she felt over JC's ex calling her. It didn't help that she had no idea the calls were happening. *But this is JC*, she thought. *She wouldn't do anything to hurt me, and I have nothing to worry about.*

"Well," JC said as she unwrapped her sandwich, "for the most part, she wants to go to dinner."

Feeling a pinch of worry, Bella forced her voice to remain even. "And do you want to do that?"

JC was quiet for a moment, clearly thinking over her answer. "I think that I do," she finally answered. "But if I do agree to meet her, I want you to come with me. Would you be willing to do that?"

Bella wasn't sure exactly how she felt about JC's request, but she was smart enough to know the right answer. "Yes, I would be," she said, then picked up her e-reader again. "But for now, I think I'd rather focus on eating my sandwich, this great book, and wonderful day than get anxious over dining with Chris."

Leaning closer, JC kissed her cheek. "Thank you," she said before folding her towel to use as a pillow and lay back. "And I agree. Let's not let anything take away from this."

. . .

Lying on the blanket, soaking up the sun, JC felt fantastic. On one side of her, Bella sat enjoying the book on her Kindle and on the other, Roxie lay on the warm sand asleep. *This is perfect,* she thought, knowing at some point they needed to get going if they wanted to reach the shrimp truck before it closed but not ready to leave yet. Although JC had thought her life was near perfect before the fateful kayaking tour where she found Bella again, everything was so much richer with the woman in it. Things were simply falling into place both with finding Roxie and Bella being able to write from the house.

For a brief moment, after her phone rang and she saw it was Chris, JC worried the wonderful day might be in trouble, but thankfully, that didn't happen. Although the decision to include Bella in dinner plans had been spontaneous, JC was glad she asked her to join in a meeting with Chris. In JC's mind, the get together was not intended to be romantic, and Bella joining them would ensure Chris knew it too.

Suddenly, JC's stomach growled loud enough to make Roxie raise her black and white head. Bella giggled. "Am I to assume that means you're hungry?" Bella said. Rubbing her tanned stomach, JC smiled. "I see," Bella continued. "Well, I'm about starving too, but I ignored it to keep reading this exciting story."

JC laughed. "I don't want you to starve. Let's pack up and hit the road. I bet Roxie could also use a bowl full of fresh water."

"Then let's go," Bella said. "And you can show me this fabulous shrimp truck everyone raves about."

In a few minutes everything was back in the jeep. Roxie drank plenty, and then JC loaded her up like she had ridden with them a million times before. Everything was perfect. Reaching for Bella's hand as they started their way back on the highway north, JC loved it when the woman gave it a gentle squeeze. "Thank you for all of that," Bella said softly. "Being on the beach with you and Roxie was one of the best times I've ever had."

"Me too," JC said with a smile. "We will come back soon. But now, time to go for some amazing food." When Bella didn't respond immediately, JC looked at her and saw she had turned to gaze out the passenger window at the lush, green foliage passing by on the side of the road. Her sudden change from happy to pensive made JC frown. "Everything okay?"

Bella hesitated before letting out a trembling sigh that immediately made JC's chest tighten with worry. "JC," she said, not looking at her. "I can't seem to find a good time to say this, so I will say it now."

Furrowing her brow, JC glanced over. "Okay," she said. "I don't think I like the sound of that, but let's have it then."

Bella shoulders sagged and she shook her head. "Oh, I hate this, but my editor called."

When she didn't immediately continue, JC glanced over again. "Okay," she said. "She's called before. What is different this time?"

Rubbing her forehead as if trying to banish what she had to say, Bella answered. "I need to go back to the mainland. There's a literary conference I am committed to attending and…" Her voice drifted off, clearly leaving off the part she hated to say the most.

"And?" JC asked, trying to stay calm even though her heart pounded.

Grasping JC's hand tighter, Bella turned in her seat. "I know you're going to think this has something to do with Chris calling you and the idea of going to dinner with her, but that's simply bad timing. I still want to do that." She gave a little laugh. "Actually, I kind of need to do that or I might go a little crazy knowing you are at dinner with her."

JC still didn't quite follow. "Bella, what are you trying to say?"

With a sigh, Bella held JC's hand tighter. "I'm trying to say I need to go home to Portland. By the end of the week."

28

*B*iting her lip as JC pulled into the restaurant's parking lot where there were going to meet Chris, Bella fought back her nervousness. She hadn't felt so anxious in a long time. *And there's no reason to be,* she thought. *This is only a woman who is an old friend of JC.* Still, she swallowed hard. *Well, and one she slept with.* That was the part Bella struggled with the most. Even though JC had reassured her many times any romantic feelings for Chris were long over, and deep down Bella believed her, she still worried. JC was a fantastic woman, and there seemed no way Chris wouldn't still have feelings for her. *So, what is her agenda?* As JC found a space and turned off the engine, Bella hoped they were about to find out.

JC reached for Bella's hand and turned in her seat to face her. Clearly seeing the anxiety on Bella's face, she leaned closer and kissed Bella's cheek. "Have I told you how fantastic you look tonight?" JC whispered against her skin, and Bella laughed.

"About a hundred times," she answered, but the compliment helped her relax. She had picked the yellow sundress because she knew JC liked it.

JC smiled. "Well, I mean it every time. The color looks incredible on you."

"I'm glad you like it," Bella said. "I wore it just for you."

"And I love that about you," JC said. "Are you ready to do this?"

Taking a deep breath, Bella nodded. "I'm as ready as I'm ever going to be," she said. "I hope this is a good idea."

JC looked into her eyes. "I know it will be. I want to make sure everything is perfectly clear for all three of us."

"Thank you," Bella said. The words meant a lot to her. Knowing she would be leaving the island in a few days, JC's reassurances were even more important. *Of course, Chris's vacation could be over soon and she will be long gone before I leave,* she thought. *And then I truly will have nothing to worry about.*

Letting go of her hand, JC got started to get out of the jeep. When Bella followed suit, the woman glanced back. "Wait," JC said. "Don't get out yet." Not sure what was happening, but trusting her, Bella waited. After a second, JC was at her door and opening it with a flourish, holding out her hand for Bella to take. "I always wanted to do that. I hope you don't mind."

Smiling, Bella took her offering and stepped out. "I absolutely don't mind," she said with a laugh. "Very chivalrous." She knew the playfulness was JC's way of helping her relax, and she appreciated it sincerely.

With a twinkle in her eyes, JC interlaced their fingers and kept hold of Bella's hand as they walked through the restaurant's glass front doors into a beautiful foyer. Even though they had been to the establishment for dinner once before, the sight still took Bella's breath away. "This is always so incredible," she said, pausing to scan the creativeness of the space. One entire wall was an elaborate aquarium filled with colorful fish swimming around rocks of various sizes and shapes. Aquatic plants in a variety of greens waved gently in the artificial current. "I'm glad you picked here."

"I know you like this place," she said, letting go of her hand and slipping her arm around Bella's waist to pull her a little closer. Bella loved the possessive feel of it. "And I want you to be okay tonight. Maybe even enjoy the evening."

Not entirely convinced that was possible, Bella forced a smiled. "You're always so thoughtful," she said while that sliver of worry nagged her again. *How could anyone let this amazing woman get away?* she thought. *And how will I make sure she stays mine while we are miles apart?*

Before any answer could come to her, the restaurant host welcomed them. "Just two?" she asked picking up a couple of menus from the host's station.

"Actually," JC said. "We are meeting someone and planned to connect with her at the bar."

"Of course, not a problem," the host said with a nod. "I will show you the way unless you know where it is?"

"Thank you, but we know," JC answered before leading Bella to the restaurant's cocktail area. As they turned the corner, Bella's eye immediately landed on Chris. Sitting on a stool, she stirred a fruity-looking drink. The woman looked fresh, almost tropical, in a sleeveless light blue blouse that offset her tanned, toned arms and cream linen pants. *And way too attractive,* Bella thought in the same instant Chris noticed them and waved.

WALKING into the bar area of the restaurant, JC noticed Chris waiting for them at the same time she felt Bella's body stiffen. Not exactly sure what she reacted to, but guessing it was from spotting the woman waiting for them, JC wanted to say something reassuring. Before she could, Chris slipped off her stool to greet them. "I was early so I decided to have a drink," she said, motioning to two empty seats. "Join me for one?"

"We'd love to," Bella answered before JC even had time to react. Although starting the evening with a cocktail sounded like a great idea, she was still surprised at Bella's quick response. *Liquid courage?* she wondered, wishing the woman didn't feel like she needed it. Even though Chris was her ex-girlfriend, and they had some history, JC's feelings were never as strong as they were toward Bella. Still, no matter how she tried to express that fact, Bella couldn't seem to quite believe it.

Chris smiled, warm and inviting. "That's perfect," she said, taking her stool, and JC knew her well enough to tell her words were genuine. Whatever reasons the woman had for being back on Oahu, JC felt the intentions were good. The fact she wanted to catch up with JC was a little bit of a surprise, but then there never was animosity between them. As she had explained to Bella, the two had wanted different futures and, in the end, went their separate ways.

Not sure about the protocol as to who should sit where JC let Bella make the next move and was glad when she took the middle stool. Sitting between the two women might have been awkward. "What are you drinking?" Bella asked, plucking a short menu from the countertop while JC sat. "It looks fruity and fun."

"It's called a Lava Flow, actually," Chris replied, stirring the red and white mixture with her straw. "Have you ever had one? They are very sweet but taste excellent." She chuckled. "But you have to be a little careful. It's easy to forget they have alcohol in them."

Bella shook her head. "I've never had one, but I think I'll try it," she said before glancing at JC. "What about you?"

JC shrugged, not a fan of sugary tasting drinks but

wanting to go with the flow of the suddenly chatty Bella. "Sure, why not?" She couldn't help but notice Chris's raised eyebrow but was happy when the woman didn't comment on JC saying yes to the fruity cocktail. Instead, Chris turned her attention to flagging down the bartender to order.

"Three Lava Flows, please," she told him, and once the man was off making their drinks, JC watched Chris refocus on them. "So. I'm glad we were able to all get together. Where did the two of you meet?"

"Kayaking tour," JC answered with a smile. "You wouldn't believe my surprise when I realized Bella was in my group."

"Talk about a blast from the past," Bella said with a laugh. "I'm standing in the parking lot trying to think of an excuse to bail on my rash decision to go on the adventure, and then there was JC."

Furrowing her brow, Chris looked from one to the other of them. "Wait," she said. "Somehow you knew each other?" Then, JC saw a light go on in Chris's eyes. "Oh, I understand now. You're The Bella from college."

Bella looked at JC. "The Bella?" she asked, and JC wasn't quite sure how to respond. Chris's comment surprised her. *Using 'The Bella' seems to be sending a clear message,* she thought. *Did I let the memory of my college crush impact my relationship with Chris?* Luckily, before JC had to say a word, their order arrived, and after some back and forth discussion, the drinks went on Chris's tab.

After taking a sip, Bella smiled. "This is very good," she said. "And I can see what you mean. You'd never know there was anything dangerous in here."

"Exactly," Chris said before looking pointedly at JC. "What do you think?" Knowing Chris took some pleasure in JC drinking something she wouldn't usually order, she held her eye as she tried the Lava Flow.

The sweetness from the strawberries, coconut, and

pineapple was a lot, but not horrible. "Not too bad," she said. "Never replace a good beer, though."

"That's what I thought you would say," Chris said with a laugh, and out of the corner of her eye, JC noticed Bella watching them interact.

A slight flush on her cheeks, Bella cleared her throat to interrupt. "So, Chris, how long are you here in Hawaii?" she said, clearly cutting to the chase, and Chris continued to smile.

"Actually," she said after taking another sip from her straw. "I've missed the island and I've decided I want to move back here."

29

At Chris's sudden announcement, Bella nearly spit out her mouthful of Lava Flow. Then, in an effort to swallow the frozen drink, she started to choke, and it was all she could do to get the sugary mix down before starting to cough. Thankfully, JC rubbed Bella's back, and the soothing touch seemed to help.

When the attack subsided, Chris touched Bella's shoulder. "Hey," she said. "I didn't say that to surprise you. That wasn't my intention."

"Well, what is your intention?" JC asked in a cooler tone than Bella had ever heard her use, and she was thankful the woman asked the question. The idea Chris would be moving back to Oahu sounded an alarm in Bella's mind.

Clearly noticing JC's tone as well, Chris leaned back a little on her stool. "All right," she said. "I can see this has upset everyone but let me clarify. I am very seriously *considering* moving back to Oahu. No official decision has been made."

Finally finding herself able to talk, Bella blurted a question before she could stop her racing thoughts. "Because of JC?"

Playing with the straw in her drink, Chris didn't look at her. "No," she said. "I'm thinking about it because my fiancée is being stationed here."

The tightness in Bella's chest loosened at the word fiancée. "So, you'd be moving back here with your partner?" she asked, not entirely convinced JC was not part of the equation.

"Exactly," Chris said, refocusing on Bella. "My girlfriend is in the military, and she will be stationed here for the next three years."

Out of the corner of her eye, Bella saw JC pick up her Lava Flow. "Then this warrants a celebration," she said, the friendliness back in her voice. "Congratulations on your engagement."

Liking the direction JC took the conversation, Bella lifted her drink too. "I agree," she said. "That's very exciting." Chris looked at JC and then to Bella with a slight smile on her face that Bella thought bordered on a smirk. *Good,* she thought. *I want her to recognize where things stand, and that JC is with me.*

After a pause, Chris nodded. "Thank you," she said. "She's an amazing woman, and I'm very lucky."

"Where did you meet?" Bella asked before bravely taking another sip of her drink, hoping Chris's answer wasn't another bomb.

At that question, Chris's smile became genuine. "I met her in San Diego. She took one of my technical writing classes." She shrugged. "And one thing led to another. We'd been together for over a year, and she asked me to marry her when she found out about being relocated to Hawaii."

"Have you found a job here yet?" JC asked, and Chris shook her head as she lifted her drink to finish it off.

"Not yet," she said. "That's why I'm hesitating." Chris drank, allowing Bella to process what the woman was telling them. *JC's ex-girlfriend may or may not be moving back, but if she does, it will be with her fiancée,* she thought. *So, why do I keep feeling like Chris has some hidden agenda?* There was also the situation where Bella was leaving the island soon, which was something Chris didn't know about. *Will that help her make up her mind?*

"It's a big move," JC said, and Bella watched Chris meet JC's eyes.

"I made a big move once before, and it turned out to be a mistake," she said, and the tightness in Bella's chest ramped up again. Bella wasn't naïve enough not to catch the reference to the fact she left JC behind when they broke up.

The statement hung in the air before JC put her arm around Bella's waist. "I believe everything worked out precisely as it should have," JC answered, and Bella was thankful she recognized how upsetting the conversation made her. Chris nodded and met Bella's eyes. Bella couldn't miss the message in the woman's gaze. *She realizes how lucky I am*, Bella thought. *And even though she has a fiancée, and I imagine they are happy, she still has regrets over JC.*

Finally, Chris looked away. "Yes," she said. "Everything did. My fiancée is a wonderful woman, and I can't wait for you to get to know her."

DRIVING them home after a delicious dinner of seafood spaghetti complemented perfectly with an excellent bottle of red wine, JC reflected on how the evening had gone. After a somewhat rocky start over cocktails, things smoothed out once they were seated in the dining room. She wasn't sure what to make of Chris's bombshell that she was moving back to Oahu. *Contemplating moving,* she thought, correcting herself. Unfortunately, always one for the dramatic, the way Chris announced it was more than a little unfair to Bella. That had been no accident, and she knew it as she took the ramp onto the freeway. *For whatever reason, Chris wanted to get under my skin. I just don't know why.* Regardless, JC wasn't happy about the maneuver.

JC had sensed Bella noticeably relaxing when Chris elaborated on why she was thinking about moving to the island. If she was being honest, it calmed her too. Although JC would never share the information with Bella, she had her own concerns about why Chris might be moving back and trying to seek her out. Their breakup had been polite for the most part, but JC struggled for a while with the hurt and disappointment of Chris's choice. *And now I have Bella in my life again*, she thought. *Even if I didn't, there never will be room for Chris on my horizon. I need to make sure both women always know that.*

The best thing to come out at dinner was learning Chris was a big fan of Bella's bestselling novel. "Oh, wow," Chris said. "I have read your book so many times. Promise me when we meet again that you will be willing to sign my paperback copy."

"I would be happy to," Bella had said with a blush. JC knew she struggled to believe people loved her work, and the unexpected praise from Chris no doubt caught her off guard. Luckily, the conversation had been a nice segue onto safer topics about how JC's business was booming and the story about finding Roxie. When the waiter offered dessert, Chris declined. "I actually have a few little things still to do tonight," she said before leaving rather abruptly. In JC's opinion, it was just as well as they had run out of safe things to talk about.

"What are you thinking?" Bella asked, and JC glanced at her. The woman was quiet since they got into the Jeep, but then so was JC. Clearly, they were both lost in their thoughts. *No doubt she is reflecting on the evening as well*, she thought. *There is a lot to process.*

"I'm thinking that all in all, dinner went well," JC said. "How about you?"

Bella nodded. "Chris seems nice enough," she said. "I imagine we can all be friends at some point." She hesitated and then took JC's hand. "I look forward to meeting her fiancée."

There was definitely an emphasis on the word fiancée that JC did not miss. "Yes, so do I," JC said, rubbing her thumb over the back of Bella's hand. "Assuming Chris even moves to the island. She had a big decision to make."

When Bella hesitated for a second, JC realized Bella might be facing a similar decision someday and wanted to clarify. "That is true," Bella finally said before JC could say anything more.

Ready to change the subject from Chris and difficult decisions but not wanting to end their evening quite yet, JC decided to try something fun. "What do you say we make a detour before getting to the house?" JC said with a grin. "Roxie will be okay for another few minutes."

Bella smiled back. "I'm happy to go anywhere with you," she said. "You know that."

Loving how good Bella's words made her feel, she lifted Bella's hand and kissed the back. "Thank you," she said. "I was thinking, since we didn't have dessert at the restaurant, I know of a fun little ice cream parlor not too far from the house that we haven't tried yet. They should still be open."

"I think that sounds wonderful," Bella said, and JC was happy to see whatever Bella had on her mind seemed to be put on hold for the moment. Although JC was no fool and realized a conversation about the woman's leaving soon was inevitable, she hoped it could wait another night. In less than week, Bella would have to attend the conference, and it would be up to her to decide what came afterward. For tonight though, she would enjoy their time and try to make each moment as special as she could.

30

*D*istracted to the point she kept misplacing things, Bella tried to pack the two large suitcases she had brought from the mainland. Patient as always, Roxie watched from her bed in the corner of the room. Bella tried to ignore the gentle brown eyes tracking her every move, but she couldn't help feeling guilty. Leaving JC was hard, but it would be tough to leave Roxie as well. They had bonded while spending the last few weeks together, with Bella writing and Roxie sleeping at her feet. Among many topics during the previous five days, JC and she talked about what exactly they would do with their new pet. Even with the flyers and posts online, no one ever stepped forward to claim her. One option was for Bella to take her back to Portland, but even then it would have to be after the conference. Ultimately, they decided Roxie would do best staying with JC in Hawaii. After a few phone calls, JC devised a plan for the dog to stay in the office with a new part-time helper during the day. "Until I teach her to ride on a kayak with me," JC had said with a wink, and Bella believed the woman just might.

Overall, JC was very understanding about everything,

but Bella could not miss the hurt look in her eyes whenever they talked about being separated for longer than a few weeks. Bella simply did not know what she was going to do after the literary conference. In so many ways, she didn't want to leave and struggled with her mixed emotions. She missed her family, her house, and her friends back on the mainland. Somehow, she needed to find a way to make her two worlds meet. "What am I going to do?" she asked Roxie, who patted the floor with her tail. Reaching to rub the wonderful animal behind the ear, Bella sighed. "I love you too, and I know if you could tell me the answer, you would."

Finding it too depressing to keep packing her suitcase, Bella decided to call her editor and give her a quick update. Settling into one of the patio chairs, she pressed Joanie's number. The woman answered on the second ring. "Don't tell me you're canceling," she said, and Bella had to laugh at her abrupt answer, even though there was a hint of desperation in the woman's voice.

"Well hello to you too," she said, smiling. She loved Joanie and knew the woman only had Bella's best interest in mind. "You know you have a bad habit of doing that."

"Only with you," the woman said. "No one else keeps me on pins and needles like you do."

There was enough humor in Joanie's voice for Bella to know she was only partially serious. "I will be coming back tomorrow morning," she said. "I decided to go home for a couple of days before the conference and pack different clothing."

"Wise choice," Joanie said, then Bella heard her hesitate for a beat. "But I know this is hard for you."

Closing her eyes for a moment, Bella tried to keep her emotions in check. "You have no idea," Bella replied. "I feel like a part of my heart is breaking."

"But the separation doesn't have to be forever," her editor said. "Unless that's what you've decided on."

"No, definitely not that. We both want to find a way to work this out."

"Good," Joanie said. "Because you've never sounded happier. Still, I'm guessing she'll want to stay on Oahu because of her business."

Bella shook her head. "I would never let her make any other decision than to stay here and do what she loves," she said. "It really comes down to what do I want to do."

"And?" Joanie asked. "What do you want to do?"

"Try to have a long-distance relationship I guess," Bella answered. "There's no easy solution to this, and JC promises she will come to visit me in a couple of months." The idea of not seeing JC or Roxie for a couple of months made Bella's stomach hurt. As she looked around the quaint house with the beautiful yard, glimmering swimming pool, and wonderful patio, she thought she was crazy for even considering leaving. But then again, she thought of home and felt divided.

"Hey," Joanie said gently. "There's nothing wrong with slowing down your relationship and spending time apart."

A tear slipped down Bella's cheek. "You're right," she said. "But I love her and don't want to lose her."

"I know," her editor said. "I know."

Holding Bella's hands, JC kissed the woman tenderly on the lips and savored the moment. They were outside the terminal at Inouye International Airport in Honolulu. In a few moments the person she realized she cared most for in the world was going to walk through the doors into the terminal and fly away. Although JC had dealt with tough things in her life, somehow that moment seemed like the hardest. Letting Bella go with only a promise they would talk to each other every day was a challenge. *But not a test,* she thought. *I trust in our relationship. Bella wants to keep us together as much as I do.* "Fly safe," JC said as she pulled back and looked into the woman's eyes. "And text me the minute you land."

Bella squeezed JC's hands. "You know I will," she said, and there were tears in her eyes that made it even harder for JC to say goodbye. She leaned in and kissed her once more before letting go of her hands.

Tears stung her eyes too. "Don't miss your flight," she said, and Bella nodded, taking hold of her suitcases.

She started to walk away. "I'll miss you."

"I'll miss you more," JC said with a smile. Bella laughed, but there was a melancholy tone to the sound, and then she disappeared through the sliding doors into the airport.

Letting her chin fall to her chest, JC let out a long sad breath. *I hope I'm not making the biggest mistake in my life*, she thought. *Maybe I should have gone with her. At least to the conference so that we could still be together.* But it wasn't that easy, and she knew it. She had responsibilities in Hawaii and not only Roxie but her Oahu Paddle Adventures business. Even if she wanted to, JC couldn't exactly cancel all her tours and close the doors at a moment's notice. *No, I would never do that.*

Instead, she would carry on and start taking Roxie with her to the office every day. She would be fine with someone to take her out a few times while JC was giving tours. With a two-hour break between the morning and afternoon excursions, she could give Roxie lots of attention. She also had high hopes of teaching her to ride on a kayak with her. With Roxie's love of the water and no fear of the ocean, there was a strong possibility the dog could adapt to it. Watching videos on YouTube of other dogs surfing and kayaking, she knew it was certainly possible. *And Roxie is a really smart dog*, she thought as she walked toward the parking garage. In life anything was possible, and that went beyond what the amazing dog they found could do. She also believed she and Bella would find a way to work things out.

Even though there would have to be sacrifices made by one or both of them, she would be patient. Just then her phone chimed, and she pulled it from her pocket. There was a text message from Bella. "At the gate," she said. "Missing you like crazy already." JC prepared to reply when a new text made her pause. "Am I making the right decision?"

JC stared at the screen for a moment, unsure exactly what to say. Her mind believed Bella was making the right decision and that she had to live her own life. But in her heart, she was afraid. *Was this only a fling in a tropical paradise?* she wondered. *Could she possibly love me as much as I love her?* Finally, she typed back. "Everything will be all right," she wrote, then considered what to add, wondering why she hadn't said it to her before she walked away into the terminal. Hoping her indecision hadn't made her too late, she typed an additional note. "Because I love you."

A message came right back. "I love you more."

31

"Well, look at you all tan," Bella's older sister said with a smile as she walked toward her in the baggage claim area at the Portland International airport. "And I like the highlights in your hair. Did you do that on purpose?"

"Hanna," Bella said, beaming back. "I missed you." They pulled each other into a hug, and Bella held on tight for a minute before letting go to watch for her luggage. "And no, it was simply being outside in the Hawaii sunshine."

"Well, it looks fabulous," Hanna said, looking her up and down. "You look great."

"Thank you," Bella answered. She had missed her sister, perhaps more than anyone else at home. Being close in age, they were often mistaken for twins, although Bella playfully reminded people that she was the much younger sister. Hanna was one of the reasons Bella was so conflicted about her future. Even though they emailed back and forth regularly throughout all of Bella's travels, there was always something special when they were in the same place. A fact that was interesting because their lives could not be more different.

While Bella tried to make sense of her life, Hanna had a family with a wonderful husband and children—two rambunctious boys. Bella's sister's life was all about baseball games, family picnics, and supporting her husband's career as a police officer. Bella often thought Hanna was a perfect role model for future moms.

"And honestly, I think Hawaii really agreed with me," Bella said with a laugh. "And it's pretty much impossible to spend time there and not get a tan."

Hanna lifted an eyebrow. "Sitting around your friend's pool probably helped with that," she said, making Bella's smile widen. She had yet to give all the details about JC to her sister, but Hanna clearly guessed enough to be more than a little curious about the new woman in Bella's life. "I expect a full story of what you were up to when you were supposedly on Oahu to find your muse."

Bella laughed. "I think I did find her, actually," she said as she spied her luggage coming around on the carousel. *But how much do I want to share about my relationship with JC?* Bella wondered. *Things are so up in the air.* Although she and Hanna were close, they didn't necessarily talk about the details of their intimate lives. Bella had no ideas about Hanna's life outside of what she could see regarding her sister's marriage and family. Everything looked perfect, but it was impossible to know for sure.

It wasn't so much Bella wanted to keep the specifics of her relationship with JC a secret. Her sister knew Bella met an old college friend while going on a kayaking adventure, but not the fact it was wanting to explore more with JC that made her extend her trip. Unfortunately, she let it slip that she moved into the friend's fantastic house but explained the separate bedroom arrangement. At the time, she thought

Hanna bought her clarification, but after the pool comment, she wasn't so sure. Bella had avoided revealing to Hanna that they had taken it further and were much more than friends. *Or even that I am sure I am in love with JC and considering moving to be with her,* she thought. Although Hanna was always supportive, even she might question such a big decision so soon.

They each grabbed a large roller bag and headed for the exit. As she followed Hanna out the revolving door, Bella felt her phone vibrate in her back pocket. Grabbing it with her free hand, she smiled when she saw a new message from JC. They had sent a few back and forth as soon as she landed, but this message seemed to include a picture. While they waited to cross the lanes of traffic, Bella opened it to see JC and Roxie on the beach beside a kayak. "We're going to give this a try," the text said. "I'll keep you posted. P.S. We both miss you like crazy."

"I miss you too and send more pics," was all Bella managed to type before they were on their way again. Thinking of the image of JC and Roxie about to try something fun made Bella long to be with them even more. Being away was already hard and only made her more unsure about what to do with her life.

FINALLY HEARING Bella had arrived safely, JC relaxed. When the first text came in after the plane landed and everything was fine, she decided it was time to head for the beach with Roxie. Since it was early enough in the afternoon it felt like a good time to teach her how to ride on a kayak and hopefully distract herself from missing Bella. *And maybe distract Roxie too,* she thought. The dog had stayed right beside her since she got back from the airport as if aware JC was sad from missing the absent Bella. *I wonder what she thinks. She's an intelligent animal and watched Bella pack, so maybe she gets what's happened.* The activity would do them both good.

Going to a quiet beach where few people visited because the waves were almost nonexistent, JC had packed one of her largest kayaks to try her experiment. Once they were on the sand, JC knelt in front of the dog. "Okay, Roxie," she said to the attentive black and white animal in a bright yellow lifejacket. "There's nothing to be afraid of, and I promise I'll keep you safe."

Never losing eye contact, Roxie simply panted under the warm sun, clearly ready to do whatever JC asked. After settling the kayak firmly into the sand and attaching a lead to the back of Roxie's jacket, JC coaxed Roxie forward. Pausing, she set up a quick picture of her and Roxie to send to Bella. *Just a little reminder of what we look like,* she thought, sending the text. Her plan was to send lots of photos and keep Bella thinking about them.

After stowing her phone in the dry bag, JC took out treats for Roxie's training. She immediately had the dog's rapt attention. With the treats and JC's encouraging words, Roxie came closer, taking a moment to smell along the side of the two-seater ocean kayak, and then without much more prompting, jumped on. She scrambled a little on the slippery surface but caught herself and sat while never taking her eyes off JC's hand holding the treat. With a laugh at the dog's antics as well as impressed, JC gave her the reward. "Well, that took less time than I thought it would," JC said. "Let's practice you getting in the kayak a few more times and then see what happens when I get you closer to the water."

She needn't have worried. Roxie was a natural, and after getting the hang of sitting on the kayak on land, JC started to move the kayak closer to the waves. As they continued to practice, Roxie became a little more excited, trying to bound around in the water. JC could always coax her focus back with a treat. Roxie even seemed to be starting to recognize her name, which was essential to JC. The last thing she wanted was for the dog to become lost again.

Finally, they were ready to push off, and with Roxie in the front seat staring into the horizon as if she had done so a million times, JC gave the kayak a push into the gentle waves. Settling into her spot, trying not to rock the kayak, JC started to paddle them a little distance away from the shore. Clearly realizing they were moving, Roxie looked over her shoulder at JC, and she would swear the dog had another smile on her face. They spent the next hour paddling up the coastline and back. Not once did Roxie try to jump out, even when they saw a flock of seabirds running across the sand. Beyond impressed, JC drove them home, eager to try again on rougher water soon. Plus, she couldn't wait to tell Bella all about it when the woman had time to talk later that night. They made a pact that Bella would at least always call before she went to bed, if not more often. It was one way they hoped to stay connected, and already JC could hardly wait. Although it wasn't an ideal situation, for the moment, JC knew it would have to do.

32

Waking to a bird singing in the tree outside her open window, Bella smiled as she stretched her arms over her head. It was one of her favorite sounds, yet she was confused for a second when she opened her eyes. Seeing that she was not in her Hawaii bedroom, and not in JC's either, the situation took a moment to register. She was in Oregon, and what she heard were the sounds of her home. Laying on her back, Bella stared at the ceiling and contemplated life. It was the first morning without JC and drinking their coffee together, and the thought made her heart hurt a little. The woman knew exactly how Bella liked it and would bring her a mug on the patio to enjoy. The two women and Roxie in her spot on the tiles between them, enjoying the start of another magical day.

Still, she knew her long unused Keurig waited downstairs. Plus, she was smart enough to ask her sister, who had been willing to grab her a few essentials, to buy some French Vanilla creamer. Slipping out from under the covers, Bella pulled on her robe to go downstairs to the kitchen. Unlike JC's one-story house on the canals, Bella lived in the suburbs of Portland in a two-story turn-of-the-century bungalow. Although the view wasn't quite the same, and there wasn't a pool in the backyard, the property was beautiful and in a much coveted location. Buying it ten years before on her father's advice, Bella could get three times what she paid for it if she listed the house. Something that came to mind often as she decided what to do with her future.

After reaching the coffee machine and starting a cup, Bella wandered the rooms of her home. The dining room with a round table she took six months to find, the perfect antique rug to fill her living room, and all the other personal touches. *How can I leave this?* she thought. *I put my heart into it, and this house is a part of me.*

When she heard her coffee was ready, Bella perfectly doctored it with creamer and wandered into her backyard. The broad, multi-tier porch was a special place where she came up with so many ideas for her stories. Sitting in a wicker chair with a bright yellow and green cushion, Bella relaxed and looked over her yard. The oak tree in the corner was full of leaves, and they would turn a beautiful orange before falling. Of course, she would have to rake them in the fall, but it was a chore she actually enjoyed. The rhododendrons were still in bloom but starting to drop their petals, and her other shrubs gave the yard a nice green space. *I need to get a gardener in here to trim everything and get me back on track*, she thought. *And buy some annuals to plant and liven things up. Although nothing will compare to JC's backyard. That is a slice of paradise.* The comparison wasn't fair though. Oregon, although beautiful in its own right, was not the tropical paradise of Hawaii.

Sipping her coffee, Bella looked over her lawn and tried to find some answer there. *Can I leave all of this behind because I think I'm in love with someone?* she wondered. The idea of packing, moving, and selling made her stomach hurt. *And what if a few months from now we don't fit so well?* That seemed impossible because, over the last few weeks, she had never felt more connected to someone. Just like in college, JC simply "got her," and Bella felt she did the same. They were inseparable back then, and she craved JC's company when they were apart. *How in the world did I go years without acting on how I felt?* She sipped again. *I wanted her the entire time but was too scared of ruining our friendship to tell her. So much wasted time.* She paused. *Am I doing the same thing by being here now and not with her?* With a sigh, Bella simply did not have a clear answer.

At the edge of the beautiful turquoise-blue lagoon, JC watched the twelve people in the tour group frolic in the warm water. The break to swim was good as the early July afternoon was warm. Plus, they were all excellent at kayaking, good swimmers and overall confident in the water, so she wasn't worried. She could easily monitor things from shore.

"Not getting in, JC?" Blake said, coming up beside her.

JC shook her head. "Not today," she said, unsure why she hesitated. It wasn't like she hadn't been to the lagoon without Bella before over the last few weeks. She went pretty much twice a day. But this time felt different. If she was being honest, she missed Bella like crazy, and the thought of doing anything that might make her memory stronger was torture. "I'm fine on the sand. You go have fun."

Nodding, Blake didn't move toward the water and instead studied JC's face. "You okay?" he asked quietly.

JC hesitated to answer. Usually, she kept all her feelings to herself and didn't like to share but considered opening up to Blake. He was a good guy and much more than simply an employee. He worked hard to make Oahu Paddle Adventures a success. Not only was he great with the tourists, but he never turned down an extra tour, was at work early without being asked, and stayed late to rinse kayaks without a complaint. Most important, she looked at him and his girlfriend as her close friends, even though they hardly saw each other outside of work once Bella came into JC's life. She frowned. *So why haven't I sold him a share of the business?* she wondered. *He's certainly earned it, but he's never asked. Maybe it's time I found out if he would want to be a co-owner and give up some control.* She smiled. *And then I could spend more time with Bella in Oregon.*

"Really, I'm okay. I promise," JC finally said, turning her thoughts back to the present moment. "I won't lie. I'm missing Bella pretty badly."

"Yeah," Blake said, looking over the water. "I can imagine. You are really into her."

Unable to help it, JC laughed. "Into her, am I?' she said. "Is it that obvious?"

Blake shrugged but grinned too. "I'm not trying to imply anything because you're always on top of things, but…

"But what?"

"Well," the young man said, nudging his toe into the sand. "You've been a little distracted since that tour with Bella on it."

Not sure if what the man said was good or bad, JC put a hand on his tanned shoulder. "I hope it hasn't put an extra burden on you," she said. "And I promise going forward, I'll focus on everything more."

Blake patted her hand. "Naw," he said. "Nothing like that. You're always a pro in the office and on the tours, only nowadays you're ready to blow out of the office at the end of the day." He laughed. "Before she came along, we would go out for a drink sometimes, and I honestly thought you worked so hard that you slept there."

He wasn't far off. In order to build the business, JC put every waking hour into it. Countless nights she stayed late to work on things. There was more to success than simply putting out a shingle and hoping people noticed. Ads had to be placed on Google, Facebook pages to update and Instagram posts to interact on, not to mention conventional ads everywhere. *Including the one in the brochure that led Bella back to me,* she thought, feeling her heart clench. *How am I going to stand being without her?*

As if sensing her conflict, Blake made a motion toward the water. "Let's get in," he said. "It's a hot day, and the water is always refreshing. And maybe it will take your mind off things."

"Thanks, Blake," JC said, forcing a grin to lighten the mood. She knew he meant well. "But today I'm going to go sit on that rock and try to figure out my crazy life."

Blake nodded. "JC, if that works, let me know," he said. "And I'll sit on the rock next time."

33

The literary conference was exhausting, but Bella was thankful her editor insisted she go. Networking with the other authors, as well as with publishers, and especially readers, was invaluable. Her presentation on writing characters with emotion was a hit, and dozens of aspiring authors tracked her down afterward to ask follow-up questions. Bella didn't mind helping them. She was grateful her book was so popular and wanted to give back whatever she could.

After navigating the few days of panels and speakers, awards night had arrived. Forcing herself not to wring her hands in her lap under the table, Bella waited as the presenter read the names of the different books in the romance author category. The competition was fierce, and although her friends and editor kept saying her book was the best of the group, Bella couldn't quite believe it. Even if her book was a runaway bestseller with sapphic book readers, the award judges did not necessarily feel the same way. They would be much more critical and might dismiss Bella's book as too sappy or unoriginal. She felt the strongest urge to call

JC, knowing that somehow the sound of the woman's confident voice would calm her nerves. Even after only a short time together, no matter what Bella went through, she knew JC could always be counted on to be her rock. Before the tug of longing for the woman could build, they were announcing the romance novel winner.

"And this year's winner of the romance category is Bella Wood."

Suddenly the people around Bella erupted with applause and said her name. Sitting in her chair, trying to register what happened, her editor tugged at her arm. "You won, Bella," Joanie said. "That means you have to stand up and go get the award."

Moving by instinct more than anything else, Bella stood and, after hugs from Joanie and a few people at her table, she made her way to the podium. Her acceptance speech was a blur as she squinted into the bright lights illuminating the stage. Through it all, one thing remained constant—she wished JC was there to share the moment with her.

As soon as she was back at her table, she sent off a text to JC about her win, but it was not until hours later that she could sneak away to the lounge outside the bathrooms long enough to call her. "That's so amazing," JC said once Bella gave her more details. "I'm so proud of you."

Bella felt tears spring to her eyes. "I hoped you would be," she murmured, hesitating for a moment as she considered her next words. "JC, I'm sorry I didn't insist you come to this with me. Not to the author stuff, but to have you here when my name was announced. Your hug was what I needed most."

There was a beat of silence on the phone, and Bella started to say something more in case she had said the wrong thing, but then JC cleared her throat. Bella heard the emotion in it. "We can't change the past," she said. "But I hope you want me to come to the next one."

Oh, JC, I want you to come to all of them, Bella thought and had to bite her lip to keep from blurting out the words. Until that moment, she didn't realize how deeply she felt about JC and how much she wanted to ensure they had a future together. Even with all the complications around her house and her life in Oregon, nothing compared to how much she loved the woman in Hawaii.

"Bella," she heard her editor say as she came up behind her. "So, this is where you are hiding." She slipped an arm around her shoulders. "Everyone wants to talk to you, and they have copies of your award-winning book to sign. Don't leave your fans waiting."

Feeling more than a little trapped, Bella faced her editor. "Two minutes," she said. "I'm talking to JC."

"It's okay," she heard JC say in her ear. "Go work some magic. Call me whenever you're done. No matter what time."

SETTING her phone on the kitchen counter, JC thought about what Bella had said, "I'm sorry I didn't insist you come to this with me." It felt good to know she was missed because, if she was being honest, the distance was very hard on JC. Bella had confided in her that she was beyond nervous about the award ceremony and what she would say if she won. Being so far away while someone she cared about needed reassurance was challenging. More than anything, JC wanted to be there for Bella but would never have asked outright. Some things had to come at their own pace.

Going to the refrigerator, she took out a beer and grabbed the bottle opener from the drawer. With a practiced flip of her wrist, she removed the cap and took a long drink of the cold liquid before letting out a deep sigh. "Well, she won, Roxie," JC said to the dog lying on her bed in the kitchen corner. "But we never had any doubt, did we?" Roxie wagged her tail, making JC smile. It was almost like she knew what JC was saying. *Or she simply hears the happiness for Bella in my voice*, she thought. Regardless, Roxie was a good companion, and she already couldn't imagine life without her. "What do you say we go for a swim?" Roxie's ears perked up at the word 'swim.'

Although dog hair was terrible for the pool's filter, she liked having Roxie swim in the pool with her. The dog loved the water so much that once JC showed her it was okay for her to get in, it was impossible to keep her out whenever JC swam. "I thought you'd like that idea," JC said, taking another swallow. "Let me go change my clothes." While carrying the beer with her, JC walked into her bedroom and, as she was changing, heard her cell phone buzz on the kitchen counter. Hoping it was a text from Bella, she hurried back only to see the words were from Chris.

"Sorry to interrupt your evening," the text said. "But I have been thinking about our last conversation at the restaurant." When there was no more to the text, JC raised an eyebrow. Many things had come up that evening, and Chris could be referring to several topics. Not in the mood to play games and try to guess, she typed back a simple sentence. "What about it?"

There was a pause, and JC slightly regretted the harshness of her words, but she wasn't sure exactly what Chris's agenda was and didn't need any drama while Bella was on the mainland. The last thing she wanted was to send any sort of wrong impression.

Finally, the three dots on the iPhone screen started jumping, and JC knew another text was coming. "About my fiancée. She's here, and I would like the four of us to go to dinner."

JC frowned. Chris didn't know Bella had left Hawaii. *That might be for the best,* she thought. *Still, it would be the polite thing to do to accept the offer.* To be honest, she was curious about the woman Chris was engaged to, and it might work out better to meet the fiancée. It could help clear up any lingering confusion.

"All right, I'll join you for dinner," JC wrote back. "When would you like to meet?"

"Tomorrow night?"

The request seemed a little rushed for JC, but she saw no reason to put it off and sent a text back. "That works," she said. After a few more exchanges where they set up a time and location, JC finally took the impatient Roxie into the backyard. As she stood at the edge of the pool, she wondered if she should text Bella about her arrangement with Chris for tomorrow night. She knew Bella was not a fan of JC's ex-girlfriend even if there was a fiancée involved. Ideally, they would have all gone to dinner together. *But she's not here,* JC thought as she finished her beer and set the bottle on one of the small tables beside a lounger. *And I can always talk with her about it tomorrow.*

34

"So, how does it feel to be an award-winning author?" Bella's editor asked as she sat down with her at the small outdoor table. They were in the courtyard at the hotel having a brunch put on by the conference organizers. It was the last get-together before everyone left to go their separate ways. Bella would miss Joanie's company after four days of supporting each other during the nonstop whirlwind of the event. Even though she was a hard-ass editor, she did a lot more for Bella's career and was also a close friend. One who would never mince words and was always good to turn to when she needed advice. Advice like she needed this morning.

A few quick texts back and forth with JC, and Bella learned the woman planned to have dinner with Chris that evening. *And her fiancée too,* Bella reminded herself. *It's not like a romantic get-together.* Still, the entire situation with Chris nagged at her. She hated to admit she was the jealous type, but apparently she was because thinking of anyone making moves on JC made her very anxious and frankly, a little angry. "The recognition feels good," Bella finally answered, and Joanie raised an eyebrow.

"You could sound a little more enthusiastic," she said before forking a pile of scrambled eggs. "What's going on?"

Bella sighed, toying with the handle of her coffee cup, not having much of an appetite. "Just me being silly," she answered with a shake of her head. "JC's going to dinner with her ex and her fiancée tonight, and it bothers me a little."

Tilting her head, Joanie narrowed her eyes at Bella. "A little?" she asked. "Seems like more than that to me."

Bella groaned. "I know," she said. "It's all because I miss her. Not having her come with me, at least to the awards ceremony and celebration afterward, was a mistake." She let out a deep breath. "Like everything else with our relationship, it's so complicated."

Joanie chewed her food before nodding. "You two have some difficult decisions to make," she said. She set her fork down and reached for her glass of orange juice. "But if you love her as much as I think you do, it will all come together."

Feeling a little more reassured by her friend's words, Bella let herself focus on how exciting the night before had been. "It was amazing to hear my name called," she said. "I hoped for it but never expected to win."

"I told you it was likely," Joanie said, after taking a sip of her drink. "Your book is a knockout, which is why everyone is chomping at the bit for the next one." She kept her eyes on Bella. "So, we need to come up with a release date."

A trickle of anxiety made Bella even less hungry, and she pushed her plate away. "You have to read it first," she said. "And see if it's worth publishing."

Joanie leaned back in her chair. "Bella," she said. "I already know, without reading it, that it's worth publishing. You're a very talented writer."

"Thank you," Bella said, unable to keep from blushing a little, even if she only heard the praise from her editor. "I am actually really proud of this story. I put a lot of myself into it."

"And JC?" Joanie said with a sly smile.

Bella laughed, her blush growing deeper. "Maybe a little bit," she said. "It does all start with a kayaking trip in Hawaii."

Her eyes twinkling, Joanie grabbed Bella's arm. "I knew it," she said. "Another bestseller for sure."

"Let's not get ahead of ourselves," Bella said, not daring to jinx herself by saying such a thing out loud. "Let's find out what you think of it first."

Digging back into her breakfast, Joanie smiled. "It's all queued up and ready for me to read on the plane headed home. That three-hour layover in Denver will be the perfect time to read it. Then I can tell you what I think."

Biting her lip, Bella picked up her coffee, unsure how ready she was for anyone to read the book. "I can hardly wait," she said, knowing it was a little bit of a lie. "Just be gentle."

"You know I will," Joanie said. "Always."

Following the hostess onto the open terrace of the Waikiki restaurant, JC scanned to see where Chris and her fiancée waited. As she spotted them, she noticed Chris was watching for her and gave a little wave when their eyes met. Closing the distance, JC took in the scene. A table in the corner with a beautiful view of the ocean in the distance. Chris in a coral-colored summer dress with her blonde hair pulled back in a clip, looking fresh and beautiful as always. Beside her was a slightly more masculine woman in a yellow and green Hawaiian shirt and navy blue shorts. A pair of sunglasses perched on the top of her head. Her features were also attractive but in direct contrast to Chris. The fiancée had short, black hair and darker skin.

"You made it," Chris said, standing with arms open to greet JC as she reached the table. Unable to avoid the hug or else make things look awkward, JC stepped forward for a quick embrace. "It's so good to see you again."

After a beat, JC moved away to pull out her chair while nodding to the other woman. The fiancée half rose from her seat and held out a hand. "I'm Tamara," she said as JC shook her hand to return the welcoming gesture.

"It's nice to meet you," JC said as she settled into her chair.

She noticed Chris looking around. "Where's Bella?" she asked. "Didn't she come with you?"

"No," JC replied. "She is currently on the mainland at a book conference."

"Oh," Chris said with a raised eyebrow. "And you didn't go with her?"

JC paused because the question felt probing. When they had met for dinner, JC and Bella never announced their timeline to Chris. *Although I don't know what our timeline is either*, JC thought. *But the whole world doesn't need to know that.*

"Unfortunately, it was short notice, and I couldn't reschedule work, but I will next time," JC said, going on what she and Bella discussed. "Although I did miss out, because she won an award for that book you like so much."

Chris clapped her hands and turned to Tamara. "Remember I told you Bella is the author of that fantastic novel I read last summer." Chris beamed. "She promised me an autographed paperback the next time I see her." As if planning the segue, Chris returned her attention to JC. "When is she coming back?"

"I'm not sure yet," JC had to admit. "Although, I'm thinking of going to visit her in Portland." Even though her plan was vague, the idea appealed to her more and more. *Maybe even surprise her*, she thought. *I think she would like that.* "But honestly, one of my delays is what to do with Roxie."

"Who is Roxie?" Tamara asked.

JC smiled as she thought of her furry companion. "A wonderful dog," she answered, glancing at Chris. "She recently came into my and Bella's life." She liked adding the second part, not only because it felt right but because it should give Chris a hint that they were a strong, very connected couple. From the pinched look on her face, JC could tell it hit home.

Grinning, clearly oblivious, Tamara nodded. "That's great," she said. "I love dogs, and I miss having one, but it's so impractical moving around in the Army." She sighed. "When I get deployed overseas, I can't take a pet with me."

"Yes, that can be frustrating," JC said, already so attached to Roxie that she didn't want to think about not having her around. "I was in the service for a while as well and having a pet would have been impossible."

"It is," Tamara agreed. "I had a wonderful dog growing up. She lived to be fourteen, and it was one of the hardest blows of my life when she passed." Her face lit up, and she grabbed Chris's hand. "Hey, why don't we watch Roxie while JC is gone?"

Chris's eyebrows went up. "You want us to take care of a dog?"

"Not just any dog. JC and Bella's dog," Tamara said. "The condo has a great yard, and we could help them while I get my doggy fix."

"Okay," Chris said slowly, not sounding convinced, while Tamara beamed.

JC pondered the offer for a moment, and as she looked at the warmth in Tamara's brown eyes, she believed Roxie would be well cared for. "You know," she said with a smile. "That idea might work."

35

Carrying the two heavy brown paper sacks full of groceries up the three stairs from the garage, Bella sighed with relief when she deposited them on the kitchen table. *It's those two bottles of wine in there*, she said with a smile at her indulgence. *And I think it's time to open one of those right now.* After snagging a wine glass from the cupboard, she poured herself a serving of Riesling from a local winery. One of the reasons she loved living in Portland was the proximity to so many excellent vineyards. It had been a long time since she went out wine tasting, and immediately she thought about JC. *How fun would that be? Touring around with her on a sunny Sunday afternoon?* She didn't have to guess. It would be fantastic.

Thinking of the wonderful woman she missed so much, Bella checked her phone, hoping for a text. There was none, making her frown. JC had been strangely quiet all day. In fact, if she actually thought about it, JC acted a little differently all week. *Was she more distant?* she thought, as anxiety twisted in her stomach at the idea JC was losing interest in her. Although they had only been separated for three weeks, the time felt a little like forever. *A lot can change in that amount of time.* As if her subconscious was waiting for the opportunity, the image of JC's ex-girlfriend Chris rose to mind. JC assured Bella the dinner a week ago was pleasant but nothing special. From the way she described it, Tamara the fiancée was especially nice, and that had reassured Bella even more. Hopefully, Chris would keep her interests in JC in check if she had her own special someone.

After putting the milk and produce away in the fridge, Bella slipped into a kitchen chair and decided to call JC. Even with the three-hour time difference, it was late enough in the day that she would be back from the afternoon tour and likely still at the office. The call went straight to voicemail. Bella listened to the woman's confident and, in her opinion, quite sexy voice asking the caller to leave a message. "Hi there," Bella said after the beep. "I'm having a glass of Riesling and thinking of you. I hope the tours went well today, and you're headed home with Roxie soon. Miss you both so much. Please call me."

Ending the call, she put the phone on the table and tried to ignore the sense that something was off between them. Until JC called back, the best thing she could do was distract herself by making dinner. The fresh, in-season tomato, lettuce, and cucumber she bought, plus some cubes of avocado, all smothered in blue cheese, sounded tempting. If only her stomach would relax. *I'm being silly,* she thought. *Of course, JC has a good reason for being busy. I'm sure she'll tell me all about it tonight when we have our long call.*

Before she stood to start prepping the food, her cellphone buzzed with a text. Seeing JC was the sender, Bella quickly checked the screen. "Hi there," the message said. "Sorry I didn't answer. Kind of in the middle of something important."

Bella furrowed her brow. "Middle of something" sounded

strangely vague for JC, who loved to send selfies and pics of everything she was doing so Bella felt a part of it. "Do I get to hear what it is later tonight?" she sent and watched as the three dots on her screen danced to show JC was responding.

"Absolutely. If I'm not mistaken, I can tell you in about three minutes."

Still confused, Bella started to type back when an additional text popped up. "Nope. I was wrong. I can tell you right about now."

"Tell me what?" Bella wrote, trying to catch up with whatever JC was talking about. There was a long pause with no sign JC was writing back. Trying to keep from becoming frustrated, Bella left the phone on the table as she took another drink of her wine and waited. A car honked outside in front of her kitchen window. First thinking about ignoring the sound, something inside her told Bella to look. She nearly dropped the wine she carried with her when she pushed the curtain aside. A sedan sat parked at the curb and the woman climbing out of it had blonde hair pulled back in a ponytail. *Oh my God,* Bella thought as tears of joy sprang to her eyes. *It's JC.*

WALKING behind Bella through the grove of redwoods and sequoias, JC continued to be amazed at every turn. She was all for the idea when Bella suggested they try a hike through parts of Portland's famous Hoyt Arboretum. So far, Portland had proven to be a beautiful city set in a perfect location along the Columbia River. There was nothing she didn't love about it. When Bella took them on an hour's drive to the east, she was among the mountains, with majestic Mount Hood the crown jewel. An hour's trip to the west led them to the beautiful rocky shores of the Oregon coast. The city itself was alive with urban activity, and as JC experienced it, she understood why Bella loved to live there.

As they neared a broad deck nestled amongst the trees, Bella glanced back at JC. "Water break?" she asked, and although her cheeks were flushed from exertion, there was a twinkle in her eyes. *She's come a long way toward being open-minded about the outdoors since our hike to the lagoon in Hawaii,* JC thought with a smile. *And I know at least some of it is because she wants to make me happy.*

JC nodded. "Absolutely," she said. "And this looks like a great place to take some pictures."

"Oh, it is," Bella said as they reached the steps. "The Redwood Observation Deck is often used as the backdrop for weddings." JC followed her to the railing. As promised, the view was one of a kind—towering trees overlooking a bubbling creek with glimpses of brilliant blue sky. *So different than the tropics of Oahu,* she thought. *Yet no less breathtaking.*

JC slipped the small nylon backpack she wore off her shoulders. "I can see why," she said, pulling a water flask from a pocket. "So serene. I really feel like I'm deep in a forest, but downtown Portland is only a few minutes away."

Taking the flask, Bella glowed at JC's appraisal. "I love how much you seem to be enjoying my city," she said. "And I can't wait until you meet everyone tonight." Feeling a flutter of nerves, JC leaned against the rail. Even though she had met Bella's parents a few times when they visited Bella at college, it was a long time ago. They were always friendly, and she liked them, but things were very different now.

She was dating their daughter in a complicated, long-distance relationship. "You're sure meeting your family so soon is a good idea?" she asked, trying to sound playful but hoping Bella might agree. "What if they don't like me?"

Bella slid her hand through the crook of JC's arm and leaned in close. "You are the kindest, most caring person I have ever met," she said. "They are going to love you." All JC could do was sigh. *Considering how much I love Bella,* she thought. *I sure hope so.* Bella tilted her head as she studied JC's face. "You're not actually concerned about this, are you?"

Shaking her head, but with a hint at a grimace, JC wasn't sure how to answer. "Well, maybe a little," she admitted after a beat. "I want to make a good impression."

"Oh, JC," Bella said, turning so their eyes met. "I promise you, the barbeque will be great, and everyone will see why I'm so crazy about you." She gave JC's arm a light shake. "So stop worrying."

Bella's enthusiasm helped, but one question worried JC. "Okay, okay," she said with a chuckle. "I believe you." She hesitated, unsure if she wanted to bring the subject up while they stood in the middle of an evergreen grove but needed to know the strategy if not the answer. "Bella, what do I say if someone asks me about our plans for the future?"

At the question, Bella sobered a little. "Let's simply hope no one does that," she said, and after a moment, JC nodded, hoping that too.

As BELLA FINISHED the red trail loop to take them back to the Hoyt Arboretum parking lot, JC's question hung in her mind. When the woman asked how to answer any questions about their future, Bella's chest filled with both excitement and anxiety. Thinking of a future with JC made her happy beyond words but figuring out how to make it all work made Bella's stomach hurt. "Let's hope they don't ask," was all she could think to answer and then pretended to be distracted by a blue jay landing on the deck's railing. JC had been quiet for the rest of the hike though and Bella knew they couldn't ignore the problem forever. *But we don't need to discuss it right now,* she thought as she scanned the crowded lot for where they parked. The day had been perfect, and she wanted to keep it that way.

In fact, JC's entire visit was wonderful. Having her in Portland encouraged Bella to do things outside her usual routine. The places they visited, even if she had been to them before, took on a whole new perspective with JC beside her. Hours spent browsing Portland's giant, famous bookstore, riding the streetcar to the south waterfront's farmers market, and a romantic dinner thirty stories high overlooking the city were highlights she would cherish forever. There was more to it than sightseeing though. Bella found herself taking more pleasure in everything. Something as simple as cooking dinner for the two of them became a little playful, and a romantic endeavor that often included dancing in the kitchen. If Bella had been in love with JC before, the emotions were even stronger now.

As they reached the car, JC surprised Bella by putting a hand on her arm. When Bella turned to look, she saw a frown on the woman's face. "What's wrong?" Bella asked, and when JC hesitated, she thought the worst. *Are we going to have a conversation about our future right here?* she wondered as her chest tightened. *Please, not now. I'm not ready.*

Finally, JC looked into her eyes. "The hike was beautiful, and I loved every bit of it," she said before pausing again. Bella watched the woman search her face as if deliberating on what to say next. She held her breath. After a beat, JC sighed. "I guess I want to apologize. I didn't mean to make things awkward there at the end." Before Bella could respond, she gave her a quick kiss on the lips, and the old JC was back in place. "This was fun." Although she loved even the sweetest of touches from JC's mouth, Bella wasn't convinced the woman said what was truly on her mind. Still, she was afraid to dig deeper and let it go.

She touched JC on the cheek. "We are fine," she said. "I

promise I know we have things to talk about but right now, I want us to have a great time at the barbeque tonight."

"And we will," JC said with a smile. "I'll be on my very best behavior."

Bella laughed as she opened the hatchback of the car. "You are the last person I am worried about," she said. "My grandmother now…"

JC chuckled as she unslung the daypack from her shoulders. "From what you've described, I am looking forward to meeting her," she said. "Lots of personality."

"That is a good way to put it," Bella agreed, keeping her smile in place but more than a tiny bit worried that if anyone tried to pin them down on a long-term plan, it would be her ninety-three-year-old grandmother. "Gramma lives by the motto that at her age, she can pretty much say and do whatever she wants, so be ready."

36

Sitting beside Bella at the picnic table in the shaded backyard of her parents' house, JC enjoyed the pleasant evening. So far, things had been going well. Bella's parents were as warm and friendly as she remembered. If they had any questions about her intentions, they were polite enough not to press her on the subject. *But the sister and the grandmother haven't arrived yet,* JC reminded herself, taking the final sip of the bottle of excellent local Oregon beer in her hand. *There's plenty of time for things to get interesting.* She would have to wait and see.

"Did you like it?" Bella asked, motioning to the beer, and JC nodded.

"Excellent like the others I've tried here," she answered. "These hazy pale ales are growing on me." She had found another wonderful thing about visiting Bella was the huge variety of locally brewed beer available in Portland. When Bella bragged that Portland, Oregon was the microbrew capital of the world, JC had laughed, only to learn the woman was serious. A quick internet search confirmed her claim. There were no less than seventy craft breweries in the area. Tomorrow they would be going on a tour of a handful of the many ones available, and she looked forward to trying different flavorings.

"Would you like another one?" Bella asked. "I am going to run into the house and make sure Mom doesn't need a hand with anything."

JC nodded. "I do, but I'll come help with you," she said, and Bella shook her head as she stood from the table, putting a hand lightly on JC's shoulder.

"No, you stay right here," she said with a smile. "You're the guest, and I want you to relax. I'll be back in a minute."

Not used to being waited on, JC considered arguing but then smiled in return. "I'll do my best," she said and watched as the dark-haired woman she had grown so much closer to over the last week disappeared through the house's backdoor. The screen door had barely closed when it opened again, and a miniature black poodle came running out, followed closely by two boys. Dressed in Seahawk jerseys and boardshorts, the taller of the two carried a football, and he darted to the open grassy area of the yard. "Go out for a pass, Kyle," he yelled to whom JC guessed from their similarities was his younger brother.

Complying, Kyle ran toward the other corner, all the while the small, black, curly-haired dog barked and nipped playfully at his heels. "Stop it, Mitzie, and get over here," JC heard from the backdoor. "You're liable to get stepped on." Turning, she saw an older woman had also come out into the yard. She used a cane to walk slowly toward the picnic table. *This must be the grandmother*, JC thought, starting to get up and lend a hand. She had hardly moved before the woman pinned her with a look. "You don't need to get up unless you intend to carry me over."

JC blinked, not sure what to do. Considering how small and frail the white-haired woman looked, she knew picking her up would be easy enough. "I can if—" she started to say only to see a twinkle fill the elderly woman's brown eyes.

"I'm not serious," she said with a little laugh as she finished her trip to the table and lowered herself carefully to the end of a bench. "You must be Bella's friend JC."

Watching as the little poodle hopped onto the bench beside the woman, JC nodded. "Yes, ma'am," she said. "It's nice to meet you."

Running a wrinkled hand over the head of the animal beside her, the woman smiled. "It's nice to meet you too," she said. "Especially since I think you would be nice enough to let me ride piggyback."

"Oh, absolutely," JC answered, with a little chuckle. "You look a lot lighter than a kayak."

The woman started to laugh at the same time Bella, followed by her mother and who JC guessed from their resemblance was her sister, came out the backdoor with plates of food. "Gramma, what's so funny?" Bella asked, meeting JC's eye with a quizzical look.

"Oh, nothing, dear," Gramma answered, giving JC a quick wink. "I'm just getting to know your friend."

As she helped her sister carry the dinner dishes into the kitchen, Bella was beyond pleased with the state of things. So far, everything went better than she had ever hoped. "I think you've found a keeper," Hanna said as she put her load of dishes in the sink. "JC is pretty wonderful. Gramma likes her too. I can tell."

Dropping off her armload as well, Bella blushed with pleasure at the comment. "She is special," she agreed. "I don't know how I got so lucky."

Hanna smiled. "Don't sell yourself short," she said. "You deserve someone wonderful in your life."

Pausing, Bella absorbed what her sister said. "Thank you," she said, and Hanna pecked her on the cheek.

"You're welcome," she said. "Now, help me with the dessert."

The sisters carried out the dish of cobbler and French vanilla ice cream to go with it. "Oh good," Bella heard her gramma say. "A treat you probably don't often find in the islands."

JC raised her eyebrows. "Well, now you have certainly made me curious," JC said.

"Blackberry cobbler," Gramma said. "Fresh this morning. Kyle and Kevin helped me pick them."

Kyle, who sat at the table beside his grandmother, proudly held up his arm. "I only got three scratches," he said, clearly pleased with himself.

"I feel honored that you went to so much trouble," JC said, giving Kyle a wink. "And it looks like there is ice cream too."

"Yay!" the two brothers said in unison.

As Bella's sister started to serve up the plates, Bella watched Gramma fix JC with a look. "Have you had blackberry cobbler before?"

JC shook her head. "I can't say that I have."

Gramma waved a hand. "It's a weed here in Oregon," she said with a laugh. "They're almost impossible to kill. But they certainly do make for a good dessert."

Accepting her bowl full of dessert, JC grinned. "It looks delicious," she said, and Bella watched her take a bite. "Wow. I would agree. Great flavor." She glanced at Bella. "Another thing about Oregon that I really like." Bella swallowed hard. JC could not have teed up an easier segue into a conversation about Oregon versus Hawaii. The last thing she wanted to discuss tonight.

Gramma didn't miss the opportunity. "So, what do you

think of Portland overall?" she asked. Bella glanced at JC, who seemed to be studying her dish of dessert.

"I like it very much," she said after a moment, and she looked up from her food to meet Bella's eyes. "It's one of the most beautiful cities I've ever spent time in. Not only is there a lot to do, but the people here are extremely friendly, and I feel very welcome."

Nodding, Gramma toyed with her dessert. "It is one of a kind. How much longer are you staying?" she asked, and Bella set down her fork. There was too much anxiety in her stomach to eat. It seemed the conversation she was hoping to avoid was coming up.

"Just another week," JC answered. "And then I have to return to my kayaking adventure business." Before Gramma could comment, JC held her look and kept going. "I get to do something I love every day, and people pay me to do it."

"But you know the most interesting part lately?" Bella chimed in. "Our dog Roxie kayaks with her."

"What?" Kyle asked with a mouthful of dessert.

"Don't talk with your mouth full, Kyle," Hanna said.

JC grinned. "It's true," she said. "I can show you a video after we finish eating."

"That would be cool," Kyle said while Kevin nodded.

"It is cool," JC said. "She rides in the front like any other passenger." She chuckled, adding. "Except she is lousy at paddling."

Everybody laughed. "I wonder if Mitzie could do it," Kyle asked between bites.

"I'm sure she could," Gramma answered. "She's a very smart dog."

Kevin snorted a laugh. "I think she would be a shark snack."

Gramma fixed him with a look. "I think not, young man. Now, eat your dessert."

37

The evening went by smoother than JC imagined it could. As Bella let them into her house after the short drive back from the barbeque, JC smiled thinking of how everyone had laughed over Roxie in the kayaking video. Seeing her, JC missed being around the dog more than she thought she would. Never having a pet before, she hadn't considered the separation affecting her. *She's simply another thing I miss about home*, she thought, following Bella into the cute little kitchen. *And another reason deciding what to do about Bella and me is so hard.* Oregon was beautiful, and Bella's family were friendly and fun people, but in her heart JC missed her life in Hawaii.

"I know it's after nine, but would you like a glass of wine on the back porch?" Bella asked, with a smile and a twinkle in her eye. "Before a few other things, maybe?"

Feeling a glow at the prospect of what the few other things might entail, JC smiled in return. "I like the sound of all of that," she said, pulling Bella closer and wrapping her arms around her waist. "Are you sure you want the wine first?"

Bella laughed, putting her arms around JC's neck. "Isn't it worth waiting for?" she asked. "And it is such a beautiful night."

Kissing her in response, JC let their lips linger, enjoying the taste of Bella's mouth against hers. "It is indeed," she murmured after a beat. "But only one glass."

With a last peck on the lips, Bella turned away to grab glasses from the cupboard while JC fished the white wine from the fridge. In a moment, with filled glasses in hand, they were stepping onto the back porch. Before JC sat, she heard her cell phone ringing from where she left it on the kitchen counter. Doing quick math in her head, she knew it was a little after six p.m. back home. *And a strange time for someone from work to call me*, she thought with a frown, knowing they closed up shop closer to five. Plus, Blake was good about only calling her about work stuff during the early part of the day and actually had only called her twice with updates since she left the island. Not many other people had her number, and if they did, the communication was nearly always via text messages. She had an uneasy thought. *Unless it's Chris or Tamara calling about Roxie.* "Sorry, but I think I should answer that," JC said as she set her wine glass on the patio table. "I'm not sure who would call this late."

Bella nodded as JC turned toward the kitchen. Before she could reach the phone, the ringing stopped. *Dang it*, she thought, scooping it up to check the screen. *Hopefully it was nothing but spam.* Yet, when she read the name 'Blake' a quick pulse of anxiety tightened her chest. *Something must be wrong.* Rather than wait for a voicemail, she dialed back. "Hi, JC," Blake answered, and immediately she knew she was right—something was wrong. The man didn't sound like himself. *Almost like he's in pain.*

"Blake," she said. "Are you okay?"

He sighed. "Not so much," he said. "I spun out in my motorcycle and hurt my wrist in the crash."

"Oh, wow, that sounds horrible," JC said, hating that her friend was hurt but also already calculating the ramifications of having her backup out of commission. "When did it happen?"

"On my way home," Blake answered. "I called as soon as I could, but I was in the ambulance." She heard him swallow hard. "I'm sorry, but I don't think I can paddle with it like this."

JC shook her head. *Leave it to Blake to worry about me and work first,* she thought, but she did appreciate it. She would have to make phone calls to take care of tours scheduled for the next day. "Don't worry about that," she said. "Where are you now?"

"I'm in the emergency room, waiting to go back for x-rays," he answered. "Maybe if it's only a sprain, I can have them wrap it real tight and—"

"No," JC said. "We will cancel tomorrow's tours, and I'll come back on the first flight I can find in the morning. You worry about yourself."

With the backdoor open, Bella couldn't help but overhear bits of JC's side of the phone conversation. She gathered the call from Blake wasn't good. Knowing the nice young man wouldn't call JC, especially outside of work hours unless there was a good reason, Bella worried something was wrong. When the night breeze carried JC's words, "we will cancel tomorrow's tours, and I'll come back on the first flight I can find in the morning. You worry about yourself," her heart fell. The next week with JC exploring even more of Portland and the surrounding area sounded like it wouldn't happen. Trying hard not to be frustrated, because clearly something terrible had happened, otherwise JC would never leave early, Bella sipped her wine and waited.

After hearing JC hang up and then complete a second call to someone else, Bella was relieved when the woman finally joined her on the back porch again. "Sorry," JC said with a sigh as she dropped into the patio chair beside Bella. "But Blake hurt his wrist, and it sounds like it might be broken."

Bella processed her words, realizing it would be impossible to paddle a kayak in that condition. "What are you going to do?" she asked. "I mean, I overheard enough to know you have to go back, but…"

Picking up her wine, JC took a sip before answering. "I have to cancel tomorrow's tours," she said. "I called the guy helping Blake while I'm gone to have him send me the contact information for everyone signed up." She sighed. "After he sends me a text that he emailed them, I'll be spending an hour calling to disappoint people and refund their money."

"I can help with that," Bella said, hating to see the frustration on JC's normally carefree face. "We can split up the list if you want."

JC gave her a weak smile. "Thank you," she said. "Then maybe we will still have time for some of the other stuff you hinted at earlier."

Feeling a little flutter at the suggestiveness in her tone, Bella nodded. "We will definitely have time," she said, then sobered as she thought of what else she overheard. "But you're leaving in the morning?"

"I am afraid I have to," JC answered, meeting Bella's eyes with her own. Disappointment filled them. "There isn't much choice."

Bella reached for her hand and held it. "I know," she said. "There's no one to blame for what happened." She rubbed her thumb over the back of JC's hand. "It's just I'm really going to miss having you here." For a long moment, neither said anything. The question they avoided all week loomed over them. Unfortunately, Bella was no clearer on an answer of how to make everything work than before.

"Well," JC said with hesitation as she stared at their hands clasped together. "I can come back to visit soon." She lifted her eyes. "Or you can come to Hawaii and stay with me and see Roxie."

Bella blinked. "Now?" she said. "Like go with you in the morning?"

JC started to nod. "Yes," she said. "Come with me and stay for as long as you want."

Images of JC's beautiful home filled Bella's mind, and her heart melted at the idea of seeing Roxie again. *Still, I can't simply drop everything and leave*, she thought. *I have to give my parents at least some notice and set up Hanna to look after my house.* "JC," she said softly. "I can't do that. Not out of the blue."

Slowly, JC nodded, and the disappointment in her eyes was almost enough for Bella to change her mind, but then the woman was standing. "You're right," she said. "I shouldn't have put you on the spot like that." She leaned to kiss Bella, and their lips met for a second. The touch was warm and a little thrilling, like always, but Bella felt something different in it. The sensation scared her, and she was about to ask the woman what she was thinking, but then JC's phone buzzed with a text. After a glance, JC nodded. "He sent me the list. Let's go make some phone calls before it gets any later."

38

As JC finished the day's paperwork in the office at Oahu Paddle Adventures, she couldn't believe how fast the last forty-eight hours had gone. She had been able to grab a last-minute flight out of Portland, picked up Roxie from a disappointed Tamara and Chris, and taken over the tours for Blake. There hadn't been much time to talk to Bella, and if JC was honest with herself, that might have been just as well. Since the night before she left, there was a lingering feeling of frustration over the woman's unwillingness to even seriously consider coming to Hawaii at the last minute with JC. It had made their few conversations a little awkward because she hadn't been sure what to say. Luckily, with time to reflect on the evening, JC had a better perspective and looked forward to talking to Bella later that night. *So I can apologize*, she thought, shutting down the computer and turning off the lights. *I put her on the spot and then got my feelings hurt when she didn't jump at my idea to drop everything.*

"That wasn't very fair, now was it, Roxie?" she said to her canine companion as they walked out the shop's door. Roxie looked at her, mouth slightly open as if in a smile. If JC didn't know better, she would think the dog was happy to have her back home. The thought Roxie missed her made her feel warm inside. JC had missed Roxie too, and when she called Chris to let her and Tamara know she was back early, they were genuinely saddened.

When JC went to pick her up, they lingered on the front steps. "She's such a great girl," Tamara had said as she ran a hand over Roxie's furry head. "I can't thank you enough for letting us watch her. I hate that she's leaving early."

JC had knelt beside Roxie and scratched the dog's neck. "I can't tell you enough how much of a relief it has been knowing she was in good hands," JC said. "I promise you can borrow her again anytime you need a doggie fix."

"Thanks," Chris had said, smiling at Tamara. "But I think we will be getting a dog ourselves soon."

JC stood, looking from Tamara to Chris and back. "Oh, yeah?" she asked. "That's great."

Beaming, Tamara put her arm around Chris's shoulders. "We both enjoyed having Roxie so much," she said. "It was the perfect test, although finding a dog as sweet as her will be challenging."

JC had agreed at the time and as they walked to the jeep, she looked at Roxie's upturned face, and she knew she was lucky to have her. "I'm lonely enough without Bella as it is," she said. "I'm not sure what I would do without you to keep me company." Suddenly, her phone rang in her pocket, and she fished it out, hoping to see the call was from Bella. Instead, it was a random local number. She thought about answering but then let it go to voicemail. If it were anything other than a salesman trying to sell her a car warranty, she would deal with it after she got home and had a cold beer in her hand, sitting in a lounger beside the pool.

Loading Roxie into the jeep and then climbing in herself, JC was about to head home when her phone buzzed again.

This time it was a text message from the random number, and she paused to check it. The words made her heart skip a beat. "I just left you a voicemail but wanted to follow up with a text," the stranger wrote. "I think you have my father's dog."

"Then the next day, Sapphic Readers Everywhere wants you for an exclusive podcast interview on the seventeenth," Bella's editor said over the speakerphone which rested on the kitchen table.

Bella groaned as she played with her wine. "Another one. Can't we spread these out?" she asked. Joanie had finished laying out a grueling promotional schedule for the two weeks leading up to the launch of Bella's book. As excited as she was to learn the time was right to release the novel, anxiety over so much publicity had her stomach in knots. Like many writers, Bella preferred to stay out of the spotlight and was content to hide behind her laptop screen, letting her words take all the attention. Unfortunately, marketing the book dictated a certain number of public appearances. Social media and the internet fed a hungry reading audience, and Bella couldn't disappoint them. The saving grace was that it was almost entirely virtual. Aside from attending a conference once or twice a year and the occasional book signing, very little of Bella's press was in person.

Joanie sighed audibly over the phone. "We've talked about momentum," her editor said, her tone laced with a hint of exasperation. "When your book goes live online, we want everyone already lined up wanting to read it."

"Wait, I thought you said preorders looked good," Bella replied. "That's a sign people are eager to read it."

"True. But keep in mind only a small percentage of your readers will preorder," Joanie said. "Even when it's a book from you. The real sales numbers come after it's out, and then we will know if you've written another hit."

Biting her lip, Bella wasn't sure she was ready to ride the rollercoaster but knew her editor wouldn't agree to a delay. "I'll cross my fingers," Bella said, thankful when she saw another call coming through on her phone. It was JC. "Joanie, we need to finish this later. JC is calling me."

"We need to talk about that situation too," Joanie said, and Bella knew she was correct, but not right then.

Bella reached for the phone. "Later," she said. "I'll text you." Then she pressed disconnect before Joanie could say another word. A wide smile crossed her face as she joined the second call. "Hi there."

"Hey," she heard JC say, and some tension in her voice made Bella pause. *Is this about my not going with her to Hawaii?* she wondered. The lack of texts and quality phone time over the last forty-eight hours had made her worry more than only a little. Still, she had chalked that up to JC being caught up in the rush of going home and dealing with the impact of Blake's injury.

Swallowing down her anxiety, Bella took the phone off speaker and put it to her ear. "JC," she said. "Is everything okay?"

There was a pause long enough for Bella's apprehension to blossom. "It's about Roxie," JC finally answered. "Someone called and left a message. They think she is their lost dog."

Bella's heart nearly stopped. "No," she whispered. "Have you talked to them?"

"I'm afraid to call back," JC admitted with an unusual tone in her voice. At first, Bella didn't recognize it, but then realized the sound was worry. Usually, JC came across as calm and collected.

Hearing her anxious was unsettling, and at first, Bella wasn't sure how to react, but then she realized what needed to be done. "I'm sure it's a mistake," Bella said, forcing her own worries down so she could be supportive of JC. "And you can give calling back a little time."

JC blew out a breath. "But I can't exactly keep Roxie from them," she said. "It might be their dog."

Bella shook her head. "I'm not saying that you don't cooperate, but Roxie doesn't have a chip and nothing to identify her that the vet could find. All they are going off is a small photo." When JC didn't answer, Bella knew her noble girlfriend was conflicted over not responding right away. "What I'm saying is they will need to prove she is theirs. You can call them, but don't do anything drastic yet."

"Yet?" JC asked. "What does that mean?"

Bella felt a sudden resolve come over her and finally she knew what needed to happen. "Not until I get there," she said. "I'm going to hang up and call the airline and then my sister to make arrangements to have her watch the house. I want to be with you if something happens with Roxie."

There was a pause and for a second Bella thought the call had dropped, but then JC was back. "Are you sure?" she asked and there was so much emotion in her voice Bella felt a tug at her heart.

"I've never been more sure," Bella said. "I love you and I'll be there soon."

39

Helping load the last kayak onto the trailer hooked behind her jeep, JC was happy the day's final tour was over. Not that it hadn't gone well. The customers, since she returned, were all good groups. She always enjoyed working with customers who were both experienced and enthusiastic. Still, JC had a lot on her mind and places to be. Bella had sent a text that she had arrived and was at the house. It was a bummer that JC couldn't meet her at the airport, but with Blake still out with a badly sprained wrist, there wasn't anyone else to cover. *At least he didn't break it*, she thought. Currently, she had him running the office but hoped he could be back on the water in another week or two.

"Need anything else, JC?" Shaun, the second guide for the day, asked. JC liked him. He was young but resourceful and a hard worker. He interacted well with the customers, and she felt lucky to have him on her staff, even if only on an as-needed basis.

JC smiled. "I think I'm all set," she said. "Thanks for taking over the van duties today. You're a big help."

"No problem," Shaun said with a grin. "Working for you is a dream come true. Kayaking every day? Even part-time, it beats a desk job by miles."

At that, JC could agree, and it felt good knowing Shaun saw things that way. "Well, I'm glad to hear it," she said. "I'm probably going to keep adding hours to your schedule if you want the work."

"Absolutely," Shaun said. "Whenever you want me, I'll be here."

Just then, JC's phone buzzed, and she fished it from her pocket as Shaun backed away. "I'll let you know when I've finished my drop-offs," he said, and JC nodded as she checked her phone screen.

There was a text from Bella. "Miss you. Do you want me to start anything for dinner?"

JC raised an eyebrow at the question. Cooking was generally JC's area of expertise, with Bella heartily admitting she wasn't great in the kitchen. JC didn't mind the woman's limitation in that department. She enjoyed the process of making a meal and the pleasure of eating what she had created with someone she cared about. *Maybe she's trying to be especially helpful because of the stress over Roxie,* she thought, then smiled. *Or is cleverly hinting I should grab takeout?* Either reason was appreciated, although in all honesty, her stomach was feeling a little uneasy, so eating wasn't high on her list of priorities. The anxiety over meeting the man who insisted Roxie was his father's dog had her entire body tense.

The text exchange she had with him hadn't been bad. In fact, he had been very understanding when JC insisted she couldn't meet him right away. His response had surprised JC a little. If she were missing her lost dog, especially one as wonderful as Roxie, she was not so sure she would have been as patient. Regardless, they planned to meet at six p.m. that evening at the park near JC's house. Unexpectedly, Bella had rushed to Hawaii to be with her for the meeting, something that JC truly appreciated. No matter what happened with Roxie later, she would be forever grateful to the dog for motivating Bella to come back to Hawaii. It was as if the situation around meeting Roxie's possible owner was the tipping point the two of them needed to move forward. *Now I need to make the most of it,* she thought, knowing spontaneous trips back and forth were not the answer. *And find a way for us both to be happy.*

Looking at her phone, she reread the message from Bella before climbing in the jeep. Rather than write back, she called her. "Well, hello," Bella answered. "Are you already headed home?"

"Hi," JC said with a smile, loving that Bella was waiting for her at the house. "Unfortunately, not yet. I'm headed to the shop to unload the kayaks. Probably forty-five minutes?"

"Okay. JC…" Bella said, then hesitated. JC frowned, unsure what to think, but before she could say anything, the woman continued. "It feels good to be here again. Really good."

The words were music to JC's ears. "Thank you again for coming," she said, starting the jeep. "Having you here means everything."

"I know. And thank you for wanting me to come back," Bella answered, and JC paused to make sure the woman heard her clearly.

"Always, Bella," she replied. "I want you to come back always."

Walking onto the patio, Bella tried to let the serene atmosphere and scent of plumerias relax her. Even though the minute she let herself in through JC's front door and a welcoming sense enveloped her, she was a little unsettled.

Since the night they learned Blake hurt his wrist, things hadn't felt quite the same with JC. She knew it was all wrapped up in their seemingly impossible predicament over what to do with their future, but that didn't help her figure out what to do to fix it. The inevitable decisions were quickly approaching. Adding to her stress was the possibility they would have to give up Roxie to her original owner. Bella didn't even want to consider how that would impact her relationship with JC.

After sinking into a lounger, Bella sighed while she closed her eyes. JC would be home soon with Roxie, who had spent the day with Blake at the Oahu Paddle Adventure's office, and then things would be okay. Being near JC always made Bella feel better. The three of them could have dinner and then see the stranger who thought Roxie might belong to his father. She wasn't entirely clear on the details, but JC did say the man gave her a name for Roxie. She simply hadn't had the nerve to try it out with the dog yet. Tonight, when they were together, JC would call Roxie by the other name and see how she reacted. *Please don't let it be the correct name,* she wished. *Lots of dogs could look like Roxie, so let it be a mistake.*

Bella forced herself to continue to take long, slow breaths, counting to four as she inhaled, and again when she exhaled. Her shoulders were starting to loosen, and her whirling mind was calming when her cell phone rang. Startled by the sound, Bella let out a little squeak of surprise. "Dang it," she muttered, thinking of ignoring the call but then worried it was JC needing something. She pulled it out of the front pocket of her shorts to see the caller wasn't JC but instead her sister. When Bella landed in Hawaii, she had sent a text to Hanna to let her know she had arrived okay, so a phone call was a surprise. Trying not to let her already anxious mood run away with her, she quickly answered with a hello.

"Hi," Hanna said. "Am I interrupting anything?"

"No," Bella replied. "JC isn't home yet. Is everything okay?"

"Yes," Hanna said with an apologetic tone in her voice. "I'm sorry. I didn't mean to freak you out by calling." She laughed. "I guess I could have sent a text, but I was in a hurry."

Feeling less anxious and more curious, Bella relaxed into the cushion. "That's okay. But what's the big rush?"

"Well, I went by and checked your mail, and there's an interesting envelope," Hanna said. "Is there something you haven't been telling me?"

Bella furrowed her brow. "Not that I know of," she said, racking her brain for what might have come in the mail to make her sister curious. "Who is it from?"

"Well, it's pretty official looking and supposedly from Crown Media Productions," Hanna said, and Bella sighed. She hated to break it to her sister, but lots of junk mail came from companies with names like that, and she had learned not to get excited. Still, before she could explain, her sister continued. "So, I googled them." She laughed. "Sorry I was nosey, but it made me curious."

"I forgive you," Bella said with a smile. "But Hanna, it's probably only junk. I get fake offers to make my book into a movie every once in a while, and they are—"

Hanna cut her off. "Crown Media Productions is for real, I think. Bella, they make movies for the Hallmark Channel."

40

"Hello? Anybody home?" JC said as Roxie bounded past her into the house. Bella appeared in the patio doorway with a smile that lit up not only the room but JC's heart. It had only been a couple of days, but she had missed the woman terribly. *A lot more than I have let myself admit*, she thought. *Somehow having her in my space completes my world.*

Bella knelt to catch the onrushing Roxie. "I'm here," she said. "And I missed you so much." She scratched the dog's neck before looking at JC. "Especially you."

JC smiled as she laid her car keys on the sideboard before crossing the room to greet Bella properly. "I think I missed you more," she said as Bella stood, and they came face to face. "Can I have a kiss?"

"All that you could ever want," Bella replied before leaning in to let JC's mouth take hers. It was sweet and tender, but JC liked the feeling of promise behind the taste of her lips. A tingle ran through her at the idea of more to come. *But first,* she thought pulling back with a sigh. *The*

Roxie situation needs to be dealt with. Clearly sensing JC's shift in thinking, Bella touched JC's cheek. "It will all work out."

Nodding, JC looked away to hide the fear in her eyes. "I know," she said, then changed the subject for the moment as she walked toward the kitchen. "I didn't call anything in for dinner. Honestly, my stomach is a little uptight over the meeting we have planned for later, so nothing sounded appetizing."

"That's fine," Bella said. "I had a banana from your fruit basket when I got here and then thought about switching to wine but decided to wait until after we find out about Roxie." With the dog on her heels, Bella followed JC into the kitchen. "We only have an hour until we have to go, so let's get something to eat afterward."

Opening the fridge, JC set down her gear bag from work on a kitchen chair. "Thanks for understanding," she said before taking a glass from the cupboard and filling it with water. "I am guessing the conversation will be short." She took a long swallow. "Either he knows Roxie, or he doesn't. Or vice versa."

Bella was quiet, and JC glanced at her to see her biting her lip. "Do you want to try the name he gave you and see what Roxie does?" the woman finally asked. "Just to know?" JC had mixed feelings about her suggestion. A part of her knew it was the right thing to do to return Roxie, but another part hated the idea of losing her. Even after such a short time, she had bonded with the dog. There was no denying Roxie was special to her. Their kindred love of the ocean made the link even stronger. But most of all, having Roxie to share with Bella felt like some of the glue that held them together. As crazy as that sounded, the fact she came into their lives so soon after they met and how they both loved her so much... it was something only they shared. JC looked at Roxie who had retreated to her bed in the corner. Not having the dog would be a blow. Not that it was something they couldn't work past, but it would still be very sad, and she wished the phone call asking about Roxie had never come.

Setting down the water glass, JC went and knelt in front of Roxie. "You're right," she said to Bella. "We need to know." The dog stared her in the eye, mouth partly opened as if in her familiar smile. *She's happy we are all home together,* JC thought with a pang of sadness. *Damn, this is an intelligent dog.* Her throat tight, she had to cough to clear it before talking to Roxie. "Do you know the name… Gracie?" Roxie's head lifted a little, and her tail slowly wagged. JC felt tears sting her eyes. "You know it, don't you? You're Gracie."

Roxie's tail wagged harder, and JC heard Bella stifle a sob. "She's his dog," she said, and JC could only nod.

"Yes," she said. "I believe she is."

RIDING in the jeep's passenger seat as JC drove them to the park to meet the man who claimed Roxie was torture. As much as Bella knew it was inevitable, the fact they were about to lose the dog hurt. When JC called her Gracie, there was no doubt in Bella's mind the name was one Roxie knew. Especially after JC walked onto the patio and called the name to see how the dog would react. The excitement in Roxie's step as she went outside to join JC was unmistakable. To make matters worse, Bella thought the animal looked around expectantly as if hoping to see another human who would have shared that name with her two new friends. *She was raised and loved by someone else,* she thought. *We knew that all along, but that doesn't make this any easier.*

As they approached the small park at the edge of JC's

neighborhood, JC glanced at her. "I love you," she said. "And I've loved sharing Roxie with you. Every minute." Bella's voice caught in her throat. There was so much about Roxie that she loved but having her be a part of their shared world was the biggest.

There would be no replacing her specialness, not even if they went forward and got a puppy or a rescue from a humane shelter. "I love you too," Bella said. "You were so brave that day, rescuing her from traffic."

JC smiled. "I was probably a little crazy," she said. "But I acted on instinct."

"And that's just who you are," Bella said, looking at JC as she pulled them into the parking lot. "A good person, and I am so lucky." JC blushed at the words, but Bella meant them more than she realized. Having JC in her life was lucky, and she didn't want to lose her. *Not like we will lose Roxie*, she thought. *I can't take what I have for granted anymore. I need her.*

Before she could voice her intense revelations, JC nodded toward a parked truck at the edge of the lot. "I think that's him," she said. "He said a blue truck." As if hearing her, a man stood from where he leaned against the hood of an older model Toyota pickup. From the jeep's description JC gave him, he clearly recognized them enough to wave as they drew close and parked. JC got out first, but Bella hung back. She simply wasn't ready to face the reality of the situation yet. "Hi, are you Tony?" she heard JC ask.

Tony held out a hand. "I am," he said. "Thanks for meeting me. I know this must be hard."

"More than I could ever imagine," Bella heard JC admit as she shook his hand. "But I called her Gracie as you suggested, and she seems to know it." Without saying anything else, JC opened the back door of the jeep. Bella turned to watch Roxie, who waited almost reluctantly as Tony came into view. Roxie didn't move for a moment, and then slowly her tail wagged. It picked up speed as the man drew closer.

"Hey, Gracie," Tony said. "We've been worried about you." Bella's heart broke a little as the man scratched Roxie behind the ear. The bond was there, and there could be no doubt Tony and Gracie knew each other. "Dad will be so happy to hear you're okay."

"So, if he's your dad's dog, where is he?" Bella blurted. She knew it was rude, but things didn't seem fair at the moment, and she hated it.

She watched as Tony's shoulders slumped a little and immediately felt horrible because clearly something wasn't right. "He had a stroke a couple of months ago, and he's in a special care facility," he said. "I wanted to bring him, because I know he misses Gracie so much, but they said he wasn't ready." Tony ran a hand lovingly over the dog's head. "He will probably have to stay in a place like that from now on."

"But Roxie... I mean Gracie... can't stay with him then, can she?" JC asked, and Tony shook his head.

"No. She was staying with me," he said, studying Roxie's face. "She's such a good girl, but I travel every week for work, so I had to board her, and I know she hated it."

Bella looked at JC, and their eyes met, and she knew they were thinking the same thing. "Then, can she stay with us instead?" Bella asked, not bothering to beat around the bush. "There is always someone with her, and she seems very happy."

Tony glanced between them, uncertainty on his face. "But I'd like to take her to visit my father sometimes," he said. "So, how would that work?"

"We can make that work," JC and Bella said in unison, and then everyone was silent as the situation set in. Only Roxie moved as she wagged her tail. Bella held her breath while she waited for Tony's answer.

Finally, the man smiled. "I think that will work fine," he said. "I can tell Gracie is happy, and if you're willing to do that for me, please give her a good home. I know my father will like that."

41

After riding home in near silence as they both absorbed the news Roxie could stay with them, JC let out a long deep breath when she pulled into her driveway. Her fingers were entwined with Bella's, and at the sound of her sigh, Bella gave her hand a gentle squeeze. "Everything is okay now," the woman said in a relieved tone of her own. "And we are home again." She glanced into the backseat. "And we have Roxie." JC knew she was right but couldn't quite shake the feeling of unfinished business. But it wasn't necessarily with Roxie.

She followed Bella's look into the backseat to see the sweet face of the black and white dog that somehow had stolen their hearts. "You're right," she said. "Do you think we should start calling her Gracie?" She glanced at Bella. "Now that we know?"

Bella nodded. "Absolutely," she answered. "That would be better for her since she knows it." She smiled. "And less confusing when she visits Tony's dad."

"Yes, you are right," JC said, refocusing on the dog. "Are you okay with that too, Gracie?" Gracie surprised her with a little yip of acknowledgment, making JC and Bella laugh. "Sounds like a done deal then," JC reached for the door handle. "Now, I think I hear a beer calling my name." As the three of them trooped in the front door, JC brought up the rear. When she watched Bella turn in the living room to give Gracie a rub behind her ears, her heart was full of happiness. It was a scene she couldn't get enough of, and although things might seem rushed, JC knew in that instant what she wanted to do. It was time to follow her heart and hope her instincts were right.

As she opened her mouth to tell Bella how she wanted to spend the rest of her life with her, the woman looked up from loving the dog and caught her eye. "In all of this with Gracie, I haven't had a chance to tell you my news," she said, making JC pause, and Bella kept talking in the gap. "You're not going to believe it, but the producers of the Hallmark Channel want to make my novel into a movie for television."

JC blinked with surprise. "Bella, that's incredible," she said, forcing herself to share Bella's excitement and not let any disappointment about her missed opportunity to propose a future together show on her face. "When did you find out about it?"

Beaming, Bella moved closer. "Hanna called while I was waiting for you to come home earlier," she said, wrapping her arms around JC's shoulders. "She was checking my mail, and there was a letter in the mailbox that made her curious."

Not quite following what happened precisely but beginning to absorb what the opportunity could mean for Bella, JC put her arms around Bella's waist. "And the letter was from the Hallmark Channel?"

"Yes," Bella replied. "Well, from their production company, but the interest is clearly outlined in the letter. I have to call in the morning to set up an appointment to discuss it with one of the company's producers." She let out a nervous laugh. "Of course, I'm scare to death.

Her mind whirling with how the turn of events might impact the two of them, JC nodded. "Of course," she said, looking into Bella's eyes. "This is a really big deal." The joy that JC saw on the woman's face was enough to convince her that any declarations of affection needed to wait. "We have to celebrate. Should I get us some champagne?"

Bella laughed. "Let's not go too far yet," she said, but her voice was filled with delight. "Nothing has even been discussed. But JC, what if…" She bit her lip. "What if they really do make it into a movie? I'll reach so many new readers."

"And those will be very lucky people," JC said, not daring to let Bella doubt herself for even a moment. "You deserve this, and I couldn't be more excited for you."

Moving her face closer, JC saw Bella's eyes take on an extra flicker of passion. "Exciting for us," Bella murmured. "Everything in my life has been wonderful since I found you again." For a fleeting moment, JC thought to tell Bella everything in her heart but then let it go. The moment was about Bella's news, and what JC had to say could come later. In fact, an idea started to form in her mind, and she smiled as she closed the few inches between their faces to kiss the woman she loved.

FLUTTERING HER EYES OPEN, Bella slowly rose from a sweet dream. She and JC had been at the lagoon on the small island JC took her to when they went on that first kayak adventure together. Warm water, bright sunshine, and a very sexy JC. She smiled lazily and took in the fact she was in bed beside JC. Wrapped up with her to be exact. The woman had an arm draped over Bella and, by the sound of her rhythmic breathing, was fast asleep. Turning her head a little, she could make out the woman's relaxed face by the faintest slivers of daylight coming in between the blinds through the bedroom window—a beautiful face. Open. Welcoming. Bella loved to look at her and felt warmth fill her body.

They had toasted Bella's great news with multiple glasses of wine, and then one thing naturally led to another. Before long, they were both naked and enjoying each other in JC's bed. A pleasant blush colored Bella's cheeks as she remembered how her body reacted to JC's touch. Her mouth. Everything about her. Their lovemaking was all she ever hoped it could be and simply another thing that added to making Bella's world so wonderful at the moment. Life could not be better to the point it was almost frightening. She didn't know why she warranted such happiness, but the thought made her smile. *There I go again, not feeling worthy of joy,* she thought. *JC would be all over that negative thinking, reminding me I am more than deserving.* As always, JC was her biggest fan.

She felt a cold nose on her arm and gently turned to look at the edge of the bed to find Gracie standing there. Her tail wagged when their eyes met. "Do you need to go out?" Bella whispered to the dog, and the tail wagged harder. "Okay. Let's go." Moving with infinite slowness, Bella released herself from under JC's arm. The woman murmured something unintelligible before rolling onto her back. Bella froze until a slight snore started. Loving the comforting sound, Bella grinned as she followed Gracie out of the bedroom and across the kitchen. Opening the patio door, she let them both outside into the backyard.

Feeling the embrace of the cool predawn air and breathing in the sweet scent of plumerias, Bella walked to the edge of the pool while Gracie ran to the corner to do her business. A glance upward and she saw a sky filled with quickly fading stars. The whole thing was so welcoming, she slipped into a lounge chair and lay back against the cushions. *How can everything always seem so perfect here?* she thought with a sigh and realized that as much as she loved Oregon, and especially Portland, her heart felt happier with JC in Hawaii. Although it was too early in their relationship to make drastic changes, Bella felt a sense of calmness settle over her as she embraced the decision. There was no reason she couldn't live full-time in Hawaii, assuming JC would be open to her moving in. Although she didn't dare assume anything, she sensed Bella living there was precisely what JC wanted.

Gracie returned to her side, and Bella ran a hand over the fur on her black and white head. "You'd like it too, I bet," she murmured. "I think I wrote my best words with you beside my writing table." The dog wagged her tail, and she licked Bella's a hand as if in answer. She heard the sound of the patio door opening and glanced to see JC coming out of the house. Bella frowned. "Oh, no, did we wake you?"

"Only by being absent," JC said with a sleepy smile. "I rolled over, and you were missing from your spot."

Bella started to get up. "Then, let's go back to bed," she said. "I was just enjoying the dawn for a moment because Gracie needed to go out."

She watched JC search the sky. "It is beautiful. The first lightening of the night sky," she said, and as Bella followed her gaze, a faint trail of shooting star darted across a part of the sky.

"Wow, did you see that?" she asked, and after a beat, JC nodded.

"I did," she said. "Did you make a wish?"

Realizing she hadn't, Bella paused and then smiled as she sent a message heavenward. She finally knew exactly what she wanted.

42

After a beautiful morning enjoying each other in bed, followed by coffee together on the patio, JC was running a little late but, if she was being honest, she didn't mind. She was sitting on the bench seat in her bedroom, putting on her waterproof sandals before heading to the office for the morning's kayaking tour, when she sensed Bella in the doorway. When she didn't say anything for a moment, JC glanced up and saw her leaning against the door jamb seeming to study her. When their eyes met, she saw Bella swallow hard as if gathering her courage about something. "So, I don't suppose your afternoon tour is full today," she finally said, and JC furrowed her brow at both the strange behavior and the random statement.

"Actually, it's not," she said. "It's only one group of three." She finished with her sandals and stood with a smile. "Why? Planning to join us?" Bella bit her lip, making JC pause to really look at the woman. Something was going on. "Bella, what are you thinking?"

Bella hesitated for another moment before smiling. "Well,

try not to pass out with disbelief, but actually I do want to join you kayaking this afternoon."

Not sure what to say, JC studied the woman's face for clues as to why she would suddenly be interested in kayaking again. After the last time, Bella was pretty clear she didn't ever want to go. Still, she stood there asking about going. "I would love that," JC finally said. "But I won't lie. I am surprised by your request." She stepped closer to Bella and pecked her on the lips. "I'm sorry, but I have to go, or I'll be late. But if you're only doing it for me, you don't have to do that."

"I know," Bella said, stepping aside to let JC pass so she could grab her backpack and keys from the kitchen counter. "I want to go with you today."

JC smiled, knowing better than to second guess an excellent opportunity to spend time with Bella. "Well then I'll come home over the lunch break and get you." An idea struck her, and her eyes drifted to Gracie, who was watching them from her bed in the corner of the kitchen. "And I'll pick up Gracie too if that's okay."

She was rewarded with an even bigger smile on Bella's face as well as a tail wag by Gracie at the sound of her name. "Yes, please," Bella said. "That would be even more perfect." As ideas formed in JC's head, she had to agree. Having both Bella and Gracie with her for the afternoon would be fantastic, especially since it was a total surprise.

After kissing Bella again, JC headed for the door. "Then I'll see you both in a few hours," she said before leaving and jogging to the jeep. The morning was perfect weather, making her even happier. Unlike the last time they went kayaking, and a storm threatened, the forecast for the day was serene. Even though that trip to the island had proved to be the most important and memorable one of JC's life, she hoped another chance at it might help Bella feel more confident. There were several fantastic places around the island to explore on the water, and she would love to share them with Bella if she was willing to start kayaking.

As she drove away from the house, she couldn't quite believe what Bella suggested. No matter what the woman said, JC knew the gesture was primarily to please her. *But why so suddenly?* she wondered. *It felt like she literally came up with the idea this morning over coffee. But I need to make the most of it.* Thoughts about how to make the afternoon tour even more special formulated in her mind as she jumped on the interstate. There wasn't time to plan much, but with a bit of luck, she could get Blake, who was still on desk duty, to help make some quick arrangements for her.

STANDING on the beach watching JC and the others prepare the kayaks for departure, Bella hoped she knew what she was doing, and not only about the kayaking. There was a lot going on in her head. She was about to embark on another trip across the waves after she had basically sworn she would never do it again. The good news was the water today appeared calm. Waves lapped onto the shore in a gentle rhythm and were a far cry from what she experienced the last time. In the jeep riding over from the house, JC assured her the morning tour went as smoothly as a trip could go. "Honestly, the water is a perfect temperature, and the waves aren't even a foot high today," JC said, taking her hand as they rode toward the launching point. "And there is hardly a breeze to ruffle the ocean."

"That is exactly what I want to hear," Bella said, and as she surveyed the water from her spot on the beach, JC was right. Everything did look perfect for a trip across to the island. Gracie stood beside her. Although the dog had wanted to help everyone get ready, JC had impressed them all when she told Gracie to stay beside Bella, and she did. Still, Bella felt the excitement radiating off the dog. Her tail slowly wagged as she watched JC's every move. Gracie may have belonged to someone else earlier in her life, but there was no doubt she was JC's dog now. Their adoration for each other was sweet to watch. Luckily, the three tourists already reserved for the trip immediately fell in love with Gracie. They acted thrilled when they learned she would accompany them. The idea of a kayaking dog seemed to entertain them greatly, and Bella was eager to see it too.

But even the excitement of seeing Gracie kayaking could not erase her anxiety about what she wanted to say to JC at the island's lagoon. With no ring or anything, she didn't plan to make a big show of asking the woman to consider a life together, but it had felt appropriate to do it on the island. There could not be a much more beautiful spot. While the others on the tour swam, Bella hoped to finally have the conversation with JC about their future. The time had come to lay out her heart and be willing to make some life-changing promises. A phone call with her sister and her editor helped her confirm what she knew in her heart—living in Hawaii with JC was where she wanted to be, not only a few weeks here and there but full-time.

"Are you ready to get settled in the kayak?" JC asked as she approached Bella across the sand. Any reservations Bella had about her plans evaporated as she took in the broad smile on the woman's tanned face. There was a twinkle of excitement in her eyes that was infectious.

Bella smiled back. "As I'll ever be," she said before glancing at Gracie. "And she is very willing. I can't believe she stayed with me all this time."

JC rubbed the dog's neck. "She's a good girl," she said before looking at Bella. "Thank you for being open to letting her ride with us on the tandem kayak. It will be crowded, but

I am confident with the water so calm today, we won't have a problem with her in the middle."

"I have no doubt you know what you are doing," Bella replied, meaning every word. There wasn't anyone she trusted more than JC, and the realization only solidified her determination to convince the woman they needed to be together. She pulled at the straps of her life vest, making sure they were snug before nodding. "I'm ready."

43

Feeling better than she had in a very long time if not ever, JC smiled. The ocean was perfect. Bella sat in the front of the kayak, Gracie perched in the middle, and she brought up the rear. Paddling them through the calm waves, JC reflected on the full circle her life had come. In less than two months, the world she once considered content had blossomed into something much more magical. As she watched Bella's dark hair, pulled back into a long ponytail, sway with the rhythm of their movement, her chest filled with happiness. *I really, truly love her,* she thought. *And today, I am going to tell her exactly how much.* Luckily she had time to work with Blake on a few quick purchases, plus she had taken her partner for the day, Shaun, aside to clue him in on her simple plan.

Like the last time Bella and JC visited the island together, they would split off from the group to take the easier and faster hike to the lagoon. In the short window of alone time, JC had a very important question to ask Bella. *Let's just hope I'm not blowing things way out of proportion,* she thought, feeling the slightest twinge of anxiety that she quickly squashed. It was not the time to worry about her decision, but rather the time had come to take life by the horns and go for it. Bella loved her, she knew it, and they needed to be together, even if it meant JC had to make significant changes in her life.

As the group of kayaks started to turn to make their approach to the island, Gracie barked. Looking at where the dog focused, JC saw the flicker of a school of tiny silver fish slightly below the surface as they caught the sun. Less than an inch long and shiny as any lure, the creatures moved in unison like blades. When the hundreds of little bodies jumped and broke the surface, JC heard Bella gasp and Gracie barked again. "Stay in the kayak, Gracie," JC cautioned her dog even though she wasn't too concerned. More than anything, Gracie was showing her excitement at the spectacle.

Bella pointed the end of her paddle toward the departing fish. "Did you see those little fish?" she asked. "I've never seen anything like that. It was so beautiful."

"I did," JC said. "And I agree. The oceans are full of spectacular views." She grinned. "Maybe I'll get you to snorkel now that you're embracing kayaking."

A nervous laugh from Bella confirmed for JC their current adventure was a special event and not likely to be repeated often. "How about we focus on getting me to dry land on that little island over there for now?" the woman said.

"Your wish is my command," she said, turning them with the next wave to let it start to propel them toward the beach. The rest of the group had already made shore, and JC had no problem running them up onto the sand. Gracie immediately hopped off, with JC following to move into place to lend a hand to Bella. Next came the one tricky part of JC's plan.

She needed Bella to agree to split from the group like they

did last time, but before she could pose a question, Bella beat her to it. "Last time I didn't get to see the view from the summit, so I say we attack the trail and go the harder route. I'm in better shape now, too," she said with a smile JC couldn't contradict. JC made eye contact with her Shaun, who was clearly unsure of what to do since Bella's suggestion was the opposite of what JC had planned. She gave him a slight shrug before focusing on Bella.

With a smile, she slung the drybag they brought with them over her shoulders. "I think that's perfect," she said, and as the group started up the trail single file, she went last, hoping to come up with an idea of how to get Bella alone later.

MOMENTS before the group reached the summit of the small island, Bella was on the verge of second-guessing her decision. The hike was steeper than she estimated, and although she was more active thanks to JC's influence, a sharp climb was outside her usual comfort zone. Luckily, with JC hiking behind her and giving her murmurings of encouragement that they were almost to the top, Bella broke out of the trees to a magnificent view. The other four in the party were already oohing and ahhing the vast expanse of turquoise water laid out before them. Even though she was tired and breathing heavily, the landscape was enough to make her pause with wonder.

JC stopped beside her. "Worth it?" she asked with a hint of playfulness in her voice.

Clearly she already knew the answer from the amazed look on Bella's face. "Oh yes," Bella whispered. "I've never seen anything like it outside of photographs."

"It never gets old either," JC said. "I have seen it pretty much twice a day for years now, and I always still love that first step out from the trees to see the ocean below." Moving closer, she put her hand on Bella's back. "I'm glad you find it special too."

Reaching, Bella took JC's arm. "I really do," she said, feeling an emotional tug at the knowledge she could never ask JC to walk away from a job she loved so much. The thought only reconfirmed Bella was about to make the right decision. It was only a matter of getting down to the lagoon and finding the perfect moment.

After another few minutes, where selfies were taken, and the view was duly appreciated, Bella made ready to go with the others down the other side of the island. "Why don't you four go on ahead?" JC surprised her by saying to the three tourists and Shaun. "We can meet you in a bit."

Not sure what was happening and concerned her plans for the day were somehow in jeopardy, Bella shook her head. "I don't need to rest any longer if that's—" she started, but JC gave a shake of her head and looked pointedly at Shaun.

"We will be ten minutes behind you," she said. "Nothing to worry about."

Bella was surprised as the young man reacted as if taking a cue and started to nod. "Right," he said, motioning the others toward the path headed in the direction of what Bella assumed was the lagoon. "See you there."

Then the man winked, and Bella watched JC's face flush a little pink. *What in the world is going on?* Bella wondered, noticing as the rest of the group left that JC started to fidget with the drybag on her back. As she watched, she saw a slight tremble in the woman's hands. "JC, are you all right?" she asked, glancing at Gracie, who sniffed the edge of the bushes around them, apparently not alarmed by any of the happenings. Somehow, Bella found the behavior reassuring. *Would Gracie sense if something was wrong?*

For a moment, JC didn't answer Bella's question and only

focused on the clasps on the pack. "I think so," she finally said once the flap of the drybag was open. She drew out a white box about a foot long and half as wide. "But you're the one that will have to tell me for sure."

Bella furrowed her brow. "What do you mean?"

"This is for you," JC said, holding out the box for Bella to take. "It's a little unconventional, but I admit things were a bit last minute."

Taking the box, Bella wasn't sure what to think, but her heart started to beat faster. "What is it?" she asked, and JC motioned toward the box.

"Open it," she said, and slowly Bella did. Inside was a Hawaiian lei of purple orchids and white tuberoses. Suddenly, JC was beside her, lifting the ring of flowers from the package and facing Bella. "The Hawaiian lei is a symbol of love. I wanted to give you one today, in a beautiful spot like this, and ask you something." Feeling her breath catch, Bella waited as JC placed the lei over her shoulders and leaned in closer until their lips almost touched.

Having a very good idea of what was happening, Bella smiled. "Well, maybe you won't believe this, but I wanted to ask you something today, too," she said softly. "Someplace beautiful like this."

JC hesitated. "You did?"

"I did, and I do," Bella said with a slight nod. "So… who goes first?"

EPILOGUE

As JC picked up her backpack from the desk at Oahu Paddle Adventures to get ready to leave, she racked her brain for any last detail she might be forgetting. "JC," Blake said from where he stood patiently at the counter. "It's not like you can't call if you think of something."

After a beat, JC grinned because the young man was right. "That's true," she agreed. "And it's not like I haven't left you in charge of things before."

Blake nodded. "Exactly," he said. "I promise not to hurt myself while you're gone this time, either."

"Good strategy," JC said as she moved toward the exit. She glanced at her watch and realized that if she didn't hurry, Bella and Gracie would be waiting on her. "But don't hesitate to call if anything comes up."

"I promise," Blake called after her as JC left the building and jogged toward her jeep.

She shot off a quick text to Bella. "Leaving now."

"We will be waiting. Drive safe," came back the answer with a red heart. After sending a heart back, JC started the jeep to head home to pick up Bella and Gracie. Even though they were packed and ready to fly to Oregon early the next morning, there was one more thing that needed to be done. Smiling as she thought of it, JC quickly made her way to the house. As soon as she pulled into the driveway, the front door opened, and Bella came out with Gracie at her side. Watching the two walking toward her, JC's heart was full of happiness.

Apparently, it showed on her face because as soon as Bella and Gracie settled in the jeep, Bella leaned in to kiss JC on the cheek. "It makes me happy to see you happy," the woman whispered against her skin.

JC turned to kiss her gently on the lips. "Same," she said softly, and for a moment, their eyes lingered before she remembered they had an appointment to keep. "But we have to get going."

As JC backed out of the driveway to head to the nearby park, Bella settled into her seat. "How did it go at work? Is Blake all set?" she asked, and JC nodded.

"He is," she said. "I might have driven him crazy the last few days with all my double-checking things."

Bella laughed. "I'm sure he understood," she said. "It's a big deal."

"But it's not like he hasn't run things before," JC said.

"Not as a co-owner of the business though," Bella said, holding up a finger. "Plus, you'll be away for three months. This is different." JC considered Bella's comments. What she said was true—Blake was her new business partner and owned half of Oahu Paddle Adventures. After JC and Bella's co-proposal on the little island's overlook three months before, they had agreed to get married at some future date. For the moment they would live together, splitting time between Hawaii and Oregon. To make that possible, JC let Blake take over a big part of the kayaking company, which freed up JC to be away for extended periods of time.

As they pulled into the parking lot of the small city park, JC smiled. "You're right," she said. "And I've never been more excited about the future."

"Me too," Bella said as they parked. They had barely climbed out of the vehicle and unloaded Gracie when a van pulled up a few spaces over. 'Tropical Oasis Retirement' was discreetly lettered on the side with a pair of palm trees. JC glanced at Gracie to see if she would have a reaction and saw her tail had started to wag. It was the third time JC and Bella had met with Gracie's original owner at the park for a visit, and clearly the dog had learned to recognize the shuttle.

JC rubbed Gracie behind the ear. "Smart girl," she said, never getting used to how intelligent her canine companion was. "Let's go say hi to Frank."

Watching the television, Bella sat curled up under a quilt with JC on the couch in her house in Portland. Gracie was at their feet, and if Bella didn't know better, the dog's eyes were fixed on the television screen too. The opening credits were playing, and Bella held her breath. Then, the words she waited for filled the screen—the title of her first book, "Catching the Moment." A new Hallmark movie. Another shot followed it, and Bella's name appeared along with the author's credit. It was all enough to bring tears to her eyes, and clearly sensing her emotion, JC hugged her closer. "I still can't believe it," Bella whispered, and JC kissed her temple.

"Believe it," JC said against her ear. "Lots of people are about to learn what I already know."

Bella furrowed her brow. "What is that?"

"How amazingly talented you are," JC answered, and Bella smiled as warmth filled her. She could not remember ever being happier. The last few weeks had held one incredible milestone after another. First, she and JC, along with

Gracie, relocated from Hawaii to Oregon for an extended stay. Then, her new book was released to rave reviews and, just as her editor promised, made it to number one on the bestsellers list. The topper though was the movie based on her first novel actually got scheduled to air. Tonight, was the release at last, and her body tingled as they prepared to watch it.

As the story that came from inside her heart unfolded on the screen, Bella had trouble remembering the characters were her own creation. Throughout the show, her cell phone chimed as friends and family, and especially her editor sent her congratulatory texts. "I told you it would be special!" Joanie sent halfway through the show with a dozen smiling and celebrating emojis, making Bella laugh. Once again, the woman was able to say she was right.

When the happy ending finally unfolded between the two women in the movie, JC kissed Bella's cheek. "I'll be right back," she said, slipping from under the blanket. "Don't go anywhere."

Bella raised an eyebrow with curiosity. "What are you up to?"

With a chuckle, JC shook her head. "Be patient. You'll know in a minute," she said, disappearing around the corner into the kitchen. Less than thirty seconds later, she was back and carried a pair of champagne flutes in one hand and a chilled bottle of bubbly in the other. "I thought we needed to celebrate this special event properly."

"Oh, JC," Bella said, unable to keep the emotion out of her voice. Of everything amazing that had happened, being able to spend all her time with JC was the greatest blessing of them all. "You always think of everything." With a smile, JC opened the bottle with a pop and poured them each a glass of the shimmering liquid.

Once she had settled on the couch beside Bella again, she

held up her drink. "I'd like to propose a toast," she said, intriguing Bella even further.

"All right," she said. "What exactly are we going to drink to?"

JC's eyes held Bella's. "To you and all your success," she said, but that wasn't good enough for Bella.

"No," she said, pulling her glass back. "Not only to me. If we are going to toast, I want it to be to both of us."

A smile crept across JC's face. "I like that even more," she said. "The future has never looked brighter." She lifted her glass again. "To us."

Bella raised hers too and tapped it against JC's. "To us," she said with a smile. "And all that lies ahead."

THE END
Want more?
Sign up for my newsletter
(https://landing.mailerlite.com/webforms/landing/r2b5s6)
to keep tabs on what I am writing next.

ABOUT THE AUTHOR

Bestselling author KC Luck writes action adventure, contemporary romance, and lesbian fiction. Writing is her passion, and nothing energizes her more than creating new characters facing trials and tribulations in a complex plot. Whether it is apocalypse, horror, or a little naughty, with every story, KC tries to add her own unique twist. She has written over a dozen books (which include *The Darkness Series* and *Everybody Needs a Hero*) and multiple short stories across many genres. KC is active in the LGBTQ+ community and is the founder of the collective iReadIndies.

To receive updates on KC Luck's books, please consider subscribing to her mailing list (https://landing.mailerlite.com/webforms/landing/r2b5s6). Also, KC Luck is always thrilled to hear from her readers (kc.luck.author@gmail.com)

To follow KC Luck, you can find her at: www.kc-luck.com

THANK YOU

Enjoy this book?
You can make a big difference

Honest reviews of my books help bring them to the attention of other readers. If you've enjoyed this story, I would be incredibly grateful if you could spend a couple minutes leaving a review (it can be as short as you like) on the book's Amazon and Goodreads pages.

ALSO BY KC LUCK

Rescue Her Heart
Save Her Heart
Welcome to Ruby's
Back to Ruby's
Darkness Falls
Darkness Remains
Darkness United
Wind Dancer
Darkness San Francisco
The Lesbian Billionaires Club
The Lesbian Billionaires Seduction
The Lesbian Billionaires Last Hope
Venandi
What the Heart Sees
Everybody Needs a Hero
Can't Fight Love
Where Love Leads

IREADINDIES

iReadIndies

This author is part of iReadIndies, a collective of self-published independent authors of sapphic literature. Please visit our website at iReadIndies.com for more information and to find links to the books published by our authors.

Printed in Great Britain
by Amazon